Three Faces in the Mirror

ALSO BY JOSEPH ITIEL

Financial Well-Being Through Self-Hypnosis

The Franz Document

Philippine Diary: A Gay Guide to the Philippines

De Onda: A Gay Guide to Mexico and Its People

Pura Vida: A Gay and Lesbian Guide to Costa Rica

A Consumer's Guide to Male Hustlers

Sex Workers As Virtual Boyfriends

Escapades of a Gay Traveler: Sexual, Cultural, and Spiritual Encounters

Escort Tales: The Trophy Boy and Other Stories

Dirty Young Men and Other Gay Stories

Three Faces in the Mirror

a novel

Joseph Itiel

Author of "Escort Tales: The Trophy Boy and Other Stories"

iUniverse, Inc.
New York Lincoln Shanghai

Three Faces in the Mirror

iUniverse books may be ordered through booksellers or by contacting:

iUniverse
2021 Pine Lake Road, Suite 100
Lincoln, NE 68512
www.iuniverse.com
1-800-Authors (1-800-288-4677)

Certain of the characters in this work are historical figures, and certain of the events portrayed in it happened. However, this is a work of fiction. All of the other characters, names, and events as well as all places, incidents, organizations, and dialogue in this novel are either the products of the author's imagination or are used fictitiously.

Photo Credit: JEANINE REISBIG

ISBN-13: 978-0-595-39846-1 (pbk)
ISBN-13: 978-0-595-84249-0 (ebk)
ISBN-10: 0-595-39846-4 (pbk)
ISBN-10: 0-595-84249-6 (ebk)

Printed in the United States of America

Contents

Acknowledgements

Many thanks to Steve Kotz, who edited the first draft of the book, and to David Klein, who did the detailed, final editing. And, as always, to my friend Howard Curtis, who helped with the foreign languages. Much of my information about the philosopher Wittgenstein was derived from Ray Monk's excellent biography, *Ludwig Wittgenstein: The Duty of a Genius.*

1

Gaia, My Mother

I was born in 1965 in the Haight-Ashbury district of San Francisco, at the beginning of the hippie movement. Fortunately for me, I inherited my father's good looks and my maternal grandfather's brains. From my father I got my first name, Eloy. My mother bestowed upon me the middle name Harmony, which was a constant embarrassment.

My father died of a heroin overdose one month after I was born. He never married my mother, so my surname, Wise, comes from her. My mother has only three small photos of Domingo Herrera, my father. He was born somewhere in Mexico. Looking at his photos, one can see that he must have had a fair amount of Hispanic and Indian blood.

I look vaguely Hispanic, mostly around my eyes. Incongruously, they are green rather than brown, with very long eyelashes. I have thick eyebrows and straight black hair; the color of my skin is just brown enough to exclude me from the Caucasian classification. I stand five-nine, have a compact body, and have often been told that I am "very nicely equipped." Throughout my life, women and men alike have referred to my face, my body, and my genitals as sexy.

These days, everybody calls my mother Gaia, the Greek way of describing the Earth personified as a goddess. Early on, she had used various other first names. But when she was born in Brooklyn in 1942, her parents named her Gitel. She is the daughter of Zalman and Chaya Weiss.

According to my mother, my grandfather was a Talmudic scholar of great fame. How she wound her way from Brooklyn to San Francisco's Haight-Ashbury district, from Gitel Weiss to Gaia Wise, from an orthodox Jewish woman to the lover of a series of Hispanic drug addicts, I don't know. It was only a few years ago that my mother told me about her family. I have never met any of them. I have no brothers or sisters; the only relative I have ever known is my mother.

At a very young age, maybe in the first grade, I scored 148 on an IQ test. Embarrassingly, after that my mother always referred to me as "my son the genius." I don't know what came first: the knowledge that I was supposed to be smarter than most people, or my observation that I was, indeed, very bright, and that most of my teachers were dumber than me.

I may have been a smart kid, but I was not a happy one. Much of the time I was neglected. One of my first memories is living in a flat on Waller Street in San Francisco. I realize now that it was a commune of sorts. My mother's lover at that point was a wild-eyed, handsome Chicano who was tweaking his life away. We shared the flat with a black guy who had long, thick dreadlocks. He called me "Child" and always gave me a small piece of the brownie he was munching on. His treats made me feel happy; I suspect they contained a lot of pot. The other person in our flat was Robin. Sometimes he dressed like a man but he usually walked around in drag. He had many male visitors in his room. When they left, he always had some money. I believe he was the guy who fed us all.

My mother moved to Fairfax, in Marin County, when I was fourteen. At that time she lived with a Mexican man, Maximiliano, who was not, for a wonder, a drug addict. Unlike her other "undocumented" lovers, he did not stand on the streets of San Rafael waiting for a day job. He had come from León, an important city in the Mexican state of Guanajuato, and was a shoemaker by profession. Not a cobbler, but a guy who could make shoes. He found jobs easily, and made good money. When he lived with us, we had enough money to pay our rent and eat well. We even owned a beat-up car.

My mother never bothered to learn Spanish; she spoke English with her many lovers. They answered as best they could in their brand of English. Maximiliano liked me a lot, and, after living with us for a while, started speaking Spanish to me. I learned the language pretty fast. To this day, I speak it just like Maximiliano. When I speak Spanish I am often taken for a Mexican. Later on, Maximiliano taught me how to read and write Spanish. He lived with my mother for only eighteen months. After he left, I continued my Spanish studies and have done pretty well for myself.

I had a big crush on Maximiliano. I had been aware, even before Maximiliano, that I was attracted to men rather than women. I say "men" because boys my age bored me, and certainly did not excite me physically. Maximiliano was pretty old when he lived with my mother; maybe even over fifty. He had a lot of gray hair, which made him look distinguished. Of my mother's lovers, he was the only one who owned a suit. Sometimes on Sundays, when we went out for dinner, he would put on a coat and tie. Just seeing him dressed like this excited me sexually.

By the time my mother broke up with Maximiliano—she never lived with a lover for any length of time—my sexual preference had become permanent: an elderly, distinguished man with gray hair, preferably in a business suit. When I was about fifteen years old, I started going across the Golden Gate Bridge to San Francisco to hang out on Montgomery Street during lunch. I feasted my eyes on the procession of cute businessmen going out for a bite to eat.

Maximiliano worried about my religion, or more correctly, my lack of one. My mother told him to mind his own business. When I was a little boy, a teacher asked about my family's religion. To the great amusement of my classmates, I didn't know the answer. I asked my mother. "We're Hindus, Eloy," she told me. My teacher raised her eyebrows in exasperation when I told her I was a Hindu. Later, a black kid said to me, "You ain't no Hindu."

"How would you know?"

"Because we live in a Hindu hotel. Mr. Patel owns it. You sure don't look like you was his family."

"I don't want to be a Hindu," I told my mother when I returned from school.

We were in the midst of one of her lovers' crises. "Oh, Eloy, stop bothering me with things that don't matter. If you don't want to say that you're a Hindu, say you're Jewish.

"Because the Jewish religion goes from mother to child. So, since I'm your mother, and I was born Jewish, you're one too. So be a Jew, not a Hindu, for all I care."

"I don't want to be Jewish because they don't have Christmas." I don't think my mother would have fussed over Christmas of her own accord. But it was a big deal for her lovers, so we did celebrate that holiday. Once a year, I would get two or three gifts.

"You know what? Tell your teacher that you're an atheist. God knows I have been one." The only time that I was sent to the principal's office for being a wise guy was when I told my teacher that I was an atheist.

Until we moved to Fairfax, I told everyone that I was Jewish, though I knew nothing about that religion. I knew more about Catholicism because of my mother's lovers. A few months after we moved to Fairfax, my mother asked me, "You tell them at school that you're Hispanic?"

"Yes."

"That's good. You'll get more mileage out of it. What do you say your religion is?" She had long ago forgotten our conversation about my religion.

"I say I'm Jewish."

"Well, tell them you're Catholic. It goes better with being Hispanic."

Eloy Harmony Wise was a puzzlement to his teachers. The names Harmony and Wise did not belong to my Chicano face, and the prejudice of my teachers told them my face didn't go with my brains. Without much effort on my part, I was always the best student in class.

My male fellow students didn't much care for me. I was a painfully shy loner who was awkward at sports. I was desperately ashamed of my mother and the home she kept. Most of all, I was ashamed of her drugged-out lovers. I never invited other kids to our home, and was rarely invited to theirs. I think they considered me a nerd, though this word did not exist then.

Things were different with girls. Many of them had crushes on me. People called me "gorgeous, "sexy," and "cute" all the time. Quite a few of them threw themselves at me. I had my first sexual experience with an older girl when I was thirteen. My sex with girls was half-hearted; I performed more to please them than to please myself. I often thought of older men while casually screwing a classmate. The more aloof I was, the more girls desired me.

* * *

My mother never had much time for me. Almost always, we lived in poverty and faced one crisis after another. Why my mother, who never did drugs (except mushrooms and pot, which she considered organic and therefore healthy), took up with hard-core users, I have never figured out. She explained everything to me by saying, "It's my karma." Karma? What karma? To help her lovers find heroin dealers?

This karma business was connected with my mother's affectation that she was a Hindu. There was always some guru in her life with "Baba" attached to his name. I remember Meher Baba, and Sai Baba, and other Babas whose last names I don't recall. I believe there were two aspects to her karma. On the one hand, she was sex-crazy and craved dark, macho, Hispanic men. On the other hand, she wanted them to make her suffer by making her life with them as miserable as possible.

Did my mother love me? As a boy, I didn't think so. I usually felt completely neglected. She always seemed to have her hands full with her lovers' drug or legal crises. In spite of all sorts of welfare checks and food stamps, we still were very poor. Yet she found the time to join a different cult every year. Now that I am much older, I think my mother was incapable of loving anyone. She knew how to pity; she always found pitiful men for her lovers. I was a handsome and intelligent boy who needed love, not pity. My mother simply didn't know how to relate to a child like me.

My mother was in her early twenties when I was born. She was generally considered a pretty woman. She had long brown hair, green eyes with long eyelashes, and an engaging smile. Unlike her lovers, who were invariably on the husky side, she was a petite woman. I didn't like her shrill voice. When I was young, I thought that her English was funny. Later on, I realized that her strong Brooklyn accent sounded strident in California.

Some eight years ago, my mother assumed the name Gaia. Three years later, she started working in halfway houses as a drug counselor. Simultaneously, she gave up her affairs with drug addicts. Now she often talks about her years in Brooklyn. She has even tried to contact one of her sisters back east, after almost thirty years of separation. I gather this didn't work out too well.

After my mother discovered that I was a "genius," she no longer concerned herself with my education. She made sure that I attended school, got all my vaccinations, and that my shoes had no holes in them. That always puzzled me. Usually my clothes were shabby, but my shoes were in good condition.

After we moved to Fairfax, I started tutoring younger kids in math. This brought in a bit of pocket money. Many Anglo parents shook their heads sadly as they watched a Chicano kid in shabby clothes tutoring one of their children.

For twelve years, my mother had attended a Jewish girls' day school in Brooklyn. This was the sum total of her education. I don't know whether it was her school in particular, or the generally higher level of education in the fifties, but my mother was a pretty literate person. What she lacked completely was common sense.

There was no question that I would attend college. My grades and SAT scores were so high that colleges vied with each other to have a Hispanic "genius" like me in their institution.

With the benefit of hindsight, I should have made a better choice than the University of California in Berkeley, with math as a major and philosophy as a minor. I didn't have the vaguest notion what I would do with myself after graduation. Mother never gave such matters any thought.

I had always enjoyed math. Unlike most students, I found it to be a simple discipline to follow. When I chose my minor, I really knew very little about philosophy. I had read all of Plato's dialogues and, in a childish fashion, was a great fan of his teacher, Socrates. In one of the introductions to the dialogues I discovered the expression "homoeroticism," which I managed to figure out by myself.

I fantasized being one of Socrates' students just before his execution at the age of seventy. My body, as well as my mind, would have been his. Even in this tiny fragment of philosophy, I managed to miss two essential points. "Know thyself," and "The unexamined life is not worth living," were Socrates' maxims. I never bothered to ask myself, "Who am I?"

By and large, most of my teachers were not fond of me. I was a quiet, well-behaved boy who never caused a disturbance in class. But my teachers were keenly aware that I knew how much they didn't know. When a science teacher caught himself making an erroneous statement, when an English teacher wasn't sure how to spell a word, they looked at me furtively. Had I noticed? Did I know the correct answer? Usually I did, though I kept it to myself. I hoped that my college instructors would like me better; that I could ask them questions and learn from their answers.

*   *   *

I think I should write about one more thing that happened to me before I started college.

During my last year of high school, in January 1982, I turned seventeen. At about that time, I gave up dating girls altogether. I was bored and uncomfortable with them. My fantasy of having a physical relationship with an older gentleman became an obsession. My trips to Montgomery Street in San Francisco became more frequent.

During the Easter recess, on the Thursday before Good Friday, I took the bus into the city. I stationed myself on the corner of Bush and Montgomery. A short, rotund gentleman with a neatly trimmed white beard walked toward me. He was dressed to the nines. I stepped forward and asked, as innocently as I could, "Excuse me, sir, do you know where Sutter Street is?"

For a moment the gentleman looked pensively through his bifocals, saying nothing. He was so cute! Then he said, "It's one block down from here. Are you from out of town?"

"Yes, sir. I mean no. I am from the Bay Area. I live in Fairfax, in Marin."

"And what brings you to our fair city?"

I needed to come up with an answer but couldn't think of anything. "I…I have an errand to run on Bush Street."

"But you're on Bush."

"I'm sorry, I meant Sutter Street."

"I was going out to have a bite. Will you have lunch with me?" the gentleman asked. "It'll be my treat."

"OK, I'll have lunch with you," I answered.

"Let's go to the Metropolitan. They have a very nice buffet for lunch."

We walked down Montgomery and turned right on Market. As we walked, we introduced ourselves. His name was Tom, and he worked for a brokerage house. He didn't say what he did for them. He spoke in a refined manner. I sensed that he was tense; I was even more nervous.

Inside the Metropolitan Hotel, on the second floor, was an atrium with a huge dining room. Tom looked at the menu. "You know, Eloy, the best deal is to have the buffet lunch. Today's buffet's special is swordfish. Would you like that?"

My mother's cooking was limited to chicken dishes. Except for fish sticks and tuna, we never had seafood for lunch at school. I had no idea what swordfish was. "I'll try it," I said sheepishly. I had never seen so much food concentrated in one place. There were all sorts of soups and salads and meats.

"Help yourself to whatever you want," said Tom. "You can go back as often as you want. The desserts are over there," he said, pointing to another section. I'm not big on food. But I was completely overwhelmed by the elegance of the place, the enormous quantities and varieties of food. We started eating. I really liked the swordfish. "How old are you?" Tom asked.

"Eighteen," I lied. To this day I don't know how, at that moment, I knew that this was the answer he would need to hear in order for us to proceed.

I wolfed down the delicious food. For a while both of us concentrated on the eating. Then, as if just to make conversation, he asked, "Do you have many girlfriends?"

"I did, but not any longer."

"Why is that?"

"Because I'm not interested in girls now."

"Have you ever been with a man?" he asked in a husky and tense whisper. "I mean, have your ever had sex with another man? Though I'm straight—I'm married you know—I like doing it with another man once in a while."

"I've never been with a man," I said in an equally tense voice. "But I wouldn't mind trying it."

"Does it matter to you that I'm a lot older than you? I'm sixty-one years old."

"That's OK," I answered. How could I have told him that I had been fantasizing about gentlemen like him for most of my life?

He looked at me, started to say something, and then checked himself. "Let me make a phone call to my office so they'll know that I'll be back a bit later."

We finished our food without talking. I had chocolate mousse and apple pie for dessert. He paid with a credit card. This was the first time in my life that someone paid for me with a credit card. Tom returned. "Eloy, as I told you, I'm a married man. I'm sorry that your first experience of this sort won't be as intimate as it should be. I know a place we can get a room for an hour."

We walked less then ten minutes, and came to a building with a neon sign that read: The Downtown Sauna—Private Rooms Available. It was too warm inside the building. There was a peculiar odor in the air: a mixture of chlorine, wet wood, and disinfectant. Behind the counter sat an apathetic young woman with a ring in her nose. Tom showed his driver's license, gave her some money, and was issued two towels and a key.

We entered a small room. In it was a hot tub with a Jacuzzi, a tiny steam cabinet, a shower, a twin-size cot covered by a sheet that had seen better days, and one chair. "Why don't we take our clothes off and get into the hot tub?" Tom asked.

I undressed slowly and shyly, with my back to Tom. When I was completely naked I turned around and, to my own surprise, asked him coquettishly: "Do you like what you see?"

"My, but you're well-hung!" Tom said. "Eloy, you have a beautiful body. You're really very handsome."

Tom was fatter than he had looked clothed. He had breasts like a woman. His balls hung low. His small penis was fully erect, moving strangely in a small arc as if searching for a target. I found him adorable.

Slowly, we entered the hot tub. The water was quite warm. Tom opened his arms and I flew into them, letting my head rest on his hairy chest, which was just as white as his beard. Inexplicably, I started crying. I hadn't cried in years. "It's all right, Eloy. It really is all right," Tom said, as he started kissing my face and body.

When we got out of the tub, Tom dried me tenderly. He took me by the hand and led me to the cot. I lay on top of him, my tongue penetrating into his mouth. I licked his body. I took his penis in my mouth. I hugged him so hard that he winced. "Eloy, is this really your first time with a man?"

"Yes. Don't you believe me?"

"You are very experienced for a first-timer."

"I've rehearsed this scene many times in my mind."

The one thing I wasn't sure of was whether I would like to be penetrated by another man. Once I had stuck a candle in my rear end to try this out. First it hurt a lot, and wouldn't go in. Then I lubricated it with cooking oil. It slipped in easily, as if it had been manufactured for this purpose. I almost lost it inside me. That was scary! I still had not made up my mind whether I would like another man's dick inside me. But I was pretty sure that I didn't want to screw another man. I didn't particularly like it with girls, and didn't think it would be different with a man.

Tom responded to my silent musings. "This is your first time. Let's take it easy. We'll just be oral."

When we were done, we lay on the cot holding each other. The house phone rang. Tom picked it up, listened for a moment, and said, "OK." To me he said, "They're telling us that our hour is up. I could pay for another hour but I've got to go back to work. Let's get cleaned up and dressed."

Before we left, Tom kissed me gently on the lips. "Sit down for a moment," he said, pointing to the only chair. He sat on the cot. "Eloy, how old are you really?"

"I turned seventeen in January."

"I thought you were younger than eighteen. Eloy, I have a family to worry about. Technically, you're a minor. Being with you can cause me lots of problems. I don't believe we should meet again, though you're the nicest young man I've met in a long time. You know, at the Metropolitan, I suspected that you were a hustler."

"What is a hustler?"

"A guy who does it for money."

"Why did you assume that I wanted money?"

"Because of the way you spoke in the hotel. I didn't think you liked being with older men."

"But I do! I do."

"I know, I know…Listen, this is your first time. I wish we could celebrate. I wish I could give you a gift. But I have no time. Please accept this. Open it after we part." From his coat pocket he took out a Metropolitan Hotel envelope he must have picked up there.

The envelope contained three bills. Two tens and one five.

2

The Yoga of Anal Penetration

Obtaining a student loan made me feel financially independent. I also managed to get a fifteen-hour-a-week job at the UC library. For the first time in my life, I had more than enough money for my modest needs. I moved to Berkeley, where I rented a reasonably priced small room.

I enrolled in two math courses for my major. For electives I took German and zoology. The history of philosophy course I wanted to take was already closed. It was the most popular philosophy course, taught by a legendary instructor with the quaint name of Dr. Brotbaum. His complete course ran two semesters. I would have to wait until my second year in order to start the course from the beginning. It was my advisor who suggested that I take German as my foreign language, since it would tie in with my philosophy minor.

I took the zoology course because of my fascination with animals. This included all creatures, from ants and bees to elephants and dolphins. Twice my mother had let me have a cat as a pet: a Manx kitten in San Francisco, and an older tomcat in Fairfax. To my chagrin, both cats disappeared after we'd had them for a few months. Years later, I read that cats sometimes seek out a new home if they feel too stressed in their environment. Even cats could not put up with my mother's insane household.

All of my classes, with the exception of beginning German, were huge. Students rarely got a chance to talk to their instructors. So much for my hopes of holding long conversations with them. Usually, I finished my homework pretty fast, and unless I had to work at the library, had very little to occupy myself.

My mother and I had shared a single recreational activity. Both of us liked listening to classical music. She splurged on music tapes, and had an impressive collection. I suppose I could have asked her to lend me a few tapes, but I didn't. In any case, they would have sounded awful on my portable recorder. I read a lot, and walked alone all over town. Here, in Berkeley, I felt the lack of friends even more acutely than in Fairfax. One day I went to a gay orientation group, though I was not sure I belonged there, at least by the usual standards.

There were about twenty students in the meeting of the Stonewall support group. Most of them were older than me. There were only two other men of color in the group: one black, one Asian.

We were all asked to introduce ourselves and "share." After the first few such shares, I realized that the other guys would be scandalized if they knew the age range of the partners I preferred. I just sat there quietly, mumbling that I had not had yet any experiences to share.

The conversation seemed completely irrelevant to my case. For instance, they had an obsession with the "Are you out to your family?" business. I wasn't out to my mother because for the last year she and I had just occupied the same space for part of the day. Her latest lover took up all of her time, energy, and money. I could have told her that I was a serial killer without getting a rise out of her. Being out to my family was a non-issue to me. Other concerns of the group members, like their religions' attitudes toward homosexuality, were equally irrelevant to me.

But in the end, my visit with the Stonewall support group turned out to be an important event in my life. It was at this meeting that I met Helmut.

*   *   *

Helmut introduced himself to the group as a foreign student from Germany, in his third year of chemical engineering. His English was good, though heavily accented. He was about my own height and build. His eyes were gray, his hair was flaxen, and he always wore a mischievous grin. He dressed casually, yet each item he wore must have been very expensive. The camel hair vest he wore that day—I learned later what the material was—fit him beautifully. He was twenty-three years old. I must have been uncomfortable and inattentive during the meeting because I have no clear recollection of what Helmut had to share. At the end of the meeting, I forced myself to speak to him. I told him that I was taking beginning German, and would like to practice with him if he had the time. He invited me for supper at his place the following evening.

Helmut shared an elegant two-bedroom apartment on Spruce Street, not far from campus, with another gay student. It was obviously an expensive place; I wondered how he could afford it.

"You said yesterday that you have not had any gay experiences," Helmut said during the meal. "Is this true? You must have one immediately." It took me a while to get used to Helmut's use of "must" where a native speaker would have used "should" or "need to"

"I have had only one gay experience. But I didn't feel I wanted to talk about it in the group."

"Why?"

"Because it was with a really old guy," I answered, wondering how Helmut would take this statement.

Helmut's face lit up. "Was he rich?"

"I don't know," I said. For the moment, I did not wish to go into the twenty-five dollars Tom had given me.

"You must always go only with rich men. You see, I shall be rich very soon. You know, of course, that chemical engineers are the smartest in the profession, and they make very good money. I believe they do even better in Germany than here. But, you see, I want to live well before I become rich."

"Don't your parents help you?"

"Of course they do. They pay my tuition and give me, how do you say in English?" he thought for a moment and came up with the correct expression, "an allowance of $500 a month. However, I own a sports car, a little Fiat convertible, and I pay a lot of rent. I like to dress elegantly and go to good restaurants. This sort of money you must get from wealthy old men."

"Are you a hustler, then?" I asked, taking pride in the word I learned from Tom.

"No, of course not. Hustlers stand in the rain on Polk Street in San Francisco waiting for customers. I never ask my old men for money."

"But you just said—"

"No, no. Old men don't like to give you money. But they'll help you by giving it to other parties in your name. Every month I've a big telephone bill. I call up my parents and friends in Germany all the time, you know. So I go to one of my old men and say, 'Now you must help me with the telephone bill. Otherwise they will cut it off, and you won't be able to call me, and I won't be able to see you any more.' Or I say to another old man, 'By tomorrow I must buy a textbook. I don't have the money for it. I will flunk the next quiz. Can you please write a check for the bookstore?'"

"Do you have more than one boyfriend?"

"But of course. Is this good English? 'You make hay while the sun shines.'"

"Yes, it is. But do you go to bed with them for money?"

"You see, my dear Eloy, sex and love are not like math or engineering. There is more than one answer; more than one solution. You're handsome, and so am I. We could make sex together and it would be OK. Tomorrow you or I will find another handsome guy and make sex together. But if I go to bed with an old man, he must have my youth, and I must have his money, and so we make sex together. It is not so easy for him to find another young guy who'll be nice to him like me. It is not so easy for me to find another old man, whom I would like, and who will give me everything I ask for."

Helmut saw three "old men" on a regular basis. His problem was his time allocation and his old men's possessiveness. Like me, Helmut didn't need to work very hard to get good grades, but still, school took up much of his time. The three gentlemen did not know about each other, and each felt that Helmut wasn't seeing them often enough.

"You know what I must do? I must let you have Joe. He is the nicest of the three old men, but he wants too much of my time and has only a little money to give me. He's a retired navy officer, only fifty-seven years old. He gets a big retirement check every month. He says he's financially comfortable, but I must meet someone who is better than comfortable."

"But how do you know that Joe will like me?"

"Oh, he likes young, sexy guys. He calls them 'twinkies.' You'll be his glass of tea. I mean his cup of tea. Do you know that in Europe we sometimes serve tea in a glass?"

"What does he look like?"

"How do you say in English? As…like an officer and a gentleman."

That was more than enough for me. Of course I wanted to meet Joe. But there was a problem. "I won't be eighteen until January," I said.

"I thought only Germans were so pedantic. You'll be eighteen in four months. Tell Joe your birthday is in November."

I didn't know what to make of Helmut. Except for the money thing, we were kindred souls. I was not an awkward nerd to him. He was as intelligent as me, if not more so. What I liked about him was his assertiveness (I was to discover later that he, in turn, was fascinated by my shyness). We complemented each other. Had I finally found a real friend?

When it came to money, my mother, throughout my childhood, behaved like a true hippie. She even said "bread" when she meant money. There should have been enough "bread" to go around, what with all the welfare checks we were receiving, and our odd jobs. It was her lovers who spent their own money on drugs and then had to "borrow" more from my mother to feed their habit. My mother took our poverty for granted.

Not holding wealth in high esteem may have been a trait I acquired from my mother. It would never have occurred to me to make friends with a gentleman for his money. I wanted to meet Joe, who was an officer and a gentleman, for many reasons, money not among them.

* * *

With great gusto, Helmut introduced me to gay life. We drove to San Francisco in his spiffy Fiat convertible. "You see, my dear Eloy,"—he always addressed me in this way, translating the German *mein lieber*—"you're too young to go to gay bars. Not that these bars are great fun. I think they're silly, but it's a good place to meet other gays. Therefore, you must meet your older gentlemen through introductions or through ads. Remember one very important thing. Joe is just contact number one. If you don't like him, there are thousands of other men waiting to meet you. When you're young and cute you can call the shooting."

"I think 'the shots' might be better, Helmut."

*　　　　　*　　　　　*

Joe lived in a high-security building on Post Street in San Francisco's Tenderloin district. Helmut worried about the safety of his convertible as we hunted for a parking space. This wasn't easy, since we arrived late in the afternoon on a Saturday.

Joe McDougall turned out to be a genuine Anglo. He was tall, with just a trace of a mid-life bulge. His hair was light brown, contrasted by his gray temples. He had a ruggedly handsome face, with a small, neatly trimmed mustache. He embraced and kissed Helmut, but shook hands with me formally.

Teaching math to the children of wealthy Marin county residents gave me an opportunity to see elegant and artistic homes. Joe's apartment was different. There was a place for everything, and everything was in its place. It was a no-nonsense apartment without frills. I was to find out later that it reflected Joe's character. Helmut had planned every detail of the operation. After we chatted for a while, he said, "I have to a return a video I borrowed from a friend. I'll be back in an hour; then we can go out for dinner."

Years later, I think during the Desert War in Iraq, I became familiar with the concept of debriefing. During our first meeting Joe conducted such a debriefing, a skill he must have acquired when he was an officer in the navy. He did it methodically rather than conversationally. He seemed to mentally file the information I gave him. By the time he was through with me, which coincided with Helmut's return, he had a pretty good idea of what I was all about. I answered all his questions reluctantly but truthfully, though I fudged a bit about my age.

It took me much longer to learn more about Joe. Later on I found out that he had been a pilot in the U.S. Navy, and retired from the service with the rank of commander. He was divorced, the father of two children. He had been stationed in Germany, attached to the Navy Liaison Office of NATO for a number of years, and spoke some German. As Helmut had told me, he was more interested in the youthful looks of his partners than their ethnic backgrounds. He made no secret about his instant attraction to me.

My feelings toward Joe were mixed. Physically, he was an appealing man. In his bedroom hung a framed a photo of him in dress uniform taken just before he left the service. I liked it so much that I had to force myself not to ask for a copy. On the other hand, I found him somewhat meddlesome. He wanted to know more about me than I was ready to divulge. Later I discovered that lots of gays attended discussion groups and enjoyed "sharing." I was a very private person. Actually, I had few secrets, since my life had been so uneventful. At that time, though, I was reluctant to share what little of me there was to dissect.

Exactly how it came about, I do not know. By some tacit agreement between the three of us, Helmut returned to Berkeley by himself, I stayed in San Francisco, and Joe promised to drive me to Berkeley Monday morning. He cooked a spaghetti and vegetable dinner for us, and then led me to the bedroom.

* * *

As I am writing this, twelve years later, I still cannot believe that Helmut's plan worked out so perfectly. On Tuesdays and Thursdays, after my work at the library, I would take the BART train from Berkeley to San Francisco. When the train was on time, I would arrive at the Civic Center Station at 6:43, where Joe would wait for me in his car. We would dine together at home or in a restaurant, and I would stay the night. The next morning, Joe would drive me to Berkeley in time for my first class. On weekends, I would arrive early on Saturday morning. I would use Joe's PC to write my papers until late in the afternoon. Saturday nights and Sundays we would go out, and on Monday, early in the morning, he would drive me to Berkeley.

Joe had a routine for everything. It was easy, even comforting, for me to fall in with his routines. In my childhood, everything in my life was topsy-turvy. As soon as I became a student and was on my own, things seemed to fall into place perfectly.

I was surprised by Joe's instantaneous switch from Helmut to me. I asked him about it. "It is not as complicated as you make it out, Eloy. I would have preferred a boyfriend who was less busy than Helmut. But he and I had excellent sex, he was an interesting companion, and I'm used to German guys. He told me that you wouldn't be as busy as a third-year chemical engineering student, and I'd be able to see more of you. I am not as naive as Helmut thinks. I have known all along that there were other men in his life."

"Didn't that bother you?"

"Yes, it did. But it also gave me the justification for getting it on with other guys. I hope that we'll have a monogamous relationship."

I knew absolutely nothing about the gay lifestyle. At the time, I wouldn't even have been able to answer the simple question, "Is Joe your lover?" We saw each other regularly, and had sex every night we were together. When we met Joe's friends, he always introduced me as Eloy. Sometimes, on the phone, he would say something like "My boy Eloy has just arrived." He never used the term "lover," and I did not refer to us as a couple.

I never asked Joe for anything. I needed little for myself, and it wasn't in my nature to ask anyone for help. Joe spent a lot on clothes and gadgets. We went shopping together quite often, and he would sometimes buy me a shirt or a sweater. Within half a year, my shabby wardrobe became stylish. Fellow students would sometimes compliment me on my clothes. Joe also bought me a portable stereo and many music tapes.

Once I asked Joe why he spent so much money on me. "Look, Eloy, I receive a generous pension. In a few years, I will also get a monthly Social Security check. If I have the money, I like spending some of it on you. It's a lot more enjoyable for me to do it on my own than being hustled into it by Helmut."

"You knew that?"

"Of course. You really do become wiser as you grow older. Look, when I was married, my wife almost drove me into bankruptcy with her shopping sprees. I've always been a provider. I'll say this for Helmut, he hustled me nicely. I don't mind Helmut living well, driving an expensive sports car, or dressing sharply. What bothers me is when someone tells me to give them money for sex."

"What is the difference whether you pay someone's phone bill or give them money?"

"Very big difference. Not mathematically—emotionally. To help a student out is one thing. I can always refuse to pay for an item I don't approve of. To exchange sex for money is a different matter."

During my first year in Berkeley I visited my mother a total of four times. This was at Joe's insistence. "She is your mother, Eloy, you can't just drop her," he told me early in our relationship.

The second or third time I visited her she said, "My, you've grown. Something in you has changed. Look at the way you dress. Where do you get the money to look so sharp?"

"From an old man in San Francisco." As usual, my mother did not really listen. My answer did not even draw a raised eyebrow.

Compared to most other gays, Joe had an uncomplicated relationship with his family. He was not "out to them" in a formal way. When visiting his children, he would simply take "my boy Eloy" along. We stayed in San Diego with his son's family, and in San Luis Obispo with his daughter. His family seemed to like me. When Joe's sister and her husband visited him in San Francisco and stayed the weekend in his apartment, Joe handled the situation as if our relationship was the most natural thing in the world. When I arrived at Joe's apartment, having walked from the train station, Joe simply introduced me as "my boy Eloy." His guests slept in the living room and, as always, I slept with him in his bed. Before they left, his brother-in-law even invited me to stay with his family in San Louis Obispo.

But Joe's attempts to introduce me to the gay lifestyle were less successful, both on the social and the physical level. Joe liked to dance, and assumed that a young guy like me would, too. Because I was a minor, we had to go to great lengths to sneak me into a disco. The Aquarius, on Folsom Street, had a mixed crowd of gays, bi's, and straights. Many of them did drugs. The club made a big profit on the high cover charge on weekends. The entrance to the bar was pitch dark. When the cashier worked alone, before ten o'clock, he could not make out the faces of the people he let in. He was joined by a bouncer precisely at ten.

Joe knew all of this from previous experience. Like a military maneuver, we would arrive at the Aquarius at precisely 9:50 and be let in. Since I never drank anything stronger than a Calistoga mineral water, and Joe was a generous tipper, the waiters did not mind me.

The disco did not really come to life until much later, and Joe wanted to stay until closing. I hated the place. I have two explanations for my attitude. First, I was a loner and felt uncomfortable and awkward in crowds. Second, because of my mother's lovers, I had developed a real hatred toward drugs. This anti-drug feeling extended to smoking and drinking.

But it wasn't only the smoking and drinking and drugs. How can I put it without sounding like a pompous young ass? I did not approve of my generation's music and dancing. When I read Plato's dialogues, I came across Socrates' negative opinion of the dancing and singing of the youth of his day. It excited me strangely that I, like old Socrates in ancient Athens, also didn't approve of the singing and dancing of the young. By definition, popular music is what appeals to the majority of listeners. I took pride in being in the minority. I suppose I could have danced reasonably well to the horribly loud and ugly music at the Aquarius, but I refused to engage in this nonsense. I just did not want to be like the other buffoons on the floor. I must confess, and now I feel ashamed of it, that in my mind I referred to them as "fags" and "queers," as if I were somehow different.

Joe was upset by my negative attitude and refusal to dance. He took it as an implied criticism of his own behavior. "I'm almost three times your age, have been straight for most of my life, and I enjoy dancing up a storm with a gay crowd. What gives with you?"

"I don't know, Joe. I want to be with you, not with a bunch of…crazies." I checked myself in time not to say something more offensive.

"Crazies? Do you think that you are better than these guys?"

Good question. I didn't think I was better than Joe and his friends. Rather, I knew that I was more intelligent than they were, and therefore very different. The antics of Joe's young companions were of little interest to me. Joe's older friends talked about things that were meaningless to me: the prices of homes and cars, the stock market, health problems, and, more than anything else, about their twinkies.

I never understood exactly what they meant when they called someone a twinkie. Helmut said it characterized guys who were cute, sexy, and fresh, though not necessarily handsome. Joe's older companions considered me a "major twinkie," though they deplored my reserve and criticized me for "giving attitude."

Joe's younger friends (often the twinkies of his older friends) and I definitely didn't get along. They were a motley group, and came in various colors and shapes, but they were all young. By vocation they ranged from dishwashers to graduate students. Quite a few of them were from other countries.

In my student days I could pick up a philosophy book and read it just to amuse myself. These twinkies were not into serious reading. Most of them were far from stupid; they just tried to avoid unnecessary mental exertion. They gossiped endlessly about other twinkies and talked about boyfriends, bars, actors, clothes, and jewelry, all of which bored the daylights out of me.

After a few unsuccessful forays to the Aquarius, Joe gave up on me as a dancing partner. I am afraid that I also failed him physically. The second time I was with him he tried to penetrate me. The idea appealed to me, but the physical act was something else again. "Just relax, Eloy, and let it happen," he scolded me.

I didn't know how you could relax when you were experiencing excruciating pain. "Don't make such a big issue out of it, Eloy. If there's enough Vaseline on my dick and in your ass, the rest is just good relaxation technique."

"If it is so easy for you, then why don't you let me screw you?"

I really had no desire to screw Joe. It annoyed me, though, that he expected me to do something that he refused to consent to. "It's different for me. I don't like to get screwed. You told me that you liked the idea of being fucked," he answered.

During our first month together we tried it in every conceivable position. Only once did Joe manage to climax inside me. I was in so much agony that I said something that surprised myself as much as Joe. "If you try this once again, Joe, I'll stop visiting you."

Joe wanted me to take a weekend workshop called "Upping Your Pleasure: The Yoga of Anal Penetration." The instructor had also written a book by the same title. I refused to take the workshop. I was not going to deal with my anal problems in front of a whole class. We argued a lot about it. Finally, Joe had me meet the instructor for a private consultation.

The instructor turned out to be a regular guy in his thirties. He was also a yoga teacher. I say he was a regular guy because I expected some weirdo. I explained to him that the notion of being penetrated appealed to me, but the physical act was more than I could bear. "The spirit is willing but the flesh is weak, eh?" he commented. "If you do all the exercises in my book, you'll be able to take the biggest cock up your ass and get to enjoy it."

In the style of the day, the first chapter of his book was about "making agreements with your asshole." The text started with the instruction to, "Look at your asshole in the mirror, and see how perfectly shaped it is. Sense the pleasure this beautiful orifice can give you. Now make a solemn agreement not to hurt it. The asshole, in return, will agree to allow you to experience pleasure by relaxing...by opening as wide as is necessary...by being open to receive a visitor. Open to receive and to give pleasure."

I performed all the breathing and visualization exercises in the book. I did, or at least tried to do, all the physical exercises, most of which were yoga of some sort. Though I thought the process was ridiculous, I tried to perform perfectly the most important exercise, the *uddiyana bandha*. According to the book, this would not only relax my anal sphincter but also enhance my pleasure during penetration.

A few weeks later I allowed Joe to screw me so we could try out my new skills. When he entered me I followed all the complicated procedures the book had taught me. I breathed correctly, visualized widely and wildly, and pressed down. It still hurt like hell. I did not want to go on with it. Joe's observation, "No pain, no gain," infuriated me.

Joe finally gave up on screwing me. He told me, "If I can't get what I need from you, why then, I'll have to get it from a stranger. You've only yourself to blame, Eloy."

Joe's seeing other people caused quite a bit of tension between us. Still, we stuck with each other for a whole year. Looking back at all of this, I wonder why Joe put up with me. Why had he stayed with someone he couldn't screw, who would not go dancing with him, and who was socially awkward?

I believe the answer lay in what his friend Monty called the "Eloy Paradox." Joe's older friends expected their twinkies to be weak and helpless, just as my mother wanted her lovers to be. They would cluck their disapproval of the messes their twinkies made, which needed to be straightened out by the older guys. But Joe was attracted to twinkies for their looks, not for their weaknesses. Both Helmut and I were self-sufficient, and Joe may very well have been attracted to us because of this quality.

With the exception of anal penetration, Joe and I made for compatible sex partners. And because it was so difficult for me to be penetrated, I did not catch what was then called GRID and, within in a very short time, became known as AIDS.

3

Twinkie Swapping

In describing my first year in Berkeley, I am tempted to write that it was an uneventful period in my life. But how could becoming independent, starting college, and being introduced to gay life be considered uneventful?

My studies, the job at the library, and my visits with Joe kept me in a comforting routine. I liked almost everything that happened to me. For instance, traveling with Joe to Southern California to visit with his family was a new experience that was enjoyable rather than threatening. Taking two new math courses in the second semester was an interesting challenge. How different all of this was, compared to my crazy life with my mother in Fairfax.

I did well for myself in my math courses in the first semester. I got A's in them without much work on my part. For me, they were like a continuation of high school. I was itching to get into philosophy, but had to wait until my second year, when I would be able to take Dr. Brotbaum's introductory course.

My most interesting experience was with my German course. I had always assumed that my success in learning Spanish was related to Maximiliano's efficient teaching and my attraction to him. I was not aware that I had a talent for learning languages.

Helmut was so impressed by my rapid learning of German, and by my good pronunciation, that he practiced with me on a weekly basis. With so much drilling, by the end of the first semester my German was far better than Joe's. At the end of the semester the instructor suggested that I skip one level and enroll in German III.

"My dear Eloy," Helmut told me, "with your Spanish and English, and my French, and now that both of us speak German, we can travel all over Europe next summer."

"Even if I had money for the ticket, how would I survive in Europe?"

"My dear Eloy, for a bright guy you're very naive. How do you think I managed my visit to Hawaii last year?"

"Well, tell me."

"I left San Francisco with just enough money for three nights at a cheap hotel and for incidentals. You don't smoke, so this isn't an issue for you, but I always pay for my own cigarettes—no old man must pay for them. When I'm sending my many postcards to Germany, I also must pay for them. But the rest…" Here he moved his arms broadly, dismissing the problem altogether.

"But how do you find an old man just when you need him?" Though I did not particularly care for Helmut's way of referring to his mature friends, I started using his expressions.

"This is what I did. I went to Hula's, which is an important gay bar in Waikiki. Many surfer types cruised me, but I cruised the old men. A few surfers actually started talking with me immediately, because I am so handsome and so…"

"And so modest," I said.

"No, not modest. Why must I be modest? I'm handsome, and very bright, and so are you. Let's both make hay while the sun shines! Well, the old men are shy about approaching a young male. So, boldly, I walk over and speak to them. They're so proud that a beautiful and smart young guy cruises them! So I just make conversation. I now must find an old man with whom I can stay and who has a car. I must not make sex with just any old man.

"The best old men are the ones who are used to having and spending lots of money. Not like Joe, who will prepare a budget before leaving on a trip. A merchant, a lawyer, or a dentist is fine. The lawyer I chose at the bar paid for the hotel, the meals, our flights to two other islands, and the car rental. Maybe $1,000 in one week. He left me a sealed envelope with another $350 because I was going to stay another week on my own."

"But did you like the lawyer?"

"My dear Eloy, the lawyer was a fat man over sixty. After he went home, I made sex with three young guys for the next week. The sex was OK with them, but they were not interesting to me. I like old men; if I can please them physically, it makes me feel powerful. If I have good sex and good company with an old man who must pay for everything, what I must look for is a young…dude. Is this correct?"

"It's OK."

"Well, then, you like old men just like me. Maybe more, because you never make sex with young guys. We go to Europe, see everything for free, and have good companions. What is the problem?"

I knew that I would not be able to travel to Europe with Helmut at the end of the school year. It was not only that I did not have the money. I also did not feel prepared to take on Europe and, for a want of a better word, hustle my way through the continent. Maybe, I thought, I could do it after my sophomore year.

*   *   *

Upon reflection, I realized that Helmut's cold-blooded analysis of old-versus-young was accurate. In Joe's circle, the twinkies and their masters pretty much acted according to Helmut's script. They just did not put it into words.

For example, in my case, "old man" Joe had to pay if he wanted us to do things together. We did not eat in very fancy restaurants when we went out, but still, I would not have been able to pay my own way. Twice when we traveled together we stayed at expensive hotels. Of course, Joe paid the entire bill. I could not have afforded to pay my share. If we were to go to Hawaii, a subject we had discussed, Joe would have to pay more than Helmut's old man. After all, he would also have to buy my ticket.

Maybe there was a slight difference in these cases. Joe and I were boyfriends; Helmut picked up older men who were strangers. But maybe this was only a technicality. I would find it more difficult than Helmut to pick up strangers just for sex. What I appreciated most about my relationship with Joe was his companionship. I would have been happy just to sleep next to him. He needed to have sex every time we were together.

I learned a bit about sex with strangers at Joe's instigation. After a few months with him it became obvious, from his phone conversations, that he was seeing other guys when I was not in town. His justification was that I would not allow him to screw me.

Once, when we had words about it, he said, "Look, Eloy, when Anton lived with me, we used to go to the bathhouse together. I was going to suggest to you that we do the same thing. This way you could gain more sexual experience. Who knows, you might find a better teacher than me, and learn how to get screwed.

"But with the GRID thing, I don't want to take chances, especially not with you; it seems to hit young men more than the older ones. Everybody says that multiple partners and anonymous sex are the cause of GRID. So why don't we go to the Monkey's Paw, and both of us will pick up a partner for the night. One partner is different from the many guys we would meet in a bathhouse. Anton and I called it twinkie-swapping."

Anton had been Joe's boyfriend in Germany. He visited Joe in San Francisco and stayed for almost a year. From the many Anton stories Joe told me, I believed him to be very promiscuous.

In the beginning, it was surprising that Joe, not a big drinker, felt the urge to go to a gay bar at least once a week. It took me a while to understand the various roles bars played in gay life. The Monkey's Paw, on Polk Street, was a twinkie pick-up bar. I thought it was a sad place, though Joe and his friends, young and old, raved about it. Instead of loud disco music, it featured a piano player. The clientele was evenly divided between older Caucasian men, and young guys from all over the globe. A young Vietnamese would just as likely be found there as a Canadian.

The Monkey's Paw was Joe's favorite bar. It was probably the only gay bar that would allow me in. The establishment was really a restaurant and a bar. Joe and I would take our dinner in the restaurant, and then walk from the dining room into the bar. The bar did not have a bouncer, but it would not do having customers under twenty-one walk in from the street. By coming in from the restaurant, our entrance was more discreet. Joe told me to stand at the back of the bar, but I was, of course, seen by the waiters who circulated in the crowd. Since I was with Joe and—as always—drank only Calistogas, they chose to ignore me.

I detested that bar for all the inane chitchat between the older men and the twinkies. But I was not always successful in dissuading Joe from going to the Monkey's Paw. The few times we went there, the older men were all over me, trying to lure me away from Joe. He, too, was overly friendly with the twinkies. After months of arguing, one Saturday night I told Joe, "OK, let's do the twinkie-swapping thing, though I think it's dumb."

We entered the bar separately from the dining room. By the time I ordered a Calistoga from a waiter who knew me, the first swallow arrived at my side. He was a pleasant older man with a protruding belly, maybe fifty-five years old. Less than five minutes elapsed between the moment he introduced himself to me as Henry, and the point at which he asked me to go home with him. Since I wanted to get out of the bar, I took him up on his offer. I finished my Calistoga, and left the Monkey's Paw with him. Joe was too busy cruising a Hispanic guy to notice my departure. I imagined that Henry and I would spend the evening together, talking or listening to music or whatever, eventually going to bed, and, if we liked each other, having sex.

Henry had other plans. He lived on Post Street, just a few blocks away from the Monkey's Paw. He let me into a studio apartment. A sofa bed occupying about one-third of the room had already been pulled out, in readiness for sex. He pointed to a chair in the corner. "You can put your clothes here," he said, as he started undressing.

"But," I said, "I…"

"No problem. Here's a hanger," he said, handing me one.

Well, I thought to myself, let's see how this will work out; maybe instant sex will not be so bad after all. In a few minutes, we were naked and in bed. He French-kissed me right away, and then went down on me for a short while. I suppose it would have been an enjoyable experience, had he not been in such a hurry. But I did not get a chance to consider this issue. Henry reached under the pillow and came out with a quarter coin. "We'll toss for it," he said.

"Toss?" I asked.

"Yes, your call."

Mystified, I called, "Heads."

Henry tossed the coin. It landed on the floor. Henry looked at it, and said gleefully, "Tails, you lose. I go first, then you."

"What're you talking about, Henry?"

"First I fuck you, then you fuck me."

"I don't screw, and I don't get screwed."

"Oh, that's OK. I don't believe in using condoms but, if you insist, we'll do it the new way."

"No, Henry, I don't screw or get screwed with or without a condom."

"You don't get screwed or screw?"

"Affirmative," I said, imitating Joe's speech.

I have always wondered how one cuts one's loses. Now Henry showed me. "It's OK, it's OK," he said soothingly, as if I were under some terrible strain. "We'll just put our clothes on again. Nice and easy. No hurry, none whatsoever." As he spoke, he kept dressing like a fireman when the alarm sounds. He kept looking at me to see whether I was following his example. "Now then, we'll just walk back to the Monkey's Paw. It's still quite early. You don't need to worry. Each of us will find a compatible partner. Just nice and easy."

While I wanted to get the hell out of Henry's place, the return to the bar posed a number of problems for me. I did not know whether I would be let in coming from the street. If Joe was still there he would gloat over my failure. His debriefing would pinpoint the exact cause of the evening's fiasco. If Joe had already left, presumably with a twinkie in tow, where would I spend the night? I saw only one possibility: going back to Berkeley on the train and returning Sunday morning. At the bar's entrance, I told Henry, "I want to get some fresh air before going in."

"Suit yourself," he said, as he entered the bar. He seemed happy to have gotten rid of me.

I stood there for a barely a minute. A tall, lanky man with a high-pitched voice addressed me. "Hello there. Nice evening."

The stranger was a good ten years younger than Henry. He stared at me through thick lenses. We talked about the weather for a few moments. Then he said, "My name is Roger, what's yours?"

"Eloy."

"Are you working tonight, Eloy?"

Working? I thought. Maybe he thinks I'm a bartender. No, I'm too young to be one. Then, in a flash, it dawned on me: I was standing, forlornly, opposite the hustler strip on Polk Street. He had asked, in a polite way, whether I was hustling tonight.

Since Roger's question was followed by such a long silence on my part, he must have assumed that I was too embarrassed to answer. Sweetly he said, "Don't worry about it, Eloy. We all have to make a living. I understand your situation, and I'll take care of you. Would you like to come home with me?"

I was afraid that Joe and his twinkie for the night would come out of the bar at any moment, and I did not wish to go back to Berkeley. Staying the night with Roger was fine with me.

Roger lived on Ivy Street, which was a ten-minute walk. He wanted to know everything about me. Inexplicably, I did not feel comfortable telling him that I was a freshman at UC Berkeley. "I live in the Mission District with my parents. I was born in León, Guanajuato, in Mexico, and we came to this country when I was two years old. I work as a messenger for a law firm." I came up with this particular story because a fellow student had just gotten such a part-time job.

"You're new to hustling, aren't you? I haven't seen you on the street before."

"It's only my second time." After all, I did get paid once before, I reasoned with myself. "My parents are mad at me, and I have no place to stay the night. And," I added for dramatic effect, "I'm hungry."

"Don't worry about a thing. You can eat at my place and stay the night." Even now, as I am writing this, I cannot believe that I had the nerve to put on that kind of act. But I was mad at Joe, and I really wanted to be bad. See, Joe, what your boy Eloy can do?

Roger lived in a flat in a ramshackle house. It was clean, though sparsely furnished. The walls had not been painted in years, and the Venetian blinds over the windows were tattered. Roger immediately set about preparing a sandwich for me. While waiting for the food, I noticed an open German textbook on the table and almost gave the show away. It was one of these self-teaching texts in which learners can check their exercises against the correct answers. I found a few mistakes Roger had made in verb conjugation, and pointed them out to him.

"Where did you study German?" he asked in his feminine voice.

"I'm taking a German course at City College."

"How long have you been studying German?"

"I'm just starting my second semester."

"You're doing pretty well for yourself. Are you taking any other courses?"

"Yes. A math course."

"You speak Spanish too?"

"Some."

"You're a pretty smart boy, Eloy. You shouldn't be hustling. I know the guys on Polk Street, and they can be bad news. It's not that they're bad. It's their involvement with drugs that fucks them up. Do you do drugs, Eloy?"

"I try not to." I noticed that I was enjoying my role-playing. The Eloy I was representing probably did do drugs. I regretted that I had told him my real name. It would have been easier had I given him a stage name, maybe in Spanish.

"What drugs do you do, Eloy?"

"Oh, some speed every now and then; pot, quite often. LSD once in a while. I don't shoot up, and I don't do smack." Was it really Eloy, saying all of this stuff? I wondered.

After Roger served me a tuna sandwich and a glass of milk, he motioned me to take my clothes off. As we undressed, I wondered whether the evening's previous scene would repeat itself.

He did not turn the lights out. When I was completely naked he examined my body. "You're so handsome, so beautiful. How come you're circumcised?"

I knew that Mexicans were uncut. But I was not really Mexican. My mother had told me many years ago, "I am so sorry, Harmony, that I let them mutilate you." She called me Harmony only when she felt guilty about something that she, or more frequently, one of her lovers, had done to me.

"Who mutilated me, and why?" I had asked her.

"They cut off your foreskin at the hospital, Harmony. You're Jewish, you know. The religion goes through the mother. They do that to little Jewish babies." I believe my mother made up the Jewish thing on the spur of the moment. Most likely, I was circumcised because it was the custom when I was born. I can't recall why my mother brought up that subject. But I wished then that mom would finally tell me what religion we belonged to.

To Roger I said, "It was an operation done here at General Hospital for a tight foreskin." Fast thinking, Eloy, I congratulated myself.

Roger had three sexual acts on his mind. He kissed me, then licked my body, and then blew me. I pretended to myself that I was a hustler. I observed myself going through the sex motions. It was like the job at the library, I thought. Just a task I had to perform—neither good nor bad. Who was I kidding? I climaxed the first time a few minutes after Roger started blowing me. It took both of us by surprise. Then, after another long session of kissing, licking, and blowing, Roger lay on top of me and rubbed his body against mine. "Arch your back to give me more friction," he said. He climaxed all over me.

"What's that called?"

"What?"

"The way you just came."

"Oh, the Princeton Rub. The scientific word is frottage."

Roger cleaned me with a paper towel, but I still felt sticky and gooey. I needed to go to sleep. I would take my shower in the morning. Roger, however, had different ideas. He kept blowing and licking me, causing me to climax once again. By then we must have been at it for well over two hours. "Roger, I need to sleep."

"You can sleep, baby. I am just making love to your handsome body and beautiful dick."

"Roger, I can't fall asleep while you're sucking me."

"Sure you can, baby."

He was right. I must have fallen asleep right away. I dreamed that my penis was hurting, and that it was as big as a watermelon. When I opened my eyes, the room was flooded with daylight. I put my right hand on my penis, and it *was* as huge as a melon. No, the melon was Roger's head. He had fallen asleep with my dick in his mouth. When I touched his head he woke up. “Oh, Eloy, I’m so sorry. I fell asleep blowing you.”

I took a shower and dressed. Roger made breakfast for us. By now it was 9 AM on a Sunday morning. I fumbled in my pockets for change so I could call Joe and tell him that I would be home soon. I could not call him from Roger’s place and pretend to be speaking to my parents. There were some bills in my right pocket that had not been there yesterday. I took out two twenties.

Roger said, “I know it was an overnight call, but staying the night was really your idea. I can only pay you for an hour’s work. That’s all the money I can give you. Here’s my phone number,” he said, handing me a piece of paper. “If you need some money, call me. Don’t hang out on the street.”

I was so embarrassed that I barely managed to thank him as I walked out.

* * *

How shall I put it? I took notice of the forty dollars given to me in exchange for sexual favors? Nowadays, I would probably say that a new file, named “sex = money,” was opened in my mind. It struck me that it would have taken me eight hours to make forty dollars working at the library, and then it would be income subject to deductions. Roger said that this was what he paid a hustler for an hour’s worth of work. But while I was assimilating this new information, I was also experiencing anger against Joe. Against his promiscuity in general, and his twinkie-swapping in particular.

How did I know that Mexicans were not circumcised? Thanks to G.I.F. (Gay International Friends), an organization Joe belonged to, I knew which countries practiced circumcision, the age at which it was done, and why. This information, and similar useless trivia, was what the "mature" GIF twinkie masters talked about. The twinkies busied themselves with organizing nitwitted activities, like gala drag evenings.

Joe was one of the founders of GIF, and currently its secretary. He had bought his PC for his GIF work. In theory, the organization was for contacts between gays from all over the world. In practice, the majority of the older members were middle-class Caucasians, and the majority of the twinkies were from the Far East, Mexico, and Central America.

GIF's perpetual president was Donny, an aging, effeminate, Indonesian-Eurasian twinkie. He tried, unsuccessfully, to recruit European twinkies as members. For undetermined reasons, it was Asian and Latino twinkies who were at home at GIF. I myself was an oddity. Unlike the other twinkies, I was a native English speaker who did not need GIF for social contacts. That I was the youngest member, and cute and smart to boot, did not make me popular with my fellow twinkies. Joe was one of the few members who were not gaga for Asians. Since he could not afford trips to Germany, he went to Puerto Vallarta or Acapulco for his vacations. In spite of the fact that he could not speak a word of Spanish—or because of it, who knows?—he met lots of twinkies in Mexico. The other mature members would make their annual pilgrimages to more remote twinkie lands, especially Thailand and the Philippines.

Honestly, GIF did have a rap session about circumcision! It was held at Joe's apartment, so I had to attend. I learned that in Muslim countries, like Indonesia and Malaysia, boys were circumcised around thirteen; that Japan had begun to follow the American custom after the occupation, and most babies there were circumcised; and that in other countries in the Far East circumcision was not practiced. The mystery was why, in the Philippines, a Catholic country, practically all boys were circumcised around twelve years of age. South of the US border, in Latin countries, children were not cut.

One of GIF's most obnoxious members was Jerome, a grossly obese lawyer in his fifties. Though he was universally disliked, he was an influential member. He was the editor of the GIF monthly bulletin, a job that had no other takers. Once a month, GIF had a rap session. At the end of each session, the next month's topic was decided. Once, Jerome suggested that the group discuss "The Fungibility of Twinkies" at the next meeting.

"What is fungibility?" a member asked.

"Sugar, for instance, is fungible," Jerome answered. "You borrow one sack of sugar from me today, and it'd be OK for you to repay me with another sack of the same quality of sugar next month. It doesn't need to be the original sugar because it is a fungible commodity."

"You're not only nuts, Jerome, you're politically incorrect. You mean to say that twinkie A is fungible for twinkie B?" This comment came from a member who thoroughly disliked Jerome.

"Well, if they're equally cute, then they are fungible. If you want me to be politically correct then I'll say to you that, for the twinkies, we mature men are also fungible. Of course, we need to be equally wealthy."

Jerome's suggestion was voted down. But a new verb was born, and used by all members: to funge. My anger against Joe was that he had funged me for the night. I did see, though, some logic in Jerome's theory. After all, I myself had been funged for Helmut, who, in turn, was a pro at funging his old men.

I was so preoccupied with my thoughts about the previous night that I forgot to call Joe from the street. Fortunately, he was by himself. Grinning like the cat that had just eaten the canary, he said, "I really had a delicious twinkie last night. A Dutch guy, no less. And you? Did you enjoy yourself?"

"Joe, I don't want you to call me a twinkie, and I won't ever be funged again."

"Was it that bad, Eloy?"

"No it was excellent. If you must know, I came twice and the guy wants to see me again. That's all I'm going to tell you. Just don't funge me again."

Joe realized that I was upset. He put his arms around me and said. "Eloy, to me you are not fungible. You know that I love you, don't you?"

He had never said that before. "I love you too, Joe," I said. "Please, Joe, let's not do stupid stuff." I did not tell him, though, about Roger's forty dollars.

4

José Luis Reveals Himself

Toward the end of my second semester, I resolved to travel to Europe the following summer. By then Helmut would have graduated and returned to Germany. He invited me to stay with his family in Wiesbaden. From there we would travel together throughout the continent. I would let Helmut be my guide in coming up with financial resources once we were on our trip.

Angrily, Joe said, "I can't afford to go to Germany because of the low dollar exchange rate. How will you support yourself there?"

"I'll be staying with Helmut. I need money only for the ticket and…" here I thought for a moment, "and incidentals." With my hands, I mimicked Helmut's dismissive gesture.

"I'm sure that Helmut will have a very positive influence on you, especially in helping you with your financial planning," Joe said. I believe he was jealous that I would be able to travel to places that were too expensive for him.

My desire to travel to Europe was enhanced by a strange incident on a trip Joe and I had made to Tijuana during the Memorial Day weekend. After we visited Joe's son in San Diego, we decided to spend two days in Tijuana. Joe did not want to drive in Mexico, so we took the streetcar from downtown San Diego to the border and crossed on foot.

We checked into a hotel in the Zona Rio Tijuana, an upscale neighborhood. As always, when traveling with Joe, we ended up at a shopping mall. Joe bought two pairs of shoes there: one for himself and one for me. The shoes reminded me of Maximiliano, and gave me an inspiration. I would pretend that I came to Tijuana from Maximiliano's hometown of León, Guanajuato, and that I was a native Mexican. It may have been Joe who planted that idea in my head. He had told me before we started our trip, "You'd better take your California and student IDs, and any other documents you have. Otherwise, they'll stop you at the border, thinking you're an illegal Mexican."

I ought to describe here how I maintained the Spanish I had learned from Maximiliano. All of my mother's lovers faithfully watched the Mexican *telenovelas* on the Spanish channels. Though we were poor, as soon as cable television became available, my mother subscribed to it. Unlike American soap operas, the *telenovelas* are real novels that have a beginning and, after many months and a zillion commercials, come to an end. The next night a new *telenovela* commences. In the Spanish "soaps," the bad guys are horribly evil, and the women are much worse.

As soon as I learned enough Spanish from Maximiliano, I got hooked on these programs. They were insipid, but they challenged my Spanish language skills. The only human contact I had with my mother's lovers was when they reminded me that our *telenovela* was about to begin. We would sit there together like an American father and son watching a football game. These programs not only maintained but helped increase my Spanish vocabulary.

I did not have a TV set of my own in Berkeley, and missed my Spanish soaps. When I started feeling comfortable at Joe's, I tried watching some of my *telenovelas* at his place. But Joe had his own TV programs, and resented anything foreign. "You know, Eloy, we're in America. We watch programs in English here," he told me once, when he missed twenty seconds of the beginning of his show because I was watching the end of mine.

Once his show was over I said, "My ancestors came to this continent thousands of years before England and Scotland even existed. Unlike your GIF twinkies, I'm as American as apple pie. And if your people hadn't stolen California from my people, the language here would still be Spanish."

Bemused, Joe replied, "I thought your grandparents landed in New York just before the second world war. No?"

I dismissed this argument. "This was on my mother's side. I was speaking about my father's folks." I knew nothing of my father's family history. But I liked the lines.

Joe solved the TV problem in his usual manner. "If money can help me deal with a problem, then that's what it's for," he said. He bought me a small TV. I watched my Spanish soaps in the bedroom.

In the authentic Mexican ambiance of Tijuana I was, at first, hesitant to speak Spanish. But after a few hours of listening to the language, I was eager to try out my bluff on some gullible natives. My opportunity came later that night.

"Let's go to a twinkie bar," Joe said, after we had eaten dinner.

"And if you meet a major twinkie, what will you do with me?"

"I'll think of something," Joe said.

"I'm sure you will." I agreed to go to the El Tigre disco, where Joe would be able to inspect many of Tijuana's leading twinkies. I planned on testing my Spanish there. We took a taxi to the downtown area and then walked around. Joe knew the area pretty well. Joyfully, he focused on what he took to be eager twinkies eyeing a gringo VIP with lust (more likely greed, as far as I was concerned) in their hearts.

The disco was even noisier than the ones in San Francisco. Joe was surrounded immediately by Tijuana twinkies. To them he must have looked like a stereotypical gringo. Maybe this was why he was so attractive to them. It did not bother him in the least to unscramble the twinkies' broken English.

I usually became tongue-tied in bars, and probably appeared standoffish at the El Tigre. Nobody addressed me, and I spoke to no one. After a while I grew bored. I wanted to meet and talk to regular Mexican folk, not bar twinkies and their gringo patrons. "I'm going for a walk. See you back at the hotel," I said to Joe.

Apparently, he did not mind being on his own. "Do you have money for a taxi?" he asked.

"Don't worry about me. This is my turf. I'll walk back to the hotel."

"Are you crazy, Eloy? Tijuana is a very dangerous place, and our hotel is far from downtown."

But I just walked out. It was a warm night. I took my shirt off and tied it around my waist. I loosened my undershirt, and made a small rip in it. I mussed my hair. "Now I look more roguish," I said to myself. Belatedly, I noticed that a group of young gays in front of the bar was observing my strange behavior. I took off in a hurry. In a few minutes, I was in front of a disco called El Rincón. Joe and I had stopped there earlier to check the place out.

A melancholy, Indian-looking young guy was standing outside the bar. He addressed me immediately. "Cómo te llamas?" he asked.

"José Luis," I answered. A second earlier I had not known that I would come up with a fake name. I had no idea why I did it, or what purpose it would serve.

"My name's Osmar. I'm from Guatemala. Where are you from?"

"From León, Guanajuato. I'm crossing the border tonight." This new fabrication came as a reaction to Osmar's statement that he was from Guatemala. I was certain that he was in Tijuana to smuggle himself into the United States.

"Eres de ambiente?" Osmar asked.

Am I of the ambiance? What could this question mean? After a brief hesitation I said, "Sí, soy de ambiente."

"Here we all are this way, so you can let your hair down," Osmar said. "I too want to cross the border. Maybe we should do it together."

In a flash, it dawned on me. He had asked me, in code, whether I was gay. My *telenovelas* had taught me a lot of Spanish, but not gay code words. If I did not want to give the show away, I should converse only briefly with the people I would meet. Then they wouldn't realize that I was not the Mexican José Luis I pretended to be. We chatted for a moment, and then I said, "Got to run now, see you in LA. Adíos."

"Wait, amigo," Osmar shouted as I ran off. But I was moving fast through the streets, exchanging just a few sentences with all sorts of strangers. I told everyone I spoke to that I was in a hurry because it was my night to cross the border.

Only one man noticed something strange about my speech. "*Es usted* Chicano?" he asked. Well, at least I was taken for an American-born Mexican. Little did he know that I had not spoken Spanish at home in the United States, and that my mother was a self-styled Jewish-Hindu hippie from Brooklyn.

I was so excited by my new role that I walked all the way from downtown to our hotel in the Zona Rio Tijuana. I made it a point to exchange a few words with passersby. Boldly, I flirted with a young woman who happened to be crossing the street at the same time. Were it not for my imminent border-crossing, I told her, the two of us could have had a good time. As José Luis, this was a sincere statement on my part.

The way I was dressed, no self-respecting mugger would have bothered with me. In my excitement, I forgot to tidy up before entering the lobby. The burly hotel guard stopped me immediately.

"What do you want here?" he asked gruffly.

"I'm a guest in this hotel," I answered in Spanish.

He looked at me as if I were mad. "Your room number and your name?"

"My name is Eloy Wise; I'm in room 225. My companion is Joseph McDougall." Though I spoke in Spanish, I betrayed my gringo roots by pronouncing our names the English way. That may have given the guard a clue that I might be a real gringo. With gringos, one never knew. Unlike Mexicans, who dressed to impress others, gringos wore whatever pleased their weird tastes. But the guard was not taking any chances. He asked the receptionist to call Mr. McDougall, though it was close to two in the morning.

When I arrived in the room, Joe asked, "What happened to you, Eloy?" He seemed bewildered. "You look a sight!"

"Nothing happened to me. But me is not me. Me is José Luis. And we had a wonderful time." I was flushed with excitement. Finally, I found out what it meant to be high.

"I don't know what got into you. It's late, and the desk clerk woke me up. I'm going back to bed. We can talk about all of this tomorrow."

As I lay there next to Joe I knew that my introduction to gay life was over. Now I was ready to make my own way. I liked Joe a lot and felt protected by him, but I was certain that our affair would be over soon.

I had read about people with multiple personalities. Was it considered a mental disorder? I wondered. I had already glimpsed another personality at Roger's when I pretended to be a hustler. In Tijuana, a José Luis emerged that had no relation to Eloy. Was it dangerous to have more than one personality? The Eloy who lay there speculated as to when José Luis would reveal himself again. I sensed that I—as Eloy—had little control over any other personality or personalities within me. But Eloy was eager to meet all the other players.

* * *

Outwardly, little had changed between Joe and me. Joe had no interest in getting into his partners' heads just for the exercise. To him, my strange behavior in Tijuana must have been a one-time event, not the dramatic beginning of a new chapter in my life.

We had planned on traveling to Hawaii during my summer vacation. But now I wanted to make money in the summer to save for my trip to Europe the following year. I also planned on taking a German course in the summer. Joe's solution was to find me a summer job in San Francisco, as well as enroll me at the San Francisco extension program of the University of California in Berkeley.

Things were going well for me. The course at the extension was Conversational German IV. It was generous of Joe to come up with the two hundred dollars for tuition. But then, Joe respected my studiousness. By staying with Joe in San Francisco during the summer, I would cut down considerably on my living expenses. My landlady in Berkeley agreed to charge only half the rent for the summer months.

Joe found me a job through what I called the twinkie masters' network. One of Joe's closest friends in San Francisco was Monty Newland, the owner of Global Gay Love Connections, GGLC for short. The job paid $7.50 an hour, and Monty said that he would train me to work on his computers. The good news was that Monty and I got along splendidly; he was a talkative man, given to philosophizing. The bad news was that Donny, the president of GIF, was the office manager.

Monty had established his business some three years earlier. It was a computerized matchmaking center. Needless to say, it matched twinkies to their admirers. Monty had spent most of his working life as a travel agent. Upon retirement, he combined his matchmaking business with his expertise in the travel industry. Monty had found a need, and filled it.

Monty's permanent staff consisted of four foreign-born twinkies. I was hired primarily to work on the Acapulco Gay Connection scheduled for January of the next year. In January, some fifty GGLC clients would descend on Acapulco in search of adventure. There were three hotels to accommodate them, and handsome Mexican guides to shepherd them. The phone calls and faxes to Acapulco would be my responsibility.

In a way, Monty reminded me of Tom, the man who invited me for lunch and then took me to the tricking place. In fact, he could have passed for Tom's older brother. Monty, too, was short, rotund, had a white beard, and looked at the world through thick lenses. Unfortunately, unlike Tom, he wore informal clothes. Starting in springtime, and throughout the summer, completely disregarding San Francisco's cool weather, he dressed in shorts. In spite of his casual appearance, I was attracted to him, and, I am sure, he to me. However, I was "Joe's Boy," and therefore not available to him. In any case, he was watched over by Benjie, his twenty-year-old Filipino lover, who worked at GGLC for the summer. At sixty-one years of age, Monty did not need the many hassles involved in running GGLC. But there was a certain degree of mischief in him. It pleased him that he could make money, a lot of it, out of the frivolity of his customers. He referred to them as clients.

"Pretending to search for a lover gives meaning to our clients' endless dating," Monty told me on my first day at his office. "Instead of just screwing around, their activities become a Quest for the Lover, with a capital Q and a capital L. What is wrong with just plain screwing around?"

Monty may not have been the ideal spokesperson for the screwing-around lobby. Benjie was a fiercely jealous lover who demanded, and got, the strictest monogamy. There had been other Benjie-like jealous lovers in Monty's life. His friends were amazed that guys forty years younger would invariably be so jealous. It should have been the other way—Monty should have been jealous of his youthful boyfriends.

Monty, always the philosopher, addressed this issue one day at the end of the summer: "You wonder why Benjie is so jealous of me? I have had four—no, make it five—lovers like Benjie over a period of thirty-three years. I was twenty-eight when I divorced my second wife and started my gay life. From experience, I know that I'll always be able to find a suitable boyfriend. Young Benjie hasn't had the experience of finding many older men. He has dated only one guy before me."

There was an avuncular relationship between Monty and myself. He enjoyed the role of being my gay mentor. In this respect, he filled a gap in my education. Joe did what Joe enjoyed, never bothering his head about the whys of a given situation. From Monty I learned gay theory.

*　　　*　　　*

To everyone's surprise, including my own, I became a computer ace within a few weeks. Earlier on, Helmut had told me that people were dismayed rather than awed when they witnessed genius at work. My almost instant mastery of the complicated computer system at GGLC delighted Monty. I am sure that he would have made me office manager had I agreed to work for him permanently.

Donny, the office manager, had to consult me when a computer problem arose. He was jealous of me, and not only because I was so much brighter than him. Everybody who came by felt obliged to cruise me. The more standoffish I was, which was easy enough for me to be, the more the visitors tried to make dates with me. Donny's jealousy would have been unpleasant enough, but Benjie, too, watched me like a hawk. He was dismayed by Monty's constant praise of me.

My problem with my fellow twinkies was my complete disdain for what I perceived to be their gay lifestyle: the dancing, the partying, the cruising, the endless gossiping, and the drag. I felt that they went out of their way to be shallow. I did not need or want a gay lifestyle. For me, being gay was primarily an emotional bond and, secondarily, a physical union with an older man. And that was it. I had nothing but contempt for stereotypically gay social activities. The GIF twinkies had a tough time defining me. They could not take away from me my looks or my brains, and regarded me as the ultimate snob. In reality, I may have been just socially awkward or unaware.

But I was not only critical of my fellow twinkies. The older guys also made no sense to me. Joe, afflicted with tinnitus from the propeller noises he had been exposed to for many year as a pilot, went to the discos with cotton balls stuffed in his ears. He was not the only older man to do so. Why, I wondered, would people expose themselves to music they tried to block out?

Early in our relationship, Joe had asked me whether I thought I was better than other gay guys. An honest answer would have been, "Not better, but more logical." It was my impression that GIF members young and old participated in activities they did not care for. This struck me as foolishness.

* * *

My first college summer vacation turned out to be successful in every respect. I did quite well in my German class. I waited impatiently to show off my conversational skills to Helmut. He had gone off to Key West and the Caribbean with one of his old men. From there he was going to fly to Europe, where he would spend the summer with his family.

I considered giving up math and majoring in German, though Monty urged me to take up computer science. For the coming fall semester, I had Dr. Brotbaum's philosophy course and beginning German literature lined up. Just for the heck of it, I enrolled in a computer programming course as well. When Monty saw my new class schedule, he offered me a part-time job at GGLC. He suggested that I work at the office on Tuesdays and Fridays from four until eight in the evening at $8.25 an hour. The offer, and my acceptance of it, infuriated Benjie. It was understood that part of the time I would work alone after the office closed. However, Benjie knew that Monty often worked late. It was quite likely that at times he and I would be alone together.

Benjie had little to worry about. I enjoyed Monty's company because he was the brightest of the twinkie masters, and had interesting insights into gay life. But I was not going to be unfaithful to Joe with his best friend. I resigned my library job, and accepted Monty's offer. Joe was content with this new arrangement. It would give him two additional nights with me each week.

By the end of the summer, I knew that I would have the funds to travel to Europe the next year.

5

Harmony Makes Himself Known

Dr. Brotbaum's course, "The History of Philosophy," was held in a hall accommodating some two hundred students. His course was immensely popular, but it took me a while to understand why. When he entered the lecture hall, I perceived him to be an ungainly man. He was of medium height, thin, and somewhat stooped. With no regard for the warm September weather, he wore a black suit much too large for his frame. His face was gaunt, his black hair thinning, and his nose long and pointed. He had a mild case of acne; these teenage pimples looked incongruous on his face.

When Dr. Brotbaum started speaking, his accent reminded me immediately of Helmut's speech pattern. But there was an additional singsong quality in Dr. Brotbaum's speech that I could not identify. As often as not, he pronounced *th* like an *s*. I am not sure everybody understood that, when Dr. Brotbaum spoke of "esics," he was referring to ethics.

"To study the history of philosophy," Dr. Brotbaum started, "just to learn which philosopher held what views would be of little value. More important would be to know how the philosophers' views affected the world they lived in, and what influence their thinking had on future generations.

"Throughout history philosophers did, indeed, have an immense influence on mankind, or, as fashion dictates, I should say on 'humankind.'

That this is true you can observe for yourselves simply by looking at the countries belonging to the communist bloc. Whose philosophy is the official cornerstone of the various communist regimes?" At this point Dr. Brotbaum stopped his discourse, raised his head, and looked at us expectantly. In my experience, no other instructor posed questions when dealing with so many students.

From the floor came a number of answers: Lenin, Stalin, and Marx. "It is Karl Marx, a graduate of Jena University in Germany, whose philosophy is officially acknowledged as the cornerstone of present-day communism. Marx received his doctorate for his thesis on Epicurus, whose philosophy we shall study. What English noun is derived from Epicurus?"

Again he looked expectantly at us. Timidly, I raised my hand. No other students had raised theirs. Dr. Brotbaum nodded in my direction. "Epicure." I said. Dr. Brotbaum repeated my comment to the entire class so they would all hear what I said. "Very good, Mister…?"

"Wise," I said. "E. Harmony Wise." I had no idea why I said this. I had never, ever, done so before.

"And, Mr. Wise, what does 'epicure' mean?" he asked.

"A person with refined tastes," I replied.

"Correct, Mr. Wise."

"Take another philosopher. He was the spiritual father of the human potential movement, and of all these fashionable consciousness-raising seminars. Who was he?"

Nobody knew. "I'll give you a hint," Dr. Brotbaum said. "He was a Frenchman."

My hand went up. Dr. Brotbaum nodded to me. "Jean Jacques Rousseau?" My answer was more of a question.

"Very good, Mr. Wise." He remembered my name!

"It would behoove us, as we are studying Rousseau, to examine whether he himself conducted his life according to his teachings. To do otherwise would be treating philosophers differently than, say, politicians. As a matter of fact, Rousseau, who had an enormous influence on modern education, gave away his newborn children like so many unwanted kittens."

As Dr. Brotbaum continued weaving history, philosophy, and language into an ever-expanding tapestry of knowledge, I started to understand why he was so popular with students. He gave his entire lecture without looking at any notes. He appeared to be prompted by an invisible device. He never uttered an "ah," resorted to a gratuitous "you know," or stopped in mid-sentence to collect his thoughts. His way of teaching mesmerized me. I wanted to become a sponge, absorbing all the knowledge gushing out of Dr. Brotbaum.

"Many philosophers have held that the purpose of philosophy is to philosophize," Dr. Brotbaum said. "Socrates, the father of dialectic philosophy, interpreted the role of the philosopher more actively. He became, in his own words, a gadfly, trying to force the citizens of Athens to think properly. He wanted, he said, to be like a midwife, helping others give birth to their own ideas. His enemies swatted the gadfly. They charged Socrates with teaching subversive ideas to the young. For doing that he was condemned to death.

"We shall be studying the history of philosophy. In this course we concern ourselves mostly with Western philosophies. Yet you must not imagine that the forefathers of Western philosophy are merely dead thinkers. Their ideas live on, and influence us daily. Plato was Socrates' student and disciple, and the founding father of Western Philosophy. In his *Republic*, he described an ideal state, a place that did not then, and most likely never would, exist. This kind of place we call a…?"

Dr. Brotbaum looked expectantly at the students. Two hands went up, mine and another student's. Dr. Brotbaum recognized a female student. "Utopia," she said.

"Utopia is correct. The etymology of this word is Greek, though the word itself was coined much later by Sir Thomas More. And what does this word mean?"

I was the only one to raise a hand. "Mr. Wise?"

"Nowhere."

"Yes, Mr. Wise. 'Nowhere,' roughly speaking, is correct. Plato envisioned a benevolent autocracy where, for instance, the arts would be censored to protect the young, and eugenics—selective breeding—would be practiced. Plato believed that a state like this would serve society best. By living in such a state, individuals would have a better life. Is there in existence, nowadays, a state based on a similar philosophy?"

A few hands, including my own, were raised. Dr. Brotbaum did not accept the answers he received from the other students. "No, the USSR and Cuba are not modeled on Plato's principles. Their regimes don't even pretend to be benevolent. Mr. Wise?"

Finally, my reluctant membership in GIF bore fruit. I had become an expert on global human geography. "Singapore," I said.

"Good, Mr. Wise. Very good. Yes, Singapore tries, after a fashion, to be a benevolent autocracy. And, not unlike Plato's notions in his *Republic*, the government of this small island state tries to match men and women with similar intelligence and of the same race for marriage and breeding purposes. Whether Singapore's masters are also philosophers, as Plato required the rulers to be, is another matter altogether."

At some point during Dr. Brotbaum's lecture, I fell in love with him. I wanted to become his student and disciple, and, in time, his philosophy buddy. I have always dreamed of an older man as my life partner.

The sex ritual that Joe demanded of me whenever we slept together was all right with me. But I also yearned for my intellect to mate with one worthy of it. I would be honored if Dr. Brotbaum's intellect merged with mine.

Joe was a handsome man. Dr. Brotbaum was plain-looking; some would even call him ugly. Yet he was attractive to me because of his intellect. His physical appearance did not matter in the least.

I was dazed when the class came to an end. I remained in my seat, transfixed, watching Dr. Brotbaum exit the lecture hall. By not moving, I blocked the student sitting next to me, a beefy Anglo. "Are you some sort of genius, Mr. Wise?" he asked me mockingly, trying to mimic Dr. Brotbaum's accent. "Well, I must admit that it was quite a performance," he said. Now he spoke earnestly. "Have you ever listened to Dr. Brotbaum on KZLW?"

"No. What's that?"

"It is his *Philosopher's Corner*. That's what makes him so popular with the students."

"When? On what channel?"

"Not channel. Station. It's radio, man, not TV. Can you imagine Dr. Brotbaum, in his undertaker's outfit, sitting in front of TV cameras? Saturday, FM radio, 97.9, at nine AM."

*   *   *

Dr. Brotbaum's class was on a Monday. All week long, I looked forward to his Saturday radio show. I told Joe about it. He found out that KZLW was a National Public Radio station. "Sometimes they have good stuff on NPR. We'll listen together on Saturday."

I would have preferred listening to Dr. Brotbaum by myself. I know this sounds silly, but I did not want to share him with Joe. But since I would be at Joe's on Saturday, there was no other way.

At the beginning of Dr. Brotbaum's show, the announcer explained the format of *Philosopher's Corner*. Listeners wrote letters with questions or observations. Three such letters were selected every week. They were read to Dr. Brotbaum by the announcer, and he commented on them. The last quarter of the show was for callers to address the issues Dr. Brotbaum had discussed, or to raise any other philosophical queries.

The subjects on that particular talk show were abortion, the death penalty, and animal rights. Dr. Brotbaum's approach became obvious right away. He examined an idea the way a scientist would dissect a specimen. He did not say whether he liked or disliked an idea, approved or disapproved of it. Rather, he looked at it dispassionately, examining it for consistency. He considered what would happen if a particular idea became universal law.

"Summing up," said Dr. Brotbaum, when he discussed abortion, "if you hold that abortion is the taking of a human life, then you cannot make exceptions for rape and incest. The woman must bear the child that results from such acts just the same as if it had been conceived in conjugal love. Once you are willing to make exemptions for rape and incest, you give preference to the mother's needs, and it follows that you can morally make other exemptions in her interest."

Though he did not speak particularly fast, he seemed to have time for well-reasoned answers. He even managed to tell little anecdotes to liven up the show. When he spoke about universal law, he referred to the German philosopher Immanuel Kant. Dr. Kant was so compulsively orderly and punctual that the townspeople of Königsberg set their clocks by the time the philosopher passed their homes on his daily walk.

I was awestruck when the show ended. I looked at Joe, expecting him to be equally impressed. "Wasn't he great?" I asked.

"My, he has a heavy German accent," Joe said. "I don't see how they let him speak on public radio. But, you know, these are just opinions. Why are his opinions so much more interesting than mine? I'm a philosopher, too, you know."

I must have looked so disappointed that Joe added, "Eloy, I hope I didn't offend you. Hey, are you in love with your philosophy instructor?"

Yes, I was in love with Dr. Brotbaum.

* * *

All I wanted now was for Dr. Brotbaum to become my personal mentor. Unlike Joe and his ilk, I did not focus immediately on the sexual aspects of this imagined relationship. For instance, was Dr. Brotbaum gay? If so, did he like boyish guys or macho bodybuilders? For the moment, as far as I was concerned, Dr. Brotbaum was destined to become my mentor. I didn't worry about exactly how things would work out between us after that.

I, Eloy (or was it Harmony?), who had never planned anything in my life, now occupied myself with devising a strategy for making Dr. Brotbaum my mentor. From Joe's military books, I knew that good intelligence was the foundation of any successful strategy. I was determined to develop such intelligence. Joe, who knew a lot about the subject, had told me that one always started with the sources that were the easiest to access.

I started my intelligence gathering with Berkeley's phone directory. And there it was: Brotbaum, Eugene I., on Woolsey Street, followed by his phone number. I walked over and checked out the address. It was a small Victorian on Woolsey near College Avenue. Dr. Brotbaum lived within walking distance of the campus. From the outside, Dr. Brotbaum's house appeared to be in good condition. It had a tidy garden in the front.

Next, I wanted to know whether Dr. Brotbaum was married. I had not seen any rings on his fingers. I practiced, for a few minutes, speaking with a heavy Spanish accent, and then dialed his number.

He answered on the second ring with a hello, pronouncing the "e" in "hello" like the "a" in father.

"I'm calling from Cookie Town, USA. We're doing research for our new brand of chocolate chip cookies. May I speak with Mrs. Brotbaum?"

"There is no Mrs. Brotbaum."

I hung up the phone. Please forgive me, Dr. Brotbaum, I thought to myself. You do understand, don't you, that I must know whether there is a Mrs. in your life?

What else could I find out about Dr. Brotbaum? Well, for one, his scholastic curriculum vita was readily available. From it, I learned that he had studied at the universities of Vienna and Zurich, and obtained his PhD from the latter in 1972. Before coming to Berkeley, he had taught at Reed College in Oregon. He had also written four books.

During my first year at UC Berkeley, I had never exchanged a word with a Teaching Assistant. There were five TAs in Dr. Brotbaum's class. Now I decided to befriend them, so I could find out more about my mentor. The problem was that I just did not know how to befriend people, certainly not in a deliberate way to obtain information from them.

In his first lecture, Dr. Brotbaum had used the word harmony a number of times. Could a character named Harmony do what Eloy couldn't? Until Dr. Brotbaum's lecture, there had been no Harmony in my life. The name embarrassed me. Yet Dr. Brotbaum might take to a student named Harmony more than to an Eloy. Maybe, by assuming a different name, I could become a changed person. After all, I reasoned, it would be easier for me to become Harmony, which was one of my given names, than to appear upon the scene with a newly invented handle.

I lucked out with the TAs. The first one I approached was Ronnell, a graduate philosophy student a few years older than myself. He was a sinewy, dark-skinned black man with meticulously braided dreadlocks. I told him that my name was E. Harmony Wise, and asked him a simple-minded question about our textbook. When he answered my question, I said that I really liked Dr. Brotbaum's first lecture.

"He is terrific, isn't he? You know, Harmony, I'm taking a graduate seminar with him. My second one. I really get off on him being so different from our American instructors. He likes to teach. Sometimes I think that his role model is Socrates."

I was pleased that Ronnell had no funny comments to make about my new first name. We talked for a while. "If you want to know more about Dr. Brotbaum, speak to Danny Fleetwood. Dr. Brotbaum is his advisor for his doctoral thesis. You know, Dr. Brotbaum himself is very shy when it comes to discussing his own life. But, because of his radio talk show, he's in the public eye a lot. I don't know how this happened, but Danny has became his official spokesperson."

*   *   *

Danny was a tall Anglo in his late twenties or early thirties. One side of his face looked frozen. In time, I found out that his facial asymmetry was due to a medical condition called Bell's Palsy. This made it difficult at times to interpret his expressions. They varied from slightly sinister to quite friendly, depending which way he faced. There was a great earnestness about him when he explained a philosophical concept. In spite of his puzzling facial expression, he already looked like a young philosophy professor out of central casting.

"I believe," he said, "that I'm one of Dr. Brotbaum's closest associates at the university. I've studied under him, and have been his TA, I'm his radio program assistant, and he supervises my doctoral thesis. Let me tell you a bit about him, since you seem to be interested. Have you noticed his German accent?"

"Yes, I have. But there also is a singsong quality to it."

"The singsong is the Hungarian part of him. He was raised speaking both German and Hungarian. Dr. Eugene Istvan Brotbaum is one of the real people, not a TV docudrama hero, who was saved by Raoul Wallenberg. He was born to Jewish parents in Budapest, in 1944. He still has in his possession a document, in Swedish, German, and Hungarian, bearing the Swedish royal coat of arms and signed by Wallenberg. It states that his parents, and the baby Dr. Brotbaum, are 'under the direct protection of His Majesty, Gustavus V, King of Sweden.' That's how Dr. Brotbaum survived the Holocaust."

It sounded strange when Danny said "the baby Dr. Brotbaum." Later on, I realized that anyone who had much contact with Dr. Brotbaum assumed that even little Eugene had been a smaller version of the adult.

"So," Danny continued, "the baby Dr. Brotbaum survived the extermination of European Jews, and lived in Hungary until 1956. His father was a professor of Greek and Latin at the university in Budapest.

"From what I understand, the 1956 anti-communist uprising in Hungary eventually also turned anti-Semitic. His father fled to Austria with his family, and from there to Israel.

"They spent some five years in that country. Apparently, Latin professors were not much in demand there. From various remarks, I've gathered that the young Dr. Brotbaum had some very unpleasant experiences with Israeli boys. Eventually, the family managed to leave that country, and started to wander about Austria, Germany, and Switzerland, according to the teaching opportunities that presented themselves to Dr. Brotbaum's father.

"Dr. Brotbaum earned his doctorate from the University in Zurich. His thesis was about Erasmus of Rotterdam. You have to understand that Dr. Brotbaum focuses on vast areas of knowledge, which other mortals devote a lifetime to explore. He had also done a lot of research in medieval Muslim philosophy, I think just so that he would have an excuse for studying yet another language and culture.

"Due to Dr. Brotbaum's encyclopedic knowledge, he can teach, at a moment's notice, whatever philosophy course is needed by the university. I myself have seen him substitute for a sick colleague, lecturing without notes or preparation time."

"So what is Dr. Brotbaum's own philosophy?"

"That's a long story. Tell you what. Dr. Brotbaum hosts a symposium every second Sunday of the month from three to six PM. His graduate students and others who are interested in philosophizing are invited. It's like an open house. You can come on the second Sunday in October. Do you know the meaning of 'symposium'?"

"Well, originally, in ancient Greece, it referred to an intellectual drinking party. Symposium is the title of one of the dialogues in Plato's *Republic*. In an ordinary sense, the word means a conference to discuss some subject of importance."

I could see that Danny was impressed. "I think you'll do splendidly at the symposium. By the way, how old are you?"

"Nineteen."

"Of course, you won't be able to drink at the symposium. But there will be lots of philosophizing taking place. That'll be fun enough for you."

*　　　　　*　　　　　*

I saw little of Helmut during the fall semester. We did manage, though, to lunch together a few times. On these occasions we would plan our trip to Europe next summer.

Though Helmut looked handsome and tan, he was tired much of the time. He complained constantly that he lacked energy. We had dinner together in Berkeley on the Tuesday after Labor Day. Helmut had a nagging cough and looked pinched. I told him that he should see a doctor the next day.

I called him a few times that week to find out how he was, but always got his answering machine. He never returned my calls. Finally, I went by his house. His roommate, Arnold, let me in. "You're Eloy, aren't you?" he asked. He had met me only once. "I couldn't call you because I don't know your number. I wasn't able to get into Helmut's computer where he keeps his addresses. Helmut is in the intensive care unit at Herrick Hospital."

"What happened?"

"He has pneumonia." Arnold hesitated for an instant, and then added, "He has AIDS."

"AIDS?" I looked at him, bewildered.

"Yes, AIDS."

I knew more about AIDS than most other gays because of Joe. In his methodical manner, he had been following every bit of news about that disease. Even so, I never thought AIDS would strike one of my friends.

"Can I visit him?"

"They may give you a hard time at the ICU. Only his family is supposed to be with him. Speaking of which, I've finally managed to locate his family's phone number in Germany, and gave it to the hospital. His mother will arrive here tomorrow. I sure am glad that I won't have to be the one to explain to her about her son."

With a great deal of apprehension, I went to the hospital. It was after visiting hours, but nobody stopped me. Surrounded by mechanical devices, with tubes and needles sticking into all parts of his body, Helmut lay there, connected to a respirator. Because of the breathing tube, he couldn't speak. He did recognize me. He seemed to have shrunk, and he looked like a malnourished child. I put my hand in his, and he pressed it weakly. I stood silently by his bed for a long time. I did not know what to say or do. Finally, a nurse told me that she needed to work on the patient, and asked me to leave.

I visited Helmut early the next morning, because I was afraid to be there when his mother arrived. He looked much worse, and didn't seem to recognize me.

I had given Arnold a few phone numbers where he could reach me. That evening, Arnold called me at Joe's. "Helmut passed away at three o'clock in the afternoon." There was a long pause. Arnold was crying. My hands shook so violently that I could barely hold the phone. "There'll be a memorial service for him at the Unitarian Fellowship Hall the day after tomorrow at 10:00 AM. His mother is taking his body to Germany for burial. Finally, I was able to get into his computer and get the phone numbers of his friends. You know, he was quite a popular guy."

Arnold had managed to contact all of Helmut's friends, including his old men. The congregation at the memorial service consisted of the minister, the dean of engineering, some five or six older gentlemen, including Joe, and many male fellow students. The only woman present was Helmut's mother. She was a daintily dressed lady, in her late fifties, quite formal and stiff. Her face reflected the terrible stress she was under, but she was composed.

I don't remember what the minister said, except that he spoke a lot about Helmut's youth. Then he asked whether anyone would like to say a few words about the deceased. To my surprise, Joe rose immediately and went to the front of the room, facing the congregation.

He spoke for a while about Helmut's impressive scholastic achievements and his many friends. Then, abruptly, he shifted to another subject. "All of us here today are affected by Helmut's passing away. He died of AIDS. So that his death, at such a young age, will serve a purpose, let us dedicate ourselves, in Helmut's memory, to fight ignorance and prejudice about this disease. Let us learn more about AIDS so we can avoid spreading it, so we can fight against it, and so that, eventually, we can discover a cure for it."

The congregation was completely silent. Some people seemed uncomfortable. Helmut's mother, though, shook Joe's hand firmly and warmly at the end of the ceremony.

Encouraged by Joe's example, another old man got up and spoke about Helmut as a companion. "His friendship with me has enriched my life tremendously," he concluded. I wondered how many people in the audience understood fully the old man's praise. But it did not seem to matter. I believe everybody was still mulling over Joe's strange eulogy.

"Why did you mention AIDS at the memorial?" I asked Joe when we were in the car.

"Because, Eloy, it was a captive audience. Nobody wants to hear about a condition that afflicts queers, prostitutes, and drug addicts. Too bad that sometimes it also kills hemophiliacs. But in the end, millions of people, all over the world, will be struck by this epidemic."

I had another question to ask Joe, but I desisted. Was he worried that he might have caught AIDS by having screwed Helmut? Were Helmut's other old men worried about it?

I was so shaken by the loss of my first real friend that it took me a few days to realize that, without Helmut, my trip to Europe next summer would not be feasible.

6

Harmony Scintillates at the Symposium

Attending Dr. Brotbaum's symposium on the second Sunday of October, 1984, was the beginning of a series of experiences that would completely change my life.

To make my narration coherent, I will write about the symposium as if I had a moment-by-moment recollection of the entire event. In fact, I recall it more like pictures in an exhibition. I remember vividly certain scenes, like Dr. Brotbaum in his strange outfit, while other chunks of time are lost to me. As I am writing this, I am still in touch with the sense of belonging I felt there. At last, I found a crowd I wanted to be associated with. And, just like my mother, I found myself a guru.

Before meeting Joe and being forced to attend GIF events, I had never gone to parties. Well, maybe I went to some as a boy. But as a teenager, I made it a point not to go to parties of any kind. With GIF experiences under my belt, I felt that at least I would not make a complete ass of myself at the symposium.

One thing was clear to me before attending the event. At GIF events, I was one of the smartest and cutest twinkies; at Dr. Brotbaum's symposium, I would certainly not be the brightest participant, and nobody would care about my looks.

*　　　　*　　　　*

The door to Dr. Brotbaum's home was slightly ajar, so I just walked in. A guy in his thirties spotted me as I entered. He looked surprised to see me. "Who are you?" he asked gruffly.

"Danny Fleetwood invited me."

"Are we going to have a kindergarten symposium? Well, if Danny invited you, little boy, then go through the kitchen; everybody's in the backyard."

From the outside, it had been impossible to guess the size of the backyard. It was large enough to accommodate the twenty or so people present. I was the last one to arrive because I had made it a point to be late. Looking at the crowd, I recognized only Danny, Ronnell, and the other TAs. Everybody was in their late twenties or early thirties. There was only one woman present, and she seemed quite a bit older than the rest of the crowd. People were standing in small groups, talking to each other.

I leaned against the wall of the house and took in the scene, unsure of what to do next. It was one of those unseasonably warm days we get in Berkeley in the fall. The backyard garden was tiny, with a profusion of flowering plants.

Nobody seemed to notice me. Suddenly, from another door, Dr. Brotbaum made his appearance. He wore a plaid shirt with mother-of-pearl buttons, a bolo tie, a pair of Levi's with a wide leather belt, and fancy boots. He also wore an expensive-looking cowboy hat.

Dr. Brotbaum must have tried hard to dress in what he considered appropriate Berkeley garden-party attire. But he looked awkward and uncomfortable in this costume. As soon as he was spotted, everybody fell silent. A moment later, two TAs emerged from the kitchen. One carried cheese and bread; the other, several bottles of wine. They placed the food on a long table.

"Welcome to our first symposium of the academic year," Dr. Brotbaum said formally. "We shall follow our usual procedure. Mr. Fleetwood, at four o'clock, if you please." Then he spotted me, and pointed in my direction. "I see we have a new member here today. He's young but already learned. Let's welcome to our midst Mr. Wise, whose parents were wise enough to bestow upon him the given name 'Harmony.' As you know, Aristotle postulated that there existed a Perfect Harmony. It behooves us all to strive to find this harmony within us!" He pointed to the students who were setting up the food on a table and said, "And now, eat, drink, and make merry."

My first reaction to Dr. Brotbaum's comment about me and my name was a triumphant mental roar from the newborn Harmony. He all but shouted, "See, Eloy, you dummy, what I can do for both of us?" Then, whether it was Eloy or Harmony, I got in touch with the enormity of what had just taken place. Dr. Brotbaum had recognized me, admired the name Harmony, and spoken favorably of me to the other students!

A number of people surrounded Dr. Brotbaum. The rest started munching and drinking. The only woman in the crowd walked toward me, extended her hand, and said, "Hi, Harmony, my name is Aviva. I'm the producer of *Philosopher's Corner*. Why does Dr. Brotbaum think you're so wise?"

Aviva was a wiry woman in her forties. She had short brown hair, wore no makeup and, though friendly enough, seemed to be a no-nonsense lady. She wore jeans and polo shirt without a bra. When she spoke, I noticed an accent that I could not place. "I don't know why Dr. Brotbaum thinks I'm so wise. All I did was answer a few of his questions in class."

I was being modest. By now I had attended four of Dr. Brotbaum's lectures and answered many of his questions. A fellow student even called me "teacher's pet."

"I wonder whether it would be a good idea to have you on *Philosopher's Corner*?" Aviva asked, directing the question to herself more than to me. "You know, representing today's new students, the young generation, that sort of thing."

"I'm not a representative of anyone or anything," I replied almost defiantly, feeling alarmed at the prospect of speaking for my generation. But this was Eloy's answer. "You idiot," Harmony said silently, "you just blew your big chance for an intellectual session with Dr. Brotbaum."

Danny came over. He ignored Aviva's presence completely, speaking to me as if she were not there. "I'm glad you could come here today, Harmony. Help yourself to the food, but not the alcohol. There's some juice on the table. We start the serious part in," he looked at his watch, "thirty-five minutes." Aviva guided me to the buffet table. The jugs contained Mosel wine, and there was bread, rolls, and three kinds of cheeses. Except for Ronnell, who said hi, nobody took notice of me. At four o'clock on the dot we went into the house.

* * *

The decor of Dr. Brotbaum's living room was far removed from Berkeley in the eighties. It consisted of massive mahogany pieces. The floors were covered with Persian rugs. On the walls hung minutely executed portraits of elderly men and women, and a large seascape, all encased in ornate frames. A grand piano occupied almost one-quarter of the living room.

Incongruously, there were twenty or so cheap folding chairs arranged in a circle. Dr. Brotbaum's heavy upholstered chairs were much too large to be used for group meetings. Now these folding chairs stood in a circle next to the piano.

Danny Fleetwood, his asymmetrical face as puzzling as ever, was the chairman of the symposium. Dr. Brotbaum's role was that of an advisor. He had taken off his large hat, and seemed to be more comfortable in his cowboy outfit.

"At our last symposium, in June, we agreed to take up Vittorio's topic at our fall meeting," Danny said after we were all seated. "The title of Vittorio's topic is, 'Do Philosophers Owe a Duty to Society?' This issue is of great interest to us because of Dr. Brotbaum's radio show with the media. Vittorio, will you please elaborate."

Vittorio was a short, handsome guy with intense eyes and a dandified mustache. He wore a silk turquoise shirt. Unfortunately, when he started speaking, his good looks were marred by his crooked teeth. "The question before us is whether a true philosopher has a duty to propagate his philosophy beyond his students, his colleagues, and his university." While Vittorio's English was grammatically correct and formal, he spoke with a heavy Italian accent. "For today's discussion I have chosen, almost randomly, four philosophers to illustrate how they varied in their interpretation of their social duties.

"Socrates deliberately assumed the role of a gadfly. He buttonholed Athenian citizens to force them to think for what he considered their own good.

"On the other hand, Immanuel Kant, the enormously influential German philosopher, served for many years as a private tutor; later, he shared his insights only with his students and colleagues as, indeed, was the practice of most other philosophers.

"Karl Marx, the author of *Das Kapital*, also wrote *The Communist Manifesto* and organized the First International. He actively propagated his own radical social philosophy. He tried to convert his philosophical insights into a revolutionary reality.

"Then we have a Ludwig Wittgenstein, one of the great philosophers of this century, who took great pride in the fact that even his instructors could not understand his philosophy. He counseled his closest friends to give up philosophy, and occupy themselves with more useful subjects.

"We take for granted that a physician is duty-bound to heal the sick, a university professor to instruct his students. What duties, precisely, does the designation 'philosopher' impose on the recipient of this lofty title?"

A few moments after the discussion started, a student by the name of Steve raised his hand. He was a pretty, rather than handsome, Anglo. As soon as he started speaking, I knew by his intonation that he was a fellow gay. "I'm surprised that Vittorio chose Wittgenstein as a model for anything. Wittgenstein went out of his way to make his philosophy obscure and unintelligible. He drove his lovers to despair by his unhinged behavior. The family of one of his lovers claimed that he had actually hastened their son's death. Wittgenstein pulled the hair of his grade school students—the girls, not the boys—and was fired for physical cruelty to children. And, all in all, he was quite cuckoo."

Dr. Brotbaum was visibly disturbed by Steve's comment. "Mr. Davidson," he said to Steve, "it is disrespectful to refer to an established philosopher as 'cuckoo,' however strange his behavior might seem." Dr. Brotbaum enunciated "cuckoo" as if Steve had uttered a four-letter word. "Nietzsche, as you well know, was clinically insane for many years. But I would not dare refer to him as 'cuckoo.' Philosophers should be respectful of each other.

"As to your charges against Ludwig Wittgenstein, Mr. Davidson." Here it comes, I thought. Dr. Brotbaum won't let Steve imply that Wittgenstein was gay. But I was wrong. "Wittgenstein was a complex human being: a mystic who voluntarily fought in the Austrian army as a plain soldier during the first World War; a man who gave his enormous wealth away, and who humbled himself by seeking the forgiveness of the girls whose hair he had pulled."

"But they didn't forgive him," Steve interrupted.

"True enough, Mr. Davidson. Wittgenstein's notion, after his mystical experiences during the war, to teach primary school in the Tyrolean mountains of Austria, was an unfortunate choice. His unhappy relationships with a number of males, who may or may not have been his lovers, is also regrettable. These relationships caused a great deal of suffering to the young men, as well as to the philosopher himself."

Dr. Brotbaum's somber manner left the impression that Neitzche and Wittgenstein had been members of his social circle. Later, at home, using our textbook, I discovered that the former had died in 1900 and the latter in 1951. It gratified me that Dr. Brotbaum was willing to speak openly and in a matter-of-fact fashion about the homosexuality of one of his philosopher buddies.

I knew nothing about Wittgenstein. I decided then and there to read more about him. Halfway through the symposium I learned that at the end of our session the subject for the next symposium would be decided upon. Vittorio, who had suggested this session's topic, was, next to Dr. Brotbaum and Danny, the star of the show. For our next symposium, I coveted Vittorio's role for myself.

I had a topic in mind because I had already researched one for my term paper. However, a sophomore term paper was one thing; proposing a topic for a symposium of graduate philosophy students, in the presence of

Dr. Brotbaum, was quite another. But it was his presence that motivated me. My mind divided itself. I paid just enough attention to the discussion not to be caught off guard if someone addressed me. The rest of my mind was busy formulating my proposal for our next symposium.

"And now," said Danny, looking at his watch, "we must bring this discussion to an end, and choose our topic for the next symposium. Suggestions?"

My hand raised itself on cue. "Harmony, you have a topic to propose?" He sounded surprised.

All eyes were on me. "I think that Socrates, by not escaping from Athens and thus saving himself from an unjust death sentence, contributed to the delinquency of the Athenians. Aristotle, when he found himself in a similar position, fled Athens. 'I do not wish to give Athenians the chance to sin against philosophy twice,' has been attributed to him in this context. I suggest that we discuss whether Socrates' decision to accept the jury's verdict was ethically correct."

The Eloy in me would never have turned a phrase like "contributing to the delinquency of the Athenians." Harmony was more clever with words.

The sarcastic student who had spoken rudely to me when I came into the house responded immediately. "I really don't believe that Harmony, however wise he is, or his parents were, will have more light to shed on this topic than Socrates himself. Socrates explained to his students precisely, and at great length, why he had chosen to face death rather than flee the city. His arguments convinced them that it was a rational and moral decision. Is Mr. Wise wiser than Socrates' students?"

Danny was about to say something when Dr. Brotbaum raised his hand. Whenever Dr. Brotbaum raised his hand, everyone immediately deferred to him. "It is not as simple as you portray it, Mr. Gamzu," Dr.

Brotbaum said, addressing the last speaker. "Plato, who wrote the dialogues, had Socrates' students debating with their master and, after a long discussion, agreeing with him that his course of action was the correct one.

"This does not mean that the issue has been resolved once and for all. It was resolved by the author, Plato, in the limited time and space he allowed. Another author may have resolved it differently. Mr. Wise, or any other student, may entertain doubts about Socrates' conduct by approaching the issue in a different light. As Mr. Wise himself pointed out, no lesser a figure than Aristotle acted the opposite way under similar circumstances, and fled Athens. But, while I think Mr. Wise's topic is important, we need to listen to other suggested topics for the next symposium."

There were some other suggestions. Dr. Brotbaum, however, seemed to like mine. My proposal would be our next discussion topic!

When it was over, all I wanted to do was to be by myself and think things over. I made for the door and would have been the first one to leave, had Aviva not intercepted me. Disregarding completely our previous conversation she said, "Harmony, I want to write down your address and phone number. Come," she said, as she dragged me towards Dr. Brotbaum's study.

Two entire walls of the study were taken over by shelves stacked with books. A curved stepladder with five rungs made it possible for Dr. Brotbaum to reach the books on the highest shelves. On the third wall hung a life-size portrait of a man. It resembled a Rembrandt. In the center of the wall, facing the garden, was a large picture window. Aviva saw me looking at the painting and said, "This is Erasmus of Rotterdam. He was the subject of Eugene's doctoral thesis."

For a moment I was going to ask her who Eugene was. Then I realized that she had called Dr. Brotbaum by his first name. Danny told me that nobody, including himself, ever addressed Dr. Brotbaum by his first name.

My eyes strayed to the enormous black desk. On it stood a typewriter that one would expect to see in a museum or in an old black-and-white movie. If I had to date it, I would guess that it had been manufactured in the thirties or forties.

"This is Dr. Brotbaum's computer," Aviva said.

"Computer?"

"Well, he does all his writing using this typewriter."

"What happens when he makes a typo?"

"Good question. He doesn't make any typos. When students ask him about it, he says, 'When I play the piano I touch the right keys. Why would I not do the same on a typewriter?'"

"But how does Dr. Brotbaum save what he writes?"

"Do you know what carbon paper was used for?"

"Of course."

"Well, until very recently he 'saved' his texts by making two carbon copies of everything. Now he's more modern. He makes photocopies of everything he writes. He has to order the ribbon for his typewriter from Germany. From an antique dealer, for all I know."

Aviva, who seemed to be totally at home in Dr. Brotbaum's study, got hold of a pen and piece of paper and asked me to write down my address and phone number. I wrote down my name as E. Harmony Wise. "I'll call you pretty soon," Aviva said. "Don't get into any arguments with the other students as you leave."

"Arguments?"

"Some of them are real asses—pompous, jealous, and insecure. You know what? I'll walk you out myself."

On the way out we ran into Danny. They looked at each other with antipathy. Danny had told me that he was the closet person to Dr. Brotbaum. Was Aviva even closer? Fortunately, Aviva ushered me out without incident.

*   *   *

At home, when I reviewed the events of the day in my mind, I focused on Dr. Brotbaum in his cowboy outfit bidding us to "Eat, drink, and make merry." Was he playing two roles simultaneously? If and when I got a chance, I would ask Aviva about it. I had a feeling that I would learn more from her than from Danny. Besides being Dr. Brotbaum's producer, what was Aviva's relationship to him? I also wondered about the origin of Aviva's name. If I knew that, maybe I could place her accent. Monty was good with this kind of thing. I would ask him about it.

To Joe's great annoyance, I had returned to Berkeley on Sunday morning for the symposium. I told him only that our philosophy professor had an open house for his students. "Why would you want to attend a stuffy meeting with an instructor who speaks funny English, instead of having a good time at a GIF picnic in Golden Gate Park?"

I did not even answer his silly question. After the symposium, I resolved that anything connected with Dr. Brotbaum was not to be shared with Joe, Monty, or any other San Francisco acquaintances. I decided, as Joe would have said, to "classify" Harmony's comings and goings.

Now, because I thought it would be improper to use the same topic for both, I needed to prepare myself for the symposium next month and come up with a new idea for my term paper.

7

José Luis Herrera Plans an Acapulco Caper

I had given Aviva three phone numbers to get hold of me. One of them was at Joe's. Luckily, when she called on a Saturday, I answered the phone. "Can I speak with Harmony?" she asked. I could imagine Joe's endless questioning had he taken the call. "Harmony, will you have breakfast with me next Saturday? I'm treating."

"Of course." I was so happy to hear from Aviva that I completely forgot my schedule at Joe's. With his navy officer's mind set, he always expected me to report to him as per schedule. After I started my sophomore year, Joe's schedule became oppressive to me. It may not have been the schedule as much as Joe himself. After school and my job at Monty's GGLC, I would have preferred, at times, to go back to Berkeley instead of spending the night in San Francisco with Joe. While I filled a void in his life, he no longer added much to mine. Counterintuitively, of the two of us, he needed sex much more than I did.

My breakfast with Aviva was scheduled for 8:30 in Berkeley. That meant that I would not be able to stay with Joe Friday night. I would have to return to Berkeley after I finished with my GGLC job.

I told Joe that Dr. Brotbaum's producer wanted to meet me for breakfast. He was surprised, and wanted to know why. "I don't know why, Joe. You'll be the first one to know once she tells me."

"Why are you so fascinated with Dr. Brotbaum?"

"Because," I started answering, and then checked myself. I was not going to cast Dr. Brotbaum's pearls before swine. "There's no reason for me to tell you why I like or dislike one of my professors. You wouldn't even understand what it is all about!"

Of late Joe found himself in the same situation my schoolteachers had encountered when dealing with me. I was a lot brighter than they were. When they discovered that, they did not know what to do with me. Now Joe, like my instructors before him, had nothing to offer me. At that moment, I did not care much whether we continued being boyfriends.

"I'm sure that you'll be able to find a cute twinkie for Friday night. Preferably, a twinkie you can screw, not a dud like me."

* * *

I asked Monty about the name Aviva. He thought about it for a moment and said: "It sounds a bit like the name of the city Tel Aviv, in Israel."

"So the name is Israeli?"

"Eloy, you ought to know that the language of Israel is called Hebrew, not Israeli. Didn't you tell me once that you were part Jewish?"

I was ashamed of myself. I despised people who believed that in Mexico, people spoke Mexican, and I had just made a similar mistake. But it did make sense to me that Aviva would be a Hebrew name. I knew from Danny that Dr. Brotbaum had spent a few years in Israel as a boy. I wondered whether Aviva spoke English with a Hebrew accent.

I really wanted to impress Aviva. How would I find out whether her name was Hebrew? For a moment, I even thought of calling my mother. After all, she had studied Hebrew as a little girl. Then I got a better idea. I looked in the yellow pages under Synagogues. There was a listing for a Jewish Educational Center of San Francisco. It took one phone call to find out that Aviva was the feminine form of Aviv which, in Hebrew, means spring.

*　　　*　　　*

We met at the Berkeley Coffee House on University Avenue. Aviva wore a pair of jeans and a flannel shirt. Again, there was no trace of makeup on her face.

"The Coffee House is not my idea of a good breakfast place," she said. "But you seemed to be so uncomfortable talking to me that I wanted to make everything simple for both of us. Easy to park, and easy to reach by bus." Her foreign accent in English was pronounced but not jarring.

Of course, I could not tell her why I was so uncomfortable when she had called. After we ordered our breakfasts I asked, "Is Aviva a Hebrew name meaning spring?"

She gave me a speculative look. "That's correct. How do you know that, Harmony?"

"I researched it."

"How?"

"My boss told me about the city of Tel Aviv. I phoned the Jewish Education Center, and they told me what your name meant."

"Dr. Brotbaum likes students who question everything, and who take the initiative to seek out information. You impressed him with your criticism of Socrates. Where do you work?"

The Harmony inside my head was still rejoicing about impressing Dr. Brotbaum, when I had to confront the reality of Aviva's question. By telling Aviva the name of the outfit I worked for, I would let her know I was gay. This was the first time I'd had to deal with this issue. At college, I was just known for being an outstanding student. I was not close enough to anyone to talk about my sexual orientation. In San Francisco, I hung out only with gays. Now I had to face the coming-out issue. What was I going to tell Aviva, and would she report back to Dr. Brotbaum?

I liked Plato more than I liked his most famous student, Aristotle. But one thing that Aristotle said stuck in my mind: "One learns to be brave by performing brave deeds." Now I was going to follow one of Aristotle's precepts. "I do computer work for the Global Gay Love Connection, GGLC for short, in San Francisco."

Once again, Aviva gave me a long, speculative look. She hesitated a moment, and then asked, "Are you gay, Harmony?"

Quite timidly I replied, "Yes, Aviva."

"That's good," she said with a smile, "I'm gay too."

Aviva's reply left the door open for the big question: "Is Dr. Brotbaum gay?" But I did not dare ask it. Over the years, I have tried to analyze my reluctance to address the issue at that particular moment. Probably, there were two reasons for my not asking that question. First, I held Dr. Brotbaum in such awe that I dared not discuss his sexual preferences, though I desperately needed to know the truth. Second, as long as I did not have an answer, there was hope. Had Aviva told me that Dr. Brotbaum was straight, the prospect of having an intellectual and physical love affair with him would have collapsed.

I did ask Aviva, though, some personal questions about Dr. Brotbaum. I wanted to understand why he had worn a cowboy outfit at the symposium, and why he had told us to "eat, drink, and make merry."

Aviva was amused by my questions. "You see, Harmony, Dr. Brotbaum is not at home in English. He's a tourist in the language."

"A tourist?"

"Well, Dr. Brotbaum has studied many languages. Some of them aren't even spoken any longer. He had studied Akkadian, Aramaic, Hebrew, classical Arabic, classical Greek, Latin, Hungarian, German, French, Italian, and, of course, English. Lately, he has taken up Spanish.

"You spoke American English at home, and probably studied a little Shakespearean English at school. They aren't the same to you. Eugene always tries to use what he calls the *mot juste*, precisely the right expression for the occasion. Sometimes he doesn't realize that he's mixing old English with modern American usage."

"What about his cowboy hat?"

"Oh, that. First of all, Eugene has a precancerous skin condition, and must not be exposed to the sun. He usually wears a hat when he's in the sun for even short periods. The clothes he wears to his lectures, somber, black, old-fashioned suits, he's comfortable with. I have no idea what recreational clothes he wore in his student days in Europe. I knew him as a youngster in Israel. We attended the same high school in Be'ersheba. I met him again while he was teaching in Oregon. To make his visitors comfortable, he wants to be, when not at work, as American as…a cowboy.

"At the beginning of next year, I'd like to have guests on Eugene's show. Because he's so popular with young people, I want you to be his first guest."

"Aviva, I don't represent American youth or Berkeley students or gay men of color. I'm a loner. Very few people see things the way I do."

"You managed to do pretty well for yourself at the symposium. Your views were certainly not off-the-wall."

"Let me think about it, Aviva. In the meantime, how do I prepare for the next symposium?"

"Just do what you did last time. Read up as much as you can about the subject. It was a good scholastic maneuver when you used Aristotle's comments to support your own views. Don't let Jack Gamzu, Danny Fleetwood, and their gang cow you with their scholarship. Be as knowledgeable as they are."

"Is there bad blood between you and Danny?"

"Let me clue you in, Harmony, to what's going on at Dr. Brotbaum's court. The students surrounding him have developed a cult of sorts. Naturally, where there's a cult, there's also a hierarchy. Danny considers himself the senior student, Dr. Brotbaum's deputy or, as he puts it, his "associate." He resents my closeness to Dr. Brotbaum. Jack Gamzu is convinced that he is the most erudite student—the senior scholar. Danny is jealous of all newcomers who could potentially challenge his exalted position.

"I'm not only Eugene's friend. I'm also his producer. Public radio is a strange business. We don't care too much about ratings, but we always worry about funding. Congress gives us some money, but only after making our lives as miserable as possible. Large corporations donate funds to us for a tax deduction, and for subtle advertising. Our listeners make up the rest. We have to please three different masters. While we encourage controversy, it needs to fall into some definable niche that has a constituency.

"For instance, we have conservatives and liberals appearing on our shows. This makes for balance. But Dr. Brotbaum is neither conservative nor liberal, neither Democrat nor Republican. He is a purist. By holding views that he deems philosophically consistent—this is the key word—he has managed to piss off, at one time or another, liberals, conservatives, scholars, the Christian right, unions, what have you.

“Once, answering a caller, he commented that if we believe that burial sites must not be disturbed, then we’ve no business poking around Egyptian pyramids just because of their antiquity. All the more so, because we know that the people mummified there wished that their remains not be disturbed.

“Then, on the spur of the moment, he came up with one of his anecdotes. ‘I understand,’ he said, ‘that archaeologists are presently searching all over Mongolia for the tomb of Genghis Khan. Legend has it that Ogadai, Genghis Khan’s son, had the two thousand men who prepared his father’s tomb put to death. In turn, the executioners themselves were killed. All of that killing was done to ensure that the grave would not be found. The wishes of Genghis Khan would seem to be very clear: “Do not disturb my resting site.”’

“Eugene concluded by asking, ‘When a grave is disturbed, does it make a difference whether it is by a robber or an archaeologist? Whether the person buried inside died ten or a thousand years ago?’

“Such off-the-cuff remarks make Eugene’s shows charming. But his maddening logic ran smack into the scientists’ claims that everything from evolution to population movements, from diseases to primitive agricultural practices, can be garnered from the examination of ancient human remains. Archaeologists and anthropologists were in an uproar. Dr. Brotbaum was, after all, a fellow scholar.

“In public radio, established programs are on the air for years, and then get canned overnight. I’m protecting Eugene and myself from his own excesses. Some of his students think that I’m compromising his integrity, his philosophical purity. Also, he’s surrounded exclusively by males. I imagine they resent the influence of a woman on him.”

I had wondered about that myself. Why were there no female students at the symposium? At that point, once again, I missed my opportunity to find out whether Dr. Brotbaum was gay.

I had breakfast again with Aviva on the Sunday of the November symposium. I ran by her what my approach would be. Aviva, though, seemed to be much more interested in my computer programming class.

My experience with my computer course was the same as with all the math I had taken. As long as I applied myself, I understood whatever there was to understand. The subject was neither difficult nor easy for me. Everything just fell into place naturally. "One day, probably sooner than later, I'll make you a job offer that I hope you'll accept. It's related to your computer studies," Aviva told me. "As for the symposium, don't worry, Harmony. I'm sure that you'll hold your own."

*　　　*　　　*

I did very well for myself at the symposium. Aviva had given me good advice. I had read so much about Socrates, Plato, Aristotle, and the period's history that my line of reasoning could not be challenged by unfamiliar information. Jack Gamzu tried hard to probe for scholastic weaknesses, but found none.

Most of the participants disagreed with me. Following Socrates' reasoning, they felt that he had done the right thing by staying in Athens and being made to drink the cup of hemlock. I stuck to my guns. As an innocent person, Socrates should not have consented to his execution simply because the Athenian jury had found him guilty. I believe that Dr. Brotbaum was pleased with my performance.

When the symposium was over, I had established my qualifications to become a regular member of Dr. Brotbaum's court. But Ronnell was the only one in the group who befriended me. After the November symposium he said, "Hey, Harmony, let's hang out together sometime." From then on, once or twice a month, we would have coffee together and talk about philosophy. I considered Ronnell's invitation a milestone in my social life. I longed for friends who would be my intellectual equals.

It slipped my mind to tell Aviva not to call me at Joe's. At the beginning of December, Aviva called me there again. Unfortunately, this time, Joe answered the telephone.

"Harmony?" I heard him say. "There's no…"

"That's for me, Joe," I said.

Joe gave me a puzzled look as he handed me the phone. It was Aviva. "Hi, Harmony," she said. "How'd you like to work for me, at KLZW, a few hours a week? I need to computerize my files. After that's done, and it'll take at least three months, I'll need clerical computer help on a regular basis. We don't pay much, but the job is interesting."

The phone I was using was in the hall. Joe planted himself a few feet away, his arms akimbo, listening intently.

"Aviva, could we meet and discuss that in Berkeley?"

"Is this a bad time to speak to you?"

"Very."

"OK, how about tomorrow for breakfast?"

"Tomorrow" referred to the second Sunday in December. I had planned on returning to Berkeley in the early afternoon, so I could attend Dr. Brotbaum's symposium. Joe and I had already had words about it, because he wanted me to stay with him until Monday morning. Breakfast with Aviva would have meant not even spending Saturday night with him.

"How about lunch tomorrow?"

"OK, Harmony. See you at noon at the Berkeley Coffee House. No time now to think of a better lunch place."

"Since when are you Harmony?" Joe asked angrily, as soon as I hung up. "I thought you hated your middle name. And why does that woman keep calling you?"

I told myself, "Only certain people may call me Harmony. You are not one of them." But to Joe I said, "I changed my mind. Now I like the name Harmony. Why do you listen to my phone calls as if I was a little boy?"

"I'm your lover, Eloy. I'm entitled to know what's going on with you. I should be notified when you decide to change your name."

"You may be my lover, but you treat me like 'my boy Eloy.' I'm not your boy, I'm not your twinkie, I'm not a GIF lost soul seeking a Caucasian master. I have my own friends who take the same classes. You don't allow me to have my own life. I'm not a ring you wear around your finger twenty-four hours a day."

Part of the bitterness between us was really related to a completely different issue. Monty had suggested that I spend part of my winter vacation in Acapulco, helping with the preparations for the GGLC trip in January. "I'll pay for your ticket and hotel, and give you a per diem of thirty dollars," Monty told me. "This way you'll have a paid holiday in Acapulco, and you can put in a few hours a day to fine-tune the arrangements we've made there. Well, I suspect it'll take more than fine tuning, but you'll still have plenty of free time."

As soon as Joe heard about Monty's idea, he decided to accompany me to Acapulco. "I'll help you, since I know my way around down there," he told me. I wished to be by myself in Acapulco because I had a my own agenda there. José Luis had not disappeared. He was just hibernating. He would come out of it in Acapulco like a bear at spring time.

"I don't need the help of a non-Spanish-speaking gringo with my own people."

"You forget the little incident in Tijuana when the security guard wouldn't admit you into the hotel because you looked such a mess. We've never talked about it, but you know, you were temporarily insane. I remember distinctly that you said 'Me, Eloy, is not me.' You seem to go crazy when you're with what you call 'my people.'"

In the end, it served no purpose that I stayed the night. We fought so much that I refused to sleep in the same bed with him. I took the BART train to Berkeley early Sunday morning.

At lunch, Aviva described in detail the job she had in mind for me. I was sure I could handle it. I knew that I could successfully carry out any project related to personal computers. I would have to put in about the same amount of hours that I worked at GGLC, though my hourly pay would be two dollars less. The job would start in January.

I accepted Aviva's offer on the spot. For practical reasons alone, it would end my relationship with Joe. It would be much too complicated for me take the train to San Francisco after I finished my job in Berkeley, and Joe would not be satisfied with just weekend visits.

The fact that Aviva's job paid less than Monty's did not matter to me. I had saved over $1,500 for my trip to Germany, and had as much money as I needed. The most important thing for me was that, through Aviva's job, I would be closer to Dr. Brotbaum.

*　　　　*　　　　*

Joe had often told me that older persons dealt better with unpleasant situations than younger ones, because they had experienced similar conditions in the past. He was right. I had never broken up with a lover before, and did not know how to go about it.

I was afraid that Joe would be upset and angry when I told him the news, but he turned out to be a real gentleman about it. "Of course I'm sorry that you're leaving me, Eloy. However, everything changes, nothing is permanent, and each of us needs to do what suits them best. Let's stay friends, Eloy. The same way that I kept my friendship with Helmut."

We ended our relationship formally on the Tuesday following my meeting with Aviva. On Wednesday morning, Joe helped me move my stuff back to Berkeley.

Monty was a bit unhappy that he would be losing me. He also felt sorry for Joe. But there was one good aspect to my resignation. His boyfriend, Benjie, would stop his jealous tirades. The most important task for me to complete at Monty's was the trip to Acapulco. He himself would lead the GGLC group on their foray. He would have liked for me to go with him as an interpreter and assistant. However, since the Acapulco expedition would take place during the school year, this was impossible. The best Monty could do was to send me to Acapulco to set things up during my winter break.

The GGLC had bought out the entire space of the three gay hotels in Acapulco for the second week in January. Late registrants would be accommodated in a "gay-friendly" hotel. Monty had also rented office space in one of the hotels as his headquarters for the operation. That office, a small room with a phone and a fax machine, would be made available to me during my visit in December.

I booked myself a room at the El Faro, one of our "gay-friendly" hotels. I made the reservation by fax for a José Luis Herrera W., adding the instruction "Bill to Eloy H. Wise." I did not leave a copy of this fax in the file. I was sure that when Monty saw the bill, he would associate my name and the reservation dates and assume that "José Luis Herrera W." was a clerical error.

I was inordinately proud of my new surname. The "Herrera" was my father's family name. By adding "W," I followed the Mexican custom of using the mother's maiden name, or just the initial, as a second surname. The letter "W" is used in Spanish only for foreign words like whiskey. Therefore, José Luis Herrera W. indicated to anyone who wanted to bother about such things that the mother of señor Herrera was not a Hispanic lady.

I had no idea what José Luis Herrera W. would do with his new identity, but I wanted to give him as much freedom as possible. At the gay hotel, Eloy would work out of his office and behave like a regular tourist. At the El Faro, an anonymous José Luis, coming out of hibernation, would be free to act out his fantasies.

The notion of using my father's surname for José Luis was related to my passport application. Both Monty and Joe urged me to obtain a passport to avoid any hassles at the border. I had to go to my mother's in Fairfax to pick up my birth certificate for the application.

When I called her from Berkeley, she was in one of her down periods. She had gotten rid of her latest lover, had not qualified for food stamps for the month, and was searching for a new guru. I say "guru" because I am used to this term. Actually, this time around, she wanted to be channeled or some such. To her surprise, I told her that I would take her out for dinner, stay the night, and return to Berkeley in the morning.

She must have been impressed with my phone call, because she had my birth certificate ready. For the first time in my life, I took my mother out for dinner. I wore the sharp suede jacket Joe had given me for our first anniversary. "Eloy," she said, "you've changed so much. You dress like a preppie. You look so much like your father, Domingo. He was a real handsome man. Do you date many girls these days?"

"No, mother. I'm gay."

Without batting an eyelash she asked, "Are you sure that you're gay, not bisexual? You know, most young Mexican men are bisexual, though of course they wouldn't admit it."

I had heard the same story before at GIF meetings. I wondered how my mother knew such things, but was not comfortable asking her. "No, mom, I'm really gay."

"Well, Eloy, it's your life and you've got to do what you've got to do. But please, do be careful. These days, we all need to be very careful with our partners."

That is how I came out to my mother. I wondered whether my mother practiced safe sex, and whether she was HIV negative. I knew that some of her boyfriends shot up. But I kept my questions to myself.

8

Hustling with Angel

I planned on being in Acapulco between Christmas and New Year's day, because I felt that I would be lonely by myself in Berkeley. Monty talked me out of it. "You won't get any work done in Acapulco at that time of year," he told me. "I promise to fix you up with a special date for Christmas."

I took off from San Francisco on December 17. The trip excited me. I had done a little traveling with Joe, but never by myself. Now I was going abroad, alone and in style. Our first stop was Mazatlán, where all passengers cleared Mexican immigration. I was issued an officially stamped tourist card. Carefully, I put the card inside my new passport. We took off again and, after a short flight, landed in Acapulco. I retrieved my suitcase, and boarded a shared limousine that delivered me to my hotel.

It was late in the afternoon when I checked in at the El Faro. I told the desk clerk that I had a reservation, and that my name was José Luis Herrera.

"Welcome, señor Herrera," the clerk said. Since you're the guest of *nuestro gran amigo*, señor Eloy Wise, we booked you into a suite at no extra cost. Please fill out this form."

I had seen Joe do that a number of times when we traveled together. On the form, I stated my name as José Luis Herrera, and gave my home address in Berkeley. The next line shocked me. It asked for my nationality, passport number, and place and date of issue. My passport was made out to Eloy. H. Wise. I had no idea what I should do. At this stage, I could not retract my previous statement and say that I was not José Luis but, rather, in the clerk's words, the "great friend of the hotel," Eloy Wise himself. I did not plan for this contingency because we had not been asked these questions on the hotel registration form in Tijuana.

I must have appeared confused to the desk clerk.

Solicitously, he asked me whether I needed help. I made a big show of searching for my passport to give me more time to think, but still could not come up with anything. Finally, I put a tiny asterisk on top of José Luis Herrera. At the bottom of the form, following a second asterisk, I wrote in, barely legibly, "aka Eloy H. Wise." I was almost certain that the desk clerk would not notice the entry at the bottom of the form. If he did, he would think that the "aka" referred to the person paying for my reservation. Once in my room, I figured out how we had entered Tijuana without travel documents. I remembered that Joe explained to me that Mexican immigration control took place south of that city.

The hotel management had, indeed, given me a magnificent room. The huge living room window faced the beach. A sliding glass door opened onto a balcony. The large room was tastefully decorated in a tropical motif, with a mini-bar in one corner and a TV in another. The living room had a small bedroom attached to it with yet another TV set. I opened the sliding glass door and watched the sunset from the balcony.

I ate dinner at the hotel, and then went up to my room. The following day would be long and hard. For weeks on end, the gay hotels kept changing the rooms they had originally reserved for GGLC. Monty suspected that they were overbooking.

He instructed me to attach a room number to each visiting GGLC member, and type up a list of these numbers. He suggested that I start my job with the least reliable of the three gay hotels.

Equally urgent were our Mexican tour guides. Earlier on, through recommendations, we had engaged three young local men. We lost touch with one, the second changed his mind once he found out that he would have to lead a troop of gringos to gay bars, and the third spoke no English. The fiasco with the third guide was entirely my own fault. I had interviewed him in Spanish on the phone. I relied on his own assessment of his English capabilities. His ignorance of the language became apparent when, a week later, Monty called and tried to speak to him in English.

The following morning I checked into my little office at one of the gay hotels. I was a bit worried about my authority. I was afraid that I would be considered too young for the tasks at hand. But I did not need to worry about my age. Mexico belonged to the young. They were in charge of everything. Even the assistant manager of the hotel where I had my office was only a few years older than me.

The interviews with the prospective tour guides went well. The first one was the guy with whom we had lost contact. He heard that we were interviewing new guides, and asked me why he was fired. "Because," I told him in English, "you disappeared. The letters we wrote you were returned to us."

"Well, you see, I didn't have enough *confianza* in your organization to give you my name real. Now that I have the pleasure of meet you it's OK I tell to you my name. In Acapulco, I have to be careful or the people will murmur."

I was amused by his English. It was a literal translation from Spanish. I rehired him under his real name. He was an unmistakable twinkie. I knew that Monty would be satisfied with my choice.

I worked the entire day in my small office. I hired two additional guides. But I got absolutely nowhere trying to match GGLC guest names to room numbers. By nine o'clock in the evening, I was certain that only the general manager could help me perform this task, and he was unavailable until the next week. I called it a night.

The next day was a Sunday. I slept late, ate a big breakfast in the hotel's dining room, returned to my room, and let the genie, José Luis, out of the bottle.

For months, I (or was it José Luis?) had planned meticulously for my first Acapulco stage appearance. I knew that the Condesa Beach was the center of gay activities during daylight hours. From the El Faro, it was only a short walk to Condesa Beach. Though I had no idea to what purpose, I intended to appear at this beach as a native Mexican.

I had given a lot of thought to the way I should dress for that occasion, and had brought my wardrobe along. I put on a pair of threadbare cutoffs, and a plain white T-shirt. Underneath the cutoffs, I wore a pair of blue Speedos with black stripes. I put my bare feet into an old pair of tennis shoes. At a garage sale in Berkeley I had bought a small wooden cross with a bronze Christ. This I secured around my neck with a leather thong. Looking at myself in the mirror, I could detect no telltale gringo signs.

There was a notice in my hotel room requesting guests to take to the beach special towels available at the front desk. A ten dollar deposit was required to obtain one. I had seen these towels when guests checked them out. They were good quality towels, embossed with the hotel's name. I decided to do without one.

My skin would not be burned as easily as that of a gringo, but I could not stay indefinitely in the sun. I was sure that it would not be in character for José Luis to bring along sunscreen to the beach. In Berkeley, I had bought the same brand of sun block that Joe always used. It was strong enough to protect even albinos from the ravages of ultraviolet rays. Before dressing in my José Luis costume, I applied it liberally all over my face and body.

In my cutoff pockets I carried only a handkerchief and a comb. José Luis was supposed to use his street smarts to survive, and would not need cash. In any case, I could always walk back to the hotel if I needed money. I left the room key at the desk.

Before making my appearance at the beach, I needed to "tune" my instrument—to get my Spanish to sound authentically Mexican. Except for guides, whom I interviewed in English, I had spoken nothing but Spanish since my arrival in Acapulco. But everybody I talked to knew that I was a Chicano, and would make allowances for an occasional slip. I looked for a different audience to hone my skills.

Approaching Condesa Beach, I saw a restaurant called Betos Safari. In front of it, tethered to a post, was a playful lion cub. A small crowd was watching it. I joined in and, for some ten minutes, talked to anyone who cared to listen to me babbling about the *animalito*. Everybody must have taken me for a native speaker because not once was I asked where I was from. I was surprised that I could hold such long conversations talking about nothing. Neither Eloy nor Harmony could have accomplished that feat.

The beach itself fascinated me. In Marin County we have quite a few beaches. But nothing I had seen there compared with Acapulco. The sky here had a much deeper blue hue, the sand appeared more golden, and the sea was inviting rather then menacing.

At the gay beach were some six rows of small thatched huts facing the ocean. I found out later that they were called *palapas*. As I walked between the rows, a number of tourists called out to me. Reminiscent of

GIF, in quite a few huts sat one or two older whites with their local twinkies. Some *palapa* renters were eating; most were drinking alcohol.

Before leaving California, I had read a gay guide book and knew exactly where the natives made their camp. It was a small sandy area extending south of the *palapas* to where the beach ended abruptly, blocked by large rocks. I walked toward that area.

I passed by a dreamy looking Mexican lad sitting alone on the sand, gazing at the sea. He was somewhat younger than me, and much, much darker. He was short, and had delicate facial features and huge, brown eyes. In a boyish voice and a childlike manner he asked, "Y tú quién eres?"

"I'm José Luis," I answered. "And you?"

"Angel." As if it was the most natural question, he asked, "Do you know how to swim?"

"Not very well. I've never swum in the ocean."

"Shall I teach you then?"

"Yes, please do."

I took off my shirt, cutoffs, and shoes. I buried the wooden cross in the sand, under my clothes. Then, wearing only my Speedos, I followed Angel to the ocean. I was surprised by the warmth of the water. When we were in up to our necks Angel took my hand. "Have faith in me, José Luis. I'm a good teacher."

For the next hour, Angel taught me how to swim. I had taken only one summer swimming class at the College of Marin pool in Kentfield. The instructor there swam with his head under water except when he breathed in air. Most students, myself included, never got the hang of it. Unlike the instructor, who swam elegantly, we thrashed around wildly, our heads bobbing. Our crawl stroke resembled the frantic motions of the drowning. Angel swam as elegantly as my instructor.

Within a short time I mastered the skill of swimming with my head under water. "Shall we swim away from the shore?" Angel asked.

I was afraid. In his childlike voice, Angel reassured me. "Always have faith in me, José Luis. My name is Angel, and I'm your guardian angel."

We swam a fair distance from the shore. Angel had me turn on my back, and taught me how to float in that position by just moving my legs and arms gently. I would have stayed in the ocean all afternoon but Angel said, "You'll get a sunburn. Let's swim back, and sit in the shade."

We found a shady space under the rocks. "Would you like a drink?" Angel asked.

"Yes, please."

Angel bought soft drinks for us. We spent the rest of the afternoon lying on the sand, going into the sea, and dozing off. Not once did Angel ask where I came from, where I stayed, or what work I did. I took a nap, and when I woke up the sun was about to set. I was hungry. "I need to eat, Angel," I said.

"Let me buy you *una hamburguesa*," he said.

It felt strange accepting Angel's generosity. Most likely, between the two of us, I had much more money. Because of my masquerade, Angel might well have assumed that I was totally without means.

Angel spoke little while we were eating. As a matter of fact, much of the time he just was there with me. There was a cherubic innocence radiating from his personality. His childlike behavior could easily have been mistaken for retardation, but I knew better.

Neither Eloy nor Harmony would have had the patience to be with Angel. The less erudite but much wilder José Luis was pleasantly tranquilized by Angel's calmness. "Let's go to my home, rest a bit, clean up, and then go out," Angel suggested.

"Do you live by yourself?" I asked.

"No. I live with my godmother."

We took two buses, for which Angel paid, and then walked a good ten minutes before we reached Angel's house. It was in a rundown neighborhood. The street was paved, but there were no sidewalks. I believe it was sewage and wash water that flowed slowly in gray rivulets on both sides of the street. Angel's small house was a fairly new cement block structure.

His home consisted of one large room with an alcove at each end, that served as a bedroom. The wizened woman who welcomed us must have been in her eighties. She was a tiny person, toothless and hunched. "*Madrina*, I present to you my friend, José Luis."

I wondered how often Angel had brought strangers to the house. The *madrina* seemed not to mind. "Children, do you want something to eat?" she asked.

"We ate *hamburguesas* at the beach. We'll get cleaned up, *madrina*, take a little siesta, and then we'll eat dinner. Did you prepare *caldo* today?"

"I'm just preparing *caldo de pollo*."

"Good," Angel said to me. "When you eat my *madrina's caldo*, you'll lick your fingers."

The shower turned out to be a hose attached to a faucet in a little tin structure at the back of the house. The cold water made me shiver. Angel handed me a small, clean towel.

Angel's bed was located in one of the alcoves. We lay on it, wearing only our shorts. Angel gave me half an embrace, and immediately fell asleep. After a while, I slept. It was late evening when the *madrina* woke us up. "The *caldo* is ready, children."

We were served large bowls of soup. In each bowl was a big chicken thigh bone with lots of meat on it. In the broth floated corn, carrots, yucca, and rice. It tasted delicious. The soup was hot, and we ate it slowly. The *madrina* kept bringing corn tortillas to the table. Like her godson, she also spoke little.

There was an old clock on the wall. It was past nine. How was I going to get back to the hotel without money for a cab? "Look, Angel, I don't have any money and I…"

Angel cut me off. "I know, I know. *Tenemos que talonear.*"

He said that we needed to do something, but I did not understand the verb he had used. As far as I knew, the noun *talón* translated to "heel," but what did Angel mean when he said, "We need to heel?" If *talonear* happened to be a common verb, I would display inexplicable ignorance by asking for its meaning. So I just put myself in his hands.

"*Madrina*," Angel said, "We're going out but we'll be back much later. I hope we'll earn a few little pesos tonight."

"Go with God, children."

We walked back to the bus stop. I caught a glimpse of myself in a store mirror. Unlike Eloy, who was handsome but without spunk, and unlike Harmony, who projected the image of a good-looking, scholarly student, José Luis exuded sexual magnetism. I noticed a few women staring at me on the bus.

Again, we got off one bus and boarded another. The destination of the second bus read *zócalo*. I knew that if we rode the bus to the end of the line we would arrive at the main plaza of the city. As we turned a corner, I saw that we were on costera Miguel Alemán, which follows the shoreline. In a few minutes I would see the El Faro Hotel. For a moment I thought it might be a good idea to get off the bus there. For all I knew, talonear referred to an illegal activity like selling drugs.

But I trusted Angel. Something in me wanted to see where this adventure would take me. If need be, I was sure that Angel would give me bus fare to go back to my hotel.

Our last stop was, indeed, the *zócalo*, and we got off the bus. The plaza was lit brightly. To our left was a bandstand. The musicians had just finished, and were leaving the stand. There were lots of people milling around, most of them young. The benches were also crowded. Angel led us away from costera Miguel Alemán, toward the church at the eastern end of the park. There it was much darker. On the benches and under the trees, young couples were making out.

"Amigo," Angel said solemnly, "both of us need to make some money tonight. What you have to do is sit on one of the benches, where it's the darkest. Ignore young men and look out for mature señores. If you give them a strong look, they'll come over and speak to you. Tell them that you can help them *disfrutar*.

"They'll understand what you have in mind when you mention enjoyment. Do whatever they ask of you. Most señores are caballeros, and will pay you well. I'll meet you here later on, and we'll return to my home. God willing, between the two of us, we'll have enough money to give to the *madrina* so she can prepare a little breakfast for us, and also to take a taxi, since the buses stop running at midnight. With what is left over between us, you can buy for yourself whatever you desire. See you later."

Angel moved away into a darker section of the park. I sat on the bench contemplating the situation. I had met Angel at the gay beach but I never gave his sexual orientation any thought. To me he seemed to be as sexless as an angel. Yet the *talonear* verb must have meant the same as our English verb "hustle." I didn't quite understand how heel translated into hustle.

On the one hand, I wanted to go back to the hotel and get out of the crazy role Angel had created for me. On the other hand, now that I was already in it, wouldn't it be fun to let it play out?

A fat señor approached my bench. He was the first person in Acapulco I saw wearing a tie. As Angel had instructed me, I gave him *una mirada muy fuerte*. The man took notice of my strong look, approached my bench, hesitated briefly, and then sat right next to me. He smelled of tobacco, alcohol, and perfume. "What are you doing here so late, *joven*?" he asked.

"Señor, I'm trying to earn some money for the bus fare to go home. It's quite far from here. Also, to give a few little pesos to my *madrina*. Maybe you can help me out?"

"I'll give you some money if you gratify me, *joven*." He did not ask me my name or introduce himself. He just kept addressing me as *joven*, the Mexican custom when speaking to a young man.

"Sí, señor, I know how do this very, very well," I told him, heeding Angel's instructions. He was a man of about fifty-five with a dark complexion and strong Indian features. There was a heavy gold bracelet on his right wrist, a large analog watch on his left wrist, and a few gaudy rings on his fingers. "*Vámonos, pues*!" he said.

He led me to his car, parked in the next block. It was a well-kept Buick. He pulled away from the curb too fast, causing the tires to shriek. He took out a pack of cigarettes. "Take one, *joven*," he said as he lit up.

"Thank you, señor. But I don't smoke."

He gave me a strange look, and lit one for himself. He drove too fast, braking at the very last moment for the ubiquitous safety bumps. We drove into the suburbs. With some difficulty, he took out his wallet and extracted a small photo. "This is my señora, my two boys, and my daughter," he said. "My oldest boy is about your age. As you can see for yourself, I am normal, very normal. Very, very normal."

I wondered about his pronouncements. Had I implied that he was anything but normal? "Do you know what the *próstata* is?"

"No, señor."

"The *próstata* is inside your gut, near your asshole. It controls how fast you can piss."

Of course, he was talking about the prostate.

Prostate discussions were common between Joe and his friends. "I understand you now, señor."

"The doctor prescribed prostate massages for me. It's difficult to do by myself. I want you to massage my prostate."

"Massage? With my finger?" That didn't sound like a very appealing procedure. "*Con la verga, joven*!" he said in an exasperated tone of voice.

So that was it. After all the prostate bullshit he just wanted me to fuck him. How could I have been so stupid? Of course, if somebody pays for sex, one way or another fucking will take place. Luckily, he did not want to fuck me. I knew intuitively that José Luis was capable of performing physical feats that Eloy could not or would not have done. I believed I would be up to that assignment, though I was not looking forward to it.

After driving maybe a quarter of an hour in the suburbs, the señor slowed down. It was quite dark, and there were no street lights, but the almost full moon made it possible to see the shapes of the buildings. We stopped by a house that looked like all the others on the street. Peremptorily, the señor pressed a button. A shrill buzzer sounded. The door did not open immediately, and the señor kept his finger on the buzzer. "*Ya voy, ya voy*," we heard an irritable voice. A bald and toothless old man, wearing only a pajama bottom, opened the door. He saw me first. "What the devil do you want here at this time of night?"

Then he saw my companion. The annoyance went out of his voice. Unctuously, he said, "Ah, Don Ricardo. It gives me pleasure to welcome you to my house. As always, here you have your home."

Don Ricardo was short with him. "Which room?"

"The same as always, Don Ricardo. Sí señor, the same as always."

Ricardo gave the landlord a few bills. "Shall I show you the way, Don Ricardo?"

"Didn't you just tell me twice, 'The same as always?' I can find my own way. Just turn on the damn lights, old man." Ignoring the landlord, Ricardo took me by the forearm, and marched me upstairs. He opened the middle room, walked into it, found the floor lamp, and turned on a bulb of low wattage.

An ample, old-fashioned brass bed occupied one wall. There was a torn sheet on the mattress, and a piece of a terrycloth towel on top of a naked, dirty pillow. Next to the bed stood the lamp and a rickety old chair. This was the only furniture in the room. Ricardo undressed methodically, neatly arranging his clothes on the chair. He kept on his underwear. He motioned me to undress and put my clothes on the floor. Obediently, I took off my shirt and shoes, keeping on only my Speedos. Ricardo was a lot fatter than I imagined. The room was very warm, and I smelled his perfumed sweat. In the stuffy room, the various smells emanating from him almost gagged me.

He lay down on the bed, and was about to pull me onto it, when he got up again. From his pants he withdrew a small bottle of Johnson's Baby Oil. I looked at the bottle. Did he want a massage before sex?

He saw me looking at the bottle and probably thought that I did not know what it contained. "This here is oil, *joven*. Put a lot on your dick so you don't hurt my asshole."

"You aren't supposed to use oil-based lubricants on the condom. It can cause it to break. We must use only water-based lubricants," I recited smartly. I knew these instructions by heart, because much of the AIDS awareness literature I had read was printed in both English and Spanish.

"I'm not a woman. You won't get me pregnant. We don't need a condom."

Quoting again from the Spanish section of the AIDS literature, I said, "I practice only safe sex."

"Safe sex?"

"To prevent SIDA."

He looked at me curiously. "Have you lived in the United States?"

"Yes, I've lived in Los Angeles."

"Well, then you're as fucked up as a damn gringo. They're afraid of everything, including even cigarettes. So that's why you don't smoke! Don't you know that only *maricones* catch SIDA? I'm not a *maricón*—I'm a married man with children. You're penetrating me, so you aren't a queer either, at least not for tonight. Forget about the fucking SIDA."

"I will not have sex without a condom!"

"Then go to hell." Ricardo turned off the lamp, and was about to go to sleep. Suddenly, he got up, took his wallet and keys out of his pants, put these on the bed, and lay on top of them. A moment later he was asleep.

I put on my clothes immediately. I sat at the foot of the bed. Ricardo lay diagonally on the bed. Even had I wanted to, I could not have shared it with him. Was I going to sit in this suffocatingly warm and smelly room all night long?

I had absolutely no idea where I was. The only way I could get back to my hotel would be by taxi. I did not know whether I would be able to find a taxi outside. But even if I did, how would I pay the driver?

After a while, I decided to take my chances outside. I could not stomach being in the same room with Ricardo any longer. When I left the room I did not close the door, because I wanted to be able to slip back in noiselessly if the obsequious homeowner woke up. I was afraid he would suspect me of stealing from Ricardo. It was pitch dark. I had to be careful to move without bumping into things. Somehow, I managed to make it downstairs to the entrance door. Softly, I opened it and stepped outside. Again, I left it open just a crack, in case I needed to go back into the house. I felt a gentle nudge in the small of my back, and the door shut behind me. It must have had a spring of some sort.

I sat on the stoop contemplating my bad luck. There was no traffic on the street, the houses were all dark, and the only sound was the occasional bark of a dog. At least it was not oppressively warm where I sat, but it would be a long night. And, in the morning, how would I get back? Could I panhandle a few pesos for bus fare?

I had to pee. I walked to the side of the house. As I was peeing, there was a sharp bark from the house across the street. Other dogs started barking, too. I was sure that if I kept moving I would wake the entire neighborhood. It was then, while I was peeing, that I switched from José Luis back to Eloy. Enough was enough. The games were over now. For starters, I would become the UC college student I used to be, rather than pretending to be an Acapulco hustler.

I had already felt it before, but I became acutely aware now that I had a bad sunburn. The skin on my shoulders and back felt painful and tight. When I sat down again, I could not even lean against the door. Somehow, I managed to doze off in that awkward position. I woke up to the sound of barking dogs and an approaching car. I wondered whether I should attempt to flag it down. As if it understood my wishes, the car slowed down and came to a stop in front of the house.

9

Spanked by an Undertaker

It was a taxi with two passengers. I was still trying to figure out what I should do when the passengers emerged. The moonlight was bright enough to allow me to observe them. The shorter one, a Mexican guy, as young or even younger than me, wore only three items of clothing: a blue undershirt, a red bikini bathing suit, and a pair of huaraches, the local thongs. His undershirt was tucked neatly into his bathing suit. A comb was held in place by the bathing suit's elastic band. He was dark-skinned with coarse black hair. By GIF standards, he was a fellow twinkie.

The taller man looked like a tourist, and appeared to be in his early fifties. The two men must have noticed me but ignored my presence. The tourist asked the Mexican guy in English, "Are you sure this is a hotel?"

"Yes, is hotel. I tell true."

"How we shall return later? Is bus or taxi traveling here?" The tourist spoke English a bit like Helmut but with a different, somewhat softer, accent. I was sure he was a German speaker. His Mexican companion did not understand him.

Speaking loudly now, the man tried his luck in what I took to be French. "*Retourner*? How we shall *retourner*?"

I was frantic now because I was a afraid the taxi would take off without me. "Can I translate for you?" I asked the tourist.

"You speak English?" he asked.

"Yes, I do. *Und auch ein wenig Deutsch.*"

For a moment he looked at me as if he had seen a mirage, and was afraid it would disappear. "You also speak German? Oh, this is excellent. We shall discuss in a moment your German speaking. Is this a hotel?" he asked, pointing to the house.

"Sort of."

"Is it a nice place?"

"No, it's horrible."

"Then, of course, we must not go in!" He pondered the situation for a moment, and then asked, "Pardon me, but what are you doing here?"

"I was...I was abandoned."

"Abandoned? Oh, I understand. *Abandonné*?"

"Yes," I said. Obviously, he spoke French better than English.

"Pardon me," the tourist said. "May I allow myself to ask you a very personal question?"

"Yes. You may ask." Just don't let the taxi take off, I added silently to myself.

"Are you gay?"

"Yes."

"You see," he said pointing to his companion, "I brought this young man here, his name is Feliciano, to have some fun. Is this correct English?"

"Yes. Why didn't you take him to your hotel?"

"The way he is dressed, not elegant. Like street boy. You...how must I say this? You're OK to bring into my hotel." I saw a skeptical look on his face. I probably looked worse than the kid. Unlike him, I had lost my comb upstairs, and my hair must have been a mess. I suppose that my advantage over Feliciano was that the tourist would be able to communicate easily with me.

"Would you do me the honor to come with me to my hotel? Just for short time? I will, of course, pay compensation for your time."

"I don't want any money. I just want somebody to pay for my taxi back to Acapulco. We can go to my hotel."

"Your hotel? What is it called?"

"El Faro."

"But this is also my hotel!" He said this as if it was beyond comprehension that we should be staying at the same hotel.

"What about him?" I said pointing to Feliciano. "Oh, I shall give compensation to him. Immediately, I shall." He took out a handful of bills. "Please tell Feliciano that I do not wish to go in this hotel. We shall return to Acapulco, and I shall tell the taxi driver to take him to his house." He handed me the bills to give to Feliciano.

All the while, the kid was observing the scene. He understood pretty much what was going on. Judging by his facial expression, he was getting more and more upset. I translated the tourist's instructions as I handed Feliciano the money.

He counted the bills carefully. Apparently, it was more than he had expected. "*Vámonos, pues,*" he said, seating himself in the front seat of the taxi.

The tourist and I sat in the back seat. "Tell the taxi driver where you live," I said to Feliciano in Spanish. "We'll stop there first."

When that was straightened out, Feliciano asked me, "Is the señor taking you to his hotel?"

"Yes. He prefers someone who speaks his language."

"You speak Spanish and English. Where are you from?"

"San Francisco, California. My parents were born in Mexico. I spoke Spanish at home."

"How is business in San Francisco?"

Business? What business? Then I understood. He assumed that I was hustling in San Francisco, and this was a busman's holiday for me. "Oh, in San Francisco I'm a student at the university."

"That's good," Feliciano said. "It's difficult to make a living if you have to *talonear*. The..."

I stopped him in mid-sentence. "What does *talonear* mean?"

"*Putear*."

"Why 'heel?'"

"Because of the *vestitdas*, the ones who dress like women when they prostitute themselves."

So now I knew. *Talonear* meant to whore. No wonder gentle Angel had not used the more vulgar verb, prostitute, when describing his activities. And what was I supposed to do about Angel? Nothing, I decided. I was lucky to get a ride back to the El Faro. There was no way I could stop at the *zócalo* to say goodbye to him.

While we talked, we ignored the taxi driver completely. Of course, by that time the driver must have understood, on his own, what his three passengers were all about.

"Let me speak to the señor. I mustn't be impolite." I turned to the tourist and said, in English, "I'm sorry, I didn't introduce myself. My name is Eloy Wise."

"It is very pleasant to acquaint myself with you. My name is Bruno Hausmann. How it happens that you speak Spanish, English, and a little German?"

"I'm a student from California. I've taken a few German courses. I spoke Spanish at home as a child. Where are you from, Bruno?"

"I'm from Zurich. I make here a vacation for two weeks. I saw this young man," Bruno said, pointing to Feliciano rather than mentioning his name, "at the La Quebrada, where the young men jump into the sea from a high cliff. All evening I am thinking where I can take him to be together in private. But I may not take him to my hotel because *es passt sich nicht.* How do you say this in English?"

"It's improper." I had learned this phrase from Helmut, who used it quite often.

Suddenly, two questions popped into my mind. Had we made an agreement that Bruno could have sex with me in return for the free taxi ride? And does he have screwing of any kind on his mind? I did not mind Bruno having sex with me. He was rather cute. His extreme formality amused and even excited me. But I wasn't going to repeat the recent fiasco.

Bruno started saying something but I interrupted him. "Just so we don't have a problem later. I don't screw, and I don't get screwed."

Bruno looked at me blankly. "Screw?"

"*Vögeln*," I said. Yet another word Helmut had taught me.

Our taxi passed under a streetlight. I could see that Bruno was embarrassed. He had blushed. "Is OK. There are so many other things we can do in bed," he said.

* * *

We dropped Feliciano off on the outskirts of Acapulco. When we reached the El Faro, the taxi driver charged Bruno a small fortune. Bruno did not seem to mind. I suspected that he was preoccupied with our grand entrance into the El Faro.

There was a large mirror in the lobby of the hotel. I looked at myself. My hair was disheveled, my T-shirt stained with slimy green gook, and my tennis shoes were grubby. With my worn-out cutoffs, I looked like a real street urchin. I was certain that Bruno was glad that I would be able to get into the hotel on my own.

The clock above the reception desk read 1:07. The receptionist looked at me disdainfully. He addressed Bruno, assuming that I was his guest. "Your room number, señor?"

After he gave Bruno his key I said in Spanish, "My key please. Room 303."

The clerk looked at me in disbelief. I occupied one of the hotel's three suites. "You're staying with señor…?"

"I'm staying by myself. My name is José Luis Herrera." As soon as I gave him my name, I realized that I had introduced myself to Bruno as Eloy Wise.

Like the receptionist at the hotel in Tijuana, the clerk was suspicious of me. He checked my name against the guest list, and then pulled my registration card. "What's your home address, Sr. Herrera?"

After I told him my address in Berkeley, including my zip code, he handed me my room key with obvious reluctance. By now I was exhausted, and my back was killing me. I did not want to have to explain my multiple personalities. As we went into the elevator I said to Bruno, "I'm very tired. Tomorrow I'll explain to you about my name."

"Names," he corrected me.

When I opened the door and turned on the lights, Bruno looked at me in amazement. "But your room is bigger than mine. And much more elegant!"

"I'll explain everything tomorrow," I said.

"You are not a…What's the English word? Narcotics trafficker, are you?" He was only half joking.

I took a quick shower. The water really hurt my back. I could not stand the towel touching my skin there, and had to wait in the bathroom for my back to dry on its own. When I was done, Bruno took his shower and followed me into bed. Before I turned the lights out I told him, "Please don't touch my back. I have a terrible sunburn." Then I fell asleep.

*   *   *

I had a weird dream before the ringing of the phone woke me up. In it I saw a big white angel with a huge halo hovering above me, then swooping down and kissing me. Suddenly, even as the angel was kissing me, he laid an egg. I knew that the egg had come from the angel's prostate.

"*Guten Morgen*," a voice said in German when I picked up the receiver. It sounded like Bruno's. Last night's misadventures came back to me in a flash. Bruno is here, with me, I thought. I looked around but Bruno was gone. *"Sind sie Herr Bruno?"* I asked the caller.

Bruno answered in English. "I left your room because I wished to shower and shave myself and eat breakfast."

"Bruno, what time is it?"

"Nine twenty-two."

"Oh, my God! I'm supposed to be at a meeting at nine." On Saturday, I had made arrangements to meet with the gay hotel's general manger at nine in the morning on Monday, to sort out the GGLC room reservations.

"You work in Acapulco or you make vacation here?"

"I'll explain everything later. Can we meet in the afternoon?"

"Shall we have lunch together?"

"It's so late now. I'll be busy until one or even later."

"Well, we shall have late lunch as the Mexicans do. Do you know the Condesa Beach?"

"Of course." Only too well, I thought.

"Meet me there for lunch. I shall be in a little *Hütte*. They will bring the lunch to us from the restaurant."

There was no time for breakfast. I shaved, dressed, and took a taxi to the gay hotel. There I met with Mike, the American owner. It was hard work negotiating with him.

GGLC members had been charged by Monty according to the type of accommodations they selected. If the hotel downgraded their room assignments, Monty would have to make refunds, as well as deal with lots of complaints. I explained all of this to Mike without much success. "Well, that's your problem," he said, trying to bring this matter to an end.

"Not really. If you don't give me the rooms we've agreed on, I'm going to book the three members whose reservations you've changed into the El Faro. The rooms there may not be as charming as yours, but they're much larger, and they're right on the beach. Why do you think I am staying at the El Faro, and not in one of the gay hotels?"

I was flabbergasted by the audacity of my speech. I had not asked Monty permission to move members from one hotel to another. Never before had I spoken in such an authoritative way. Was there yet another personality, with leadership potential, as Joe would call it, lurking within me?

Mike backed down immediately. Because of the economic downturn in the United States, it would not be a good tourist season for Acapulco's hotels. He knew that the much larger El Faro would have many rooms to spare. In less than half an hour I had the room list exactly the way Monty wanted it.

I walked over to my little office and, from there, faxed the confirmed reservation list to Monty. By then it was noontime. This allowed me to work on my Condesa Beach image. In Berkeley, I had prepared José Luis's wardrobe meticulously. It never occurred to me that after only one stage appearance, Eloy would take over. The single pair of Speedos that would have served José Luis for a week was hardly what Eloy, a UC student, would wear at the gay beach. I also needed a sharp short-sleeved shirt, since I could not expose my back to the sun.

I spent too much money buying a sexy bathing suit and two shirts in a store opposite the hotel. Then I went up to my room and changed. All the while I was thinking of Angel. What would I do if I saw him at the beach?

A bond of brotherly love had been established between me, as José Luis, and Angel. When we were eating the *madrina's caldo*, I fantasized about staying in Acapulco and moving in with Angel and his *madrina*. But I also wondered whether Angel was for real. Maybe he was some sort of a symbolic representation, like the fool in a deck of tarot cards. For all of his sweetness, and the soothing effect he had on me, he, like the fool, represented danger. Did Angel get José Luis into yesterday's mess, or did José Luis create Angel as a catalyst for his escapades? And what were Eloy's obligations toward Angel?

I did not manage to come up with any solutions to these questions. I would just have to play it by ear if Angel and I bumped into each other. I used the sidewalk parallel to the beach, going beyond the gay section, until I reached the sandy expanse. There I crossed to the beach, looking for Angel. I was aware that quite a few local gays tried to size me up. My expensive beach outfit confused them. Was I a native or a tourist?

I searched for Angel for a long time but did not see him. Then I had a revelation. Angel would appear to me only when I was José Luis! Eloy was not meant to meet him. This was all right. For the rest of my stay in Acapulco, I would be Eloy.

I turned to my right, and walked toward the *palapas*. Bruno was sitting in what he called his *Hütte*. He had an athletic build. For an older man, he looked quite fit. He was a muscular man of medium height, who obviously watched his diet. Everything about Bruno was orderly. His light brown body hair ran in a narrow strip up from his belly button and then curved, with great precision, below and above his pectorals. The thinning hair on his head was combed at a perfect angle. His gray bathing suit, with red stripes on either side, looked like an ad for beachwear geared toward middle-aged executives. In spite of his great formality and rather severe facial expression, he was soft-spoken and had a pleasant voice. "*Guten Tag*, how may I call you today, José Luis or Eloy?"

While we ate lunch, I told Bruno what Joe would have called a sanitized version of the events he had witnessed the previous night. I also gave him a censored autobiographical outline. I told him I did not wish to discuss why I had been at the "hotel" the previous evening; it was too painful. I said I had been sent by my San Francisco employer, who organized gay tours, to do preparatory work in Acapulco. I explained that in California, I used the names my mother gave me; in Mexico, I preferred the Spanish names my father bestowed upon me. But I wanted Bruno to call me by my American name, Eloy, since we were speaking in English. "Now, Bruno, enough about me. Tell me about yourself."

Bruno collected his thoughts for a few moments. Or maybe he was mulling over the veracity of my story. Then he started speaking. "As I told you, I come from Zurich. There I'm a funeral director. Every winter I make vacation in Sri Lanka, very unexpensive. But now is too dangerous because of terrible political chaos. So I take charter flight to Mexico City then plane to Acapulco. I like swimming and tropical weather. And also I like young gentlemen like you with dark skin for…companions."

I felt comfortable with Bruno. He was overly formal—what else could one expect from a funeral director?—yet did not come across as self-important, as did so many of the Anglo GIF members.

We stayed at the beach until late in the afternoon. Then we went back to the hotel and cleaned up. We had dinner across the street at a fancy Mexican restaurant. I insisted that we split the bill.

Before we left the restaurant Bruno said, "We must spend the night in your room. Nobody will hear our sex-making."

My suite was at one end of the hall. The small bedroom was in back of it. If one wanted to make noise, that would be an ideal place for it. But why would our "sex-making" be so noisy? Surely Bruno would not want to listen to loud music?

We went to bed early. We were hugging and kissing each other when Bruno asked, "How is your back now?"

"A little bit better," I said.

"Good," he said. "I don't want to hurt it. Maybe your ass a little bit."

"I told you, I don't…"

"I know, I know. Something different. Please relax yourself." He was lying under me. Very gently, he started tapping my buns. It was somewhere between caresses and soft smacks. He did this rhythmically for quite a while. Ever so slowly, he increased the force of the smacks. Strangely, I felt stimulated by the cadence. All the while we were kissing and cuddling. Bruno put even more force into his smacks. Now they were almost slaps. They started making noises which grew louder as the force behind them increased. I hardly felt any pain.

Abruptly, the predictable cadence became random slapping. Two on the right cheek, five on the left, then again, much lower on the right, three resounding slaps. I was just about ready to tell Bruno to cut it out when I started to feel euphoric. I had felt like that only once before, when I had dislocated my shoulder and was given a Demerol injection.

My body understood that if I did not try to anticipate where the next slap would land, it would not hurt me much. All I had to do was to relax completely, and just let it happen. As the spanking grew harder, whatever pain I had felt initially faded away. My euphoria matched the force of Bruno's spanking.

We continued our passionate kissing throughout the spanking scene. Paradoxically, Bruno's spanking gave me a sense of well-being. Of course, there was also pain associated with it, but I had long ago stopped feeling it.

Abruptly, Bruno stopped the spanking. He changed positions, lying face-to-face on top of me. Still kissing me, he took my hand in his, and motioned me to spank his butt. In the beginning I felt awkward, almost embarrassed. Then I got into it. I applied the same random pattern Bruno had used on me. I really got off on Bruno's enjoyment of my spanking. Only after both of us climaxed by humping each other did I feel a stinging sensation in my buns. Eventually, it changed to a dull pain. I asked Bruno later, "Do you always spank your sex partners?"

"No, very, very little. Much noise. Very unpractical in hotels. Also many persons think it's perverse. Sometimes, they like me to do it, but are afraid that it is unnormal."

* * *

Unlike Joe, Bruno disdained gay watering holes, but he was big on tourist sights. Methodically, we did them all: the aquarium, the Spanish fort, the archaeological museum, and the craft stores. But most of the time we spent on the beach. Bruno was an excellent swimmer. Thanks to Angel, I could hold my own while swimming with him.

Bruno was going to stay in Acapulco over Christmas. He asked me to spend the holiday with him. "My room is paid for only until the twenty-third of the month. I don't have the money for the additional six days," I told him.

"You must be my guest. I shall pay for everything! I don't wish to be alone on Christmas."

How right my late friend Helmut had been! Old men did indeed extend their generosity willingly, without even being asked. I was delighted that he invited me. I would have been lonely in Berkeley. In deference to my benefactor, Señor Eloy H. Wise, José Luis Herrera and Bruno Hausmann were allowed to stay in the El Faro's suite until the twenty-ninth, for the price of an ordinary room. I told Bruno the story of Helmut and his death, and that I had decided not to go to Europe in the summer. On our last day together Bruno asked, "Do you still have enough money for a ticket to Europe?"

"Yes."

"Then maybe you take a charter and come visit me next summer, but not in Zurich too much. You see, Zurich is a very small town."

"Small? I thought it was very large and important." Joe knew all about Swiss bank accounts and stuff like that. He took great pride in how familiar he was with the ins and outs of Zurich's financial establishments.

"Zurich, like other Swiss cities, is a relatively small place. Fewer than half a million souls. But I don't mean it so. You see, I have to be very careful because of my job, and people in Zurich like to gossip.

"Also, as I've already told you, I live with my mother. I'm in a closet still. When I want a little fun I have to go to Lugano, which is not a very gay city. But Italian Swiss are not so formal, also less gossiping. I suggest you take a charter flight—they are the most cheap—to Zurich. I pick you up at the airport and take you to a hotel room. All paid. You rest there because of terrible jet lag. Next day we take my car and make a tour in Zurich, and then we go to the Alps and make vacation there. You like to climb in the mountains?"

"I don't know. The only mountain I've ever climbed is Mount Tamalpais in Marin County. It's very close to San Francisco, just across the Golden Gate Bridge."

"You'll enjoy in the Alps. Maybe we also drive to Lugano and even to Italy."

"Let me think about it."

Bruno told me that I was the first date, outside Switzerland, with whom he could communicate meaningfully. "My partners are often silly young men and we don't speak the same language. With you, the fun is elevated from the physical to the social, and the way we make sex, also maybe the spiritual level."

Bruno encouraged me to continue with my German studies, and try to obtain a graduate scholarship to study philosophy in Switzerland. "I shall make arrangements if you will be coming to Zurich to study. With you, it won't be easy but I can do. Much explaining to my mother and friends, but I can do. With a Sri Lankan, never."

"What is the difference? My skin is also dark."

"Yes, but not so very dark. Also facial look not so very different from European, not like Sri Lankan. We Swiss have little minds and much prejudice."

Bruno's suggestion reminded me that Dr. Brotbaum had received his PhD from the University of Zurich. Planning my studies in Switzerland, what a neat subject to discuss with Dr. Brotbaum!

* * *

I knew that Acapulco was not a typical Mexican place. I liked it not as part of Mexico, but as a city with beautiful beaches. Once I began swimming in earnest, I was fascinated by the ocean. Bruno and I spent countless hours in the water.

We visited other beaches besides the Condesa. One morning we went to Caleta Beach for snorkeling. On another day, in the afternoon, we went sailing, with a bunch of tourists, at Pie de la Cuesta. From the boat, we watched the spectacular sunset. But we spent most of our time at the Condesa Beach because it was closest to our hotel.

We kept to ourselves, and did not make friends with other *palapa* renters. The exception was Monsieur Roger Darlan of Belgium. He was another formal European gentleman in his forties. Without fail, he managed to rent an adjacent *palapa*. Bruno had spent much of his childhood in Geneva, and spoke French fluently. I suspected that Monsieur Darlan was interested in Bruno as more than just a fellow francophone, and consequently was jealous of me. To avoid even a hint of intimacy, Bruno always addressed Roger as Monsieur Darlan. His formality was reciprocated by the Belgian gentleman.

I laughed silently when I fantasized Bruno lying under the chubby M. Darlan, spanking him lustily and noisily. Roger spoke Spanish quite well, and had been in Acapulco many times. He took us to native eateries. In these restaurants I would order a *caldo de pollo*, and remember my meal at the *madrina's*.

Except for our dinners with M. Darlan, I saw little of the native scene. At the beaches, Mexicans were mostly servers and hawkers. The vast majority of the people were tourists. The exception was the Condesa beach. Amidst the gay foreigners were quite a few young Mexican camp followers. I did not mix with them at all.

There was a longing in me to merge completely, even if only briefly, with my Mexican heritage. It was not a new desire. After all, my handsome Hispanic looks were Domingo Herrera's bequest. Of the triumvirate ruling my psyche, José Luis was the personality most suited to get me in touch with the people of my forebears.

Just as I knew that Eloy would never see Angel, I was certain that José Luis would never reveal himself to Bruno. This is why I stuck to him. I took him along even when I went about finishing my GGLC assignments. But I also knew that José Luis had unfinished business in Acapulco.

10

The Wittgenstein Term Paper

It was our last full day in Acapulco. After breakfast Bruno said, "M. Darlan asked me to accompany him to go shopping for souvenirs. I, too, must buy souvenirs. I know shopping will go on your nerves and also M. Darlan incommodes you. You should go to the beach by yourself and I shall be there around midday and we shall have lunch in the *Hütte*."

True enough. Shopping for souvenirs would get on my nerves, and M. Darlan was a pain. But I was afraid that as soon as Bruno left me, José Luis would materialize to take care of unfinished business. It would be better for me, I thought, to stay in my hotel room and pack rather than go to the beach by myself. I would join Bruno later for lunch at his *Hütte*.

As I was packing, I took José Luis's cutoffs from the closet in order to put them in my suitcase. I held them in my hands momentarily and…switched personalities. In a jiffy, I was dressed in his outfit. Fortunately, I had washed the T-shirt and cleaned the tennis shoes. Ceremoniously, I hung the wooden cross around my neck. Now, once again, I was José Luis. Looking at myself in the mirror, I was pleased with my sexiness.

I walked directly to the sandy expanse beyond the gay beach. Angel was sitting almost at the same spot where I had seen him the first time. He smiled at me brightly. "Hola, José Luis. *Comó has estado*?" he asked in his childlike voice. He made no mention of our evening at the *zócalo*. I told him that I was well. He said he, too, was well.

"Do you want to go swimming?"

"Yes, very much, Angel."

"Vámonos, pues."

Just like the previous time, I buried the cross in the sand under my clothes. I went into the ocean with the same Speedos I had worn the last time. We swam far away from the shore. There we rested, just treading water. "Why don't you move in with me and my *madrina*?" Angel asked. "She likes you a lot, and would enjoy having more children in the house."

Angel used the word *niños*. To him, and to his *madrina*, he and his friends would forever be children. Playfully, he splashed some water in my face. "If you don't want to work in the *zócalo, ni modo*," he continued. "My *madrina's* brother-in-law owns a fishing boat. Tourists rent it by the day. He prepares a lunch for them and serves them drinks. He always needs someone to help out. He doesn't pay very much, but you'll get good tips."

I could see myself serving drinks to the gringos on the boat, pretending that I did not understand their language. I would astound them with the ESP of a Mexican galley boy. "Why," they would exclaim, "this José Luis character seems to read our minds. How strange it is for an uneducated Mexican to be so perceptive!" What a hoot!

Even while Eloy was enjoying Bruno's company, the José Luis part of me had formed some sort of a plan for staying in Acapulco with Angel. The plan did not call for me to live in Mexico permanently. It would just be a short escapade. I would store my suitcase at the El Faro, including my passport, ticket, and traveler's checks, and move in with Angel and his *madrina*. I would bring with me just enough cash for bus fare and incidentals. I could afford to miss a week or so of school. Then, when the escapade was over, I would retrieve my stuff from the El Faro and fly back to Berkeley.

Of my three personalities, only Harmony had a long-range plan of action: Through outstanding scholarship, I would become Dr. Brotbaum's associate. As long as we were enjoying a school vacation, Eloy and José Luis could do whatever amused them, as far as Harmony was concerned. It was all right to play little games in the *zócalo* with Angel; it was a pleasant distraction to have an affair with Bruno. That was what vacations were all about. But as soon as school started, Harmony would be there with his nose to the grindstone.

At sea, far from the shore, a swimmer hardly feels the difference between large and small waves. But the wave that lifted me up must have been very big. By the time it let me down roughly, I had switched back to Eloy. I knew, of course, that it was Harmony who orchestrated the shift. I swam over to Angel and, fighting the waves, managed to plant a clumsy kiss on his cheek. "Adíos, Angel. Take good care of yourself. I'll always love you." Using the crawl stroke Angel had taught me, I swam back to shore.

I did not have a towel, but I didn't wait on the beach to dry. I was afraid that Angel would come ashore and cause me to switch back to José Luis. I let the sun dry me as I walked to the El Faro, carrying my clothes in a bundle. I dressed just before entering the hotel. I went directly to my room. There I showered, changed into my fashionable bathing suit, finished my packing, and, about noon, arrived at the beach. Bruno had already secured a *palapa* for himself, and of course Monsieur Darlan was in the adjacent one. I knew that as long as I was with Bruno, neither Angel nor José Luis would have power over me.

Early the next morning, Bruno and I took a taxi to the airport, though his plane to Mexico City, where he would catch his charter flight, departed much later. I told Bruno that I would take him up on his offer to visit him in Switzerland next summer.

Our parting was cordial rather than emotional. Both Bruno and I knew that we would remain good friends. Unlike Joe, who wanted to have sex in the context of a relationship, all Bruno wanted was an intelligent and congenial sex buddy. I could fulfill his needs easily. I was certain that my trip to Switzerland would be a success.

* * *

I understood that, in the eighties, UC students did not date their instructors. Even dating between students and faculty members who were not their instructors was frowned upon. Though Berkeley campus social life was of little interest to me, I was aware of the powerful taboos against instructor-student romances. Even a close intellectual relationship with Dr. Brotbaum would be difficult. After a few monthly Sunday meetings at Dr. Brotbaum's, I appreciated Aviva's reference to his "court." Students really did act as if they were courtiers vying for the king's favor. If Dr. Brotbaum paid me more attention than the other students, it would arouse their jealousy.

Nevertheless, I was determined to have a romantic relationship with Dr. Brotbaum. A clandestine affair, if necessary. My strategy for seeing him privately would be to seek his advice regarding my term paper for the spring semester. I had started researching the philosopher Ludwig Wittgenstein immediately after hearing Steve Davidson's remarks about Wittgenstein's unfortunate homosexual love affairs.

Wittgenstein, who was considered by some to be the most outstanding philosopher of the first part of the twentieth century, turned out a hard subject for a term paper. His philosophical theories were so arcane that even his instructor and mentor and, ultimately, his follower, Lord Bertrand Russell, had difficulties understanding them. But Wittgenstein's application of mathematical logic to philosophy intrigued me. After getting used to Wittgenstein's cumbersome style, I understood, more or less, what he tried to convey. Fortunately, he had not written voluminously. Among all his other peculiarities was an aversion to putting his theories to paper.

But I was even more intrigued by Wittgenstein the man. He came across as the weirdest of geniuses: a brilliant philosopher who disdained his calling; an extremely wealthy man who gave away all of his money as a result of a mystical war experience; a lonely gay soul seeking love, but dispensing misery to those who gave him theirs; a school teacher who had to resign after abusing his pupils physically.

I was surprised by Wittgenstein's open homosexual relationships with two of his students. He was a full philosophy professor at Cambridge when he fell in love with a math student many years younger than himself. The love affair was not at all secretive. I wished that Dr. Brotbaum and I could behave like Wittgenstein and his students. But Berkeley in the eighties was not Cambridge in the forties.

Writing a term paper about Wittgenstein would be a major undertaking. I had a hunch that no TA would want to guide me in my research because of the difficult subject matter. I would need to see Dr. Brotbaum personally and often. From his lectures, I knew that Dr. Brotbaum took great interest in the personal lives of philosophers. All of them were his buddies. Dead or alive, Dr. Brotbaum philosophized with them. He took Aristotle to task for his opinion that slaves had a slavish nature and that therefore it behooved them to be in that position. He all but said, "How could you, Aristotle, especially you who are so concerned about ethics, hold such unworthy views?" Still, Aristotle continued to be his buddy. Dr.

Brotbaum even described him physically. "He was handsome, of slender waist, and a bit of a fop."

Wittgenstein's guilt-ridden sex life—he even kept a coded log of his masturbation activities—would be, from Dr. Brotbaum's perspective, part and parcel of his philosophical views. If I could package all of this neatly into a term paper, without undue prurience, Dr. Brotbaum might support my endeavors.

I kept the subject of my research to myself. For one, we were still in the fall semester and I was already doing my research for the spring. More importantly, though, was the audacity of my undertaking. Shortly before my trip to Acapulco, I told Ronnell casually that I was interested in Wittgenstein. "Leave this philosopher for your graduate work or your doctorate," he said. "The only person who has ever understood Wittgenstein fully was he himself, and even that's doubtful."

On another occasion Ronnell told me, "Wittgenstein was an Austrian front-line soldier during the first World War. At the end of the war he was captured by the Italians and made a POW. Throughout the war, he writes in his journal about logic and philosophy, and corresponds about it with other philosophers. He even has a mystical experience as a result of his soldiering. You'd think that, surrounded by the horrors of war, he would have some philosophical insights into this whole business. But no. All he obsesses about, as a POW, is getting his book on logic published!

"Compare Wittgenstein to his own teacher, Bertrand Russell, who got very involved in the war issue. Or just compare Wittgenstein to Dr. Brotbaum. He always applies his philosophical theories to the present conditions. Wittgenstein, when surrounded by a horrendous reality, doesn't even comment on it. All he does is his logic."

Ronnell was a political activist, involved with various black causes. I didn't tell him this, but I, too, could see myself escaping from the grim reality of war into my little world of math or logic. His comment, though, made me think. Could I raise that issue in my term paper and discuss it with Dr. Brotbaum?

*   *   *

In the meantime, I was busy with many other undertakings. Upon my return, Monty gave me a Christmas bonus of a hundred dollars and asked me to continue working for him a few hours a week. He had just opened a second office. Since I would be working at both places, Monty insisted that I learn to drive. He paid for my lessons, which I took in Berkeley. I passed the driving test the first time around.

Working out of two offices, Monty managed sometimes to give Benjie the slip and have lunch with me. I looked forward to these occasions. Monty was now my only remaining contact with the gay community.

I was satisfied with my job at KLZW. I set up various computer programs for Aviva so she and her assistants could easily retrieve whatever information they needed. Though I was quite busy doing my work, I met a lot of interesting people. Of all the public radio stations in the San Francisco Bay Area, KLZW was considered the most intellectual.

I became Aviva's protégé. As far as we knew, we were the only gays working for the station. This created a bond between us. Unfortunately, I saw little of Dr. Brotbaum because we had different schedules. But Aviva spoke to me often about him. "Eugene's spontaneous answers really worry me," Aviva told me after one of his programs aired. "I usually agree with what he has to say. But listeners want to be able to classify him as liberal or conservative, progressive or reactionary; put some label on him. Eugene cannot be labeled, because he dissects each idea on its merits without telling you whether he likes or detests it. What he needs desperately is a constituency."

"A constituency?"

Aviva had received her MA in political science from Cornell University. That fact helped explain her analogy. "Yes, just like a politician. A group of dedicated listeners and callers who support him because he represents their views. The way things are now, he's defenseless. One day he'll say the wrong thing, and the program will be canned."

Aviva was so worried about the program that she dared not change its format. For the time being, she let go of the notion that I appear on Dr. Brotbaum's show as the spokesperson for youth.

* * *

To understand Wittgenstein's life story, I needed to know much more world history than I had been taught at my Fairfax high school. I enrolled in a twentieth century history course for the spring semester to help me sort out the historical cataclysms that had dogged Wittgenstein's life. I also enrolled in two computer programming courses and a German class.

One afternoon, while I was working in my tiny office at KLZW, Aviva asked me: "Would you like to have dinner with me Friday after work? I usually cook a festive meal Friday nights."

"Sure. Thanks, Aviva."

Aviva was quite lonely these days, because she and her girlfriend had split recently. Though Aviva had to deal with lots of people as part of her job, she did not seem to have close friends. Friday evening after work, she drove me to her condominium on Dana Street in Berkeley. It was a cheerful two-bedroom apartment furnished in post-modern style. "You know, Harmony, I'm not an observant Jew at all. But I have good memories of the meals my mother cooked to welcome the Sabbath. So I, too, prepare the same dishes on Friday evenings." She added sadly, "Just three months ago there were two of us here."

"Do you ever invite Dr. Brotbaum?"

"I used to. There are some issues between us these days."

Aviva had prepared the food before going to work, and it just needed warming up. I thought Jewish women lit candles Friday evenings and recited some prayers. But Aviva just lit two candles housed in antique silver candlesticks. We listened to tapes of Israeli folk songs, which I enjoyed. The first dish we had was gefiltefish, cold fish balls with a jelly-like sauce. With it, she served a white bread twist that she called a *challah*. The fish didn't do much for me.

Then came a hearty chicken soup with noodles and vegetables. She placed the serving bowl on the table, and its smell instantly evoked Acapulco and the *madrina's caldo.* I was going to switch to José Luis right in front of her. If I did that, I knew that I would wind up at an emergency psychiatric ward. "Go away, leave us alone!" I snarled voicelessly at José Luis. I started crying uncontrollably. I am sure that this was what saved me from switching.

Momentarily, Aviva was taken aback. Nothing had happened between us to bring about this drama. Then she moved to the back of my chair and hugged me. I stood up and turned around and, suddenly, we were hugging each other. I don't recall what I said between sobs. Aviva hushed me. "It's all right, Harmony. I understand. You don't need to explain."

I had not been hugged by a woman in a nonsexual way for a very long time. As far as I could recall, my mother had never done that. On the rare occasions she kissed me, she did so formally and awkwardly. Being hugged by an older woman was a comforting experience. When we sat down again, Aviva did not mention the incident. The soup was similar to the *madrina's caldo*, though Aviva had not put any yucca in it, and instead of rice there were noodles. During the meal we just chatted. Then, after we cleared the table and she washed the dishes, she served cognac. To my great surprise, I rather enjoyed that alcoholic drink. In a worried tone she said, "You know, Eugene is going to come out of the closet." My facial expression must have betrayed me.

"Harmony?" Aviva exclaimed. Her tone implied both reproach and amusement. "There is more than one closet, Harmony. Your Dr. Brotbaum is coming out of his intellectual closet."

"I didn't know that he was in the closet."

"Eugene has written extensively about other philosophers. Until now he has managed to keep his own philosophical views to himself. Now he's coming out, and I'm afraid the shit will hit the fan."

"What's he going to say that's so controversial?"

"In this case it's not what, it's where. Public radio isn't an obscure scholastic publication. In a free society, whatever a scholar writes about is usually tolerated. If a society isn't free, the scholar, even if the masses don't understand him, may have to recant, or worse. This is, as you know, what happened to Galileo, and used to happen in the communist bloc all the time.

"It's different, though, if the scholar has a public forum at his disposal. Let's say a popular radio program. This kind of forum requires a clear and simple style. The scholar is understood, more or less, by the audience. Now his theories are bandied about by the masses.

"If the scholar has given offense to a powerful group, its members strike back. They immediately push the buttons of people who can bring pressure to bear on the scholar and his sponsors. He doesn't get tenure, his upcoming book doesn't get published, and his radio program is canceled.

The crazies have a field day. They send out hate mail, rail against him on talk shows, and some nut might even decide to kill him."

Aviva went on and on. In the beginning, I thought she was dramatizing. But then Lord Russell, Wittgenstein's mentor, came to mind. Though he was a peer of the realm, an earl, no less, he was imprisoned during World War I for his activities as a pacifist. His library was confiscated by the British government when he refused to pay a fine. Aviva had a point. The public did not bother with Russell's writings about the philosophy of mathematics because they did not understand the subject matter. Lots of people, though, took exception to Lord Russell's unpopular views about the war. These they understood only too well. And they took drastic measures just because of his opinions.

Dr. Brotbaum's views on public radio were easy enough to comprehend. I could see why the listening audience would be upset with him. His penchant for pointing out logical contradictions became obvious to his audience almost immediately. I remembered what Aviva had told me months earlier. "In our society, only teenagers have the privilege of constantly pointing out how illogical and contradictory, even hypocritical, the views of adults are.

"For Danny Fleetwood," Aviva continued, "Eugene becoming popular is a win-win situation. There'll be more glory for him than just a footnote acknowledging his contribution to his instructor's research. He will be in the limelight created for him by Eugene. If the going gets too rough, he can bail out and be known as 'Dr. Brotbaum's former associate.'

"Do you know, Harmony, what happens when you take apart concepts or ideas that the masses hold dear?" This was a rhetorical question, and Aviva answered it herself. "You make powerful enemies, that's what happens. You know that because of your interest in Socrates. The

Athenians condemned him to death just for his philosophical examination of their cherished ideas."

11

"Praying" with Takahashi-San

A few weeks after the beginning of the spring semester I made an appointment to see Dr. Brotbaum about my term paper. There were so many students who wanted to speak to him that I had to wait two weeks for a time slot.

He seemed pleased that I visited his office. "Ah, Mr. Harmony Wise," he said, emphasizing my first name, "what philosophical insights do you have today?"

"I would like to write my term paper about Ludwig Wittgenstein. This isn't an easy assignment, and I need your advice."

"Not many beginning students take up Wittgenstein." He pronounced the philosopher's name the German way so it came out Vittgenshtein. "Why did you choose him for your term paper?"

"I was discussing him with Ronnell Chase. Ronnell thinks it's strange that Wittgenstein should have survived a long and brutal war as a fighting soldier, followed by captivity as a POW, without making any philosophical observations about the subject. Wittgenstein spent the war years writing in his notebooks about logic. His main occupation in the Italian POW camp was to see that his *Tractatus Logico-Philosophicus* would be published. I agree with Ronnell that Wittgenstein's reactions to his war experiences are strange. He seems to take war as a natural phenomenon, as we in California would regard an earthquake. It is as if the fine points of logic are more important than wars."

"What would you have him do?"

"I don't know. When I first started reading about Wittgenstein, I couldn't understand why Wittgenstein was at Cambridge during the second World War. I looked him up in a number of encyclopedias, but there was no explanation. In the fifth or sixth book about him, I finally discovered the fact that Wittgenstein could not return to Austria after 1938 because under the Nazi racial laws he was considered Jewish, even though his parents had converted to Protestantism, I could have added here that none of the books mentioned Wittgenstein's homosexuality, but refrained.

"Given Wittgenstein's personal life experiences, wouldn't it have served more of a purpose had he applied his genius to the burning issues of his day, war and racism? Instead, he limited himself to writing about logic and language, and few people, philosophers included, really understood him."

"Your point is well taken, Mr. Wise. It would be unfair, though, to single Wittgenstein out. Practically all major schools of philosophy have paid little attention to the institution of war. As you say, they have taken it for granted that there always will be wars, as we in California view the inevitability of earthquakes.

"As far as Wittgenstein is concerned, he believes strongly that one cannot improve the world. One can, however, improve oneself and, through self-improvement, make the world a better place. Wittgenstein, probably more than most philosophers, attempted to change himself. This is why he gave away his enormous fortune and become a village schoolteacher.

"Mr. Wise, you fall into a common trap. Famous musicians and artists are asked routinely what they think about political and social issues.

Their answers are often simple-minded. Their skills do not always transfer. Playing a musical instrument superbly does not imply that the musician has political insights. After all, we don't ask politicians to become musicologists.

"Wittgenstein was a genius in very limited, though important area of philosophy. He was a self-deprecating man, quite aware of his shortcomings. Had he written about the war or the Nazis, his views might not have had the insights of a genius.

"We come now to your implied question, influenced no doubt by Mr. Ronnell Chase, about the social duties of a philosopher. I'd be quite interested in reading a paper dealing this issue. Would you care to write such a paper? I'll read and grade it myself."

I was disappointed. I had spent untold hours studying Wittgenstein so I could discuss his life intelligently with Dr. Brotbaum. I even enrolled in a history course to understand Wittgenstein's circumstances better. Now my project was scuttled by Dr. Brotbaum himself! I wanted to write about Wittgenstein the man, not the social obligations of philosophers. But, naturally, I promised Dr. Brotbaum to do the term paper he suggested. I was no closer now to a romantic relationship with him than before taking up Wittgenstein.

* * *

Working for Aviva allowed me to find out how *Philosopher's Corner* was produced. The station received about twenty letters a week suggesting topics readers wanted Dr. Brotbaum to discuss. These letters were turned over to Danny Fleetwood. He would choose half of them to show Dr. Brotbaum. Then he and Aviva would meet with him and decide on the three topics for the next show.

To appeal to different audiences, the topics to be discussed would be unrelated and deal with subjects of general interest. At times, though, Dr. Brotbaum would insist on looking at the entire stack of letters the station had received, and then choose one that was of special interest to him.

Aviva would rewrite the listeners' questions to make them coherent and concise. The announcer, acting as an interviewer, would read the letters to Dr. Brotbaum. He would also prepare a number of follow-up questions in case Dr. Brotbaum finished earlier than the allotted fourteen minutes per answer. But Dr. Brotbaum, without consulting any notes, never strayed from his allocated time.

The last segment of the show, calls from listeners, was monitored closely by Aviva. She would choose what she believed to be the best questions, then put the caller on the air. She would listen to the dialogue, ready to cut off offensive or crazy remarks. This part of the program scared her most, since Dr. Brotbaum's answers were never predictable.

Some time before I had started working for KLZW, Dr. Brotbaum suggested that, over a period of four weeks, a fourteen-minute segment be turned over to him for his own "philosophical examinations of social issues." Naturally, Aviva asked him what he would discuss. She told me that he replied in his "maddening logic" that, if she trusted him to reply spontaneously to questions from callers, she could also trust him with his social examination.

"You see, Harmony, I've known Eugene long enough. He has a bee in his bonnet about society establishing institutions and traditions that screw everyone without benefiting anybody. It's an all-encompassing theory that, most likely, will offend lots of listeners."

"Why now? Why hasn't he discussed or written about these issues earlier?"

"There's great resistance in academia to iconoclastic thinking, at least in the liberal arts disciplines. Instead of searching for the new, these institutions insist on researching the old. Eugene's theories aren't the stuff that university presses would hasten to publish."

* * *

At KLZW, I worked in a little cubicle adjacent to Aviva's room. Originally it may have served as a closet. It had two doors: one lead into Aviva's room, the other into the hallway. For ventilation, I kept the door facing Aviva's room open a crack. Usually, I closed it when she had a visitor, but sometimes I forgot. Aviva did not care one way or the other. If I needed to leave my cubicle I could use the other door, so my presence never bothered her.

When I came to work on a Friday, two weeks after my supper with Aviva, I entered, as always, from the hallway. The door to Aviva's room was open, and I could hear Dr. Brotbaum's and Aviva's voices. Then I saw him. He was standing, apparently about the leave. "If you don't wish to let me know the topics you'll be discussing tomorrow," Aviva said, "will you please tell me at least the general subject matter?"

"The Aztecs."

"The Aztecs?" Aviva asked as if she was not sure that she had heard correctly.

"Precisely."

Dr. Brotbaum left without another word. There was complete silence. I was sure that Aviva was trying to figure out how many Aztecs listened to the program, and how many of them Dr. Brotbaum would manage to offend. Aviva opened my door all the way. "Did you hear that?"

"Just the end"

"You're of Mexican origin. Are you an Aztec?"

I wish Aviva had not asked this. I had to suppress an urge to switch to José Luis. He certainly would have boasted that he was a direct descendant of Emperor Montezuma.

I collected myself. "I don't have the faintest idea, Aviva."

"Would you come to the studio tomorrow? I need you for moral support."

"Sure, Aviva."

* * *

I was with Aviva in the control booth. She looked down at Dr. Brotbaum who, with the interviewer, sat in a small booth with glass walls on three sides. The interviewer, who acted also as an announcer, said at the very beginning of the program: "At Dr. Brotbaum's request, we're changing the format of *Philosopher's Corner* for the next four weeks. Dr. Brotbaum will answer only two written questions, and then take calls. During the fourth segment of the show, Dr. Brotbaum will examine philosophically certain social issues of special interest to him."

The first three segments were uneventful. Even the call-ins were tame. Then it was Dr. Brotbaum's turn. "If you will bear with me for a few moments, I would like to examine Aztec society in the sixteenth century, just before the conquering Spaniards, under Hernando Cortés, all but wiped it out. The reason for my discourse about this particular subject, I will make clear later on.

"We know that the Aztecs were highly advanced in many areas. They had an amazing knowledge of astronomy, which they applied to their complicated calendar. For this they needed to be proficient in mathematics.

They had great engineering, architectural, and artistic skills. Militarily, they were a dominant force over much of what is Mexico today."

Dr. Brotbaum stopped for a moment, as if collecting his thoughts, and then added, "The Aztecs even invented the wheel, but it was used only for their children's toys." Here he chuckled momentarily.

"The dictates of their religion prescribed human sacrifices," Dr. Brotbaum continued. "The victims were mostly slaves or prisoners of war. At the time of the Spanish conquest, the Aztecs routinely sacrificed thousands upon thousands of human beings to their insatiable gods. Their constant battles with their neighbors, The Flower Wars, as they were called, were mainly to capture prisoners of war for sacrificial purposes.

"How could the Aztecs, who were so proficient in so many areas, have put in place an institution that was detrimental to every party involved, and, predictably, destined to destroy their own culture and religion?

"Let's examine who could have benefited from the Aztec human sacrifices. The victims? Most certainly not. The Aztec people? I think not. They would have benefited much more by using their captives for forced labor. The Aztec priests? Certainly, every sacrifice demonstrated their enormous power to the common Aztecs, but such demonstrations of power did not need an infinite number of victims.

"Sacrificing human beings to appease the gods was not unique to the Aztecs. It was the colossal number of victims that was an Aztec invention. The Aztecs, who excelled in mathematics, could have predicted that there would come a time when the system would be unable to sustain itself. In that they failed.

"If it benefited nobody at all, why did the clever Aztecs establish such an institution in the first place? And, more importantly, why did they let it get out of hand? It appeared to the Aztecs that for each victory their gods demanded additional sacrifices. As more human sacrifices were offered, more Aztec victories ensued. Each victory mandated another war for more victims. Far less skillful mathematicians could have figured out that this system could not go on indefinitely. In the end, a mere six hundred Spaniards, accompanied by an army of a native anti-Aztec alliance, brought down the empire.

"The thesis that I shall explore with you over the next few weeks is that all societies establish utterly useless institutions and practices. Rather than dismantle them when it becomes obvious that they benefit nobody and are, in fact, destructive, they are lovingly preserved. Emperor Moctezuma—or, as he's usually called, Montezuma—earnestly explained to Cortés that human sacrifice, which shocked even the savagely ruthless Spaniards, was a righteous and pious religious act.

"I've used the Aztecs as an example because it is easier to observe such a phenomenon in an extinct culture with which we do not have an emotional involvement. In the coming weeks we shall discuss such institutions and practices in contemporary societies."

Dr. Brotbaum raised his right hand to signal the announcer that he was through. The latter made a few comments about programs to be aired later on in the day, and the show came to an end. When the program was over, and Dr. Brotbaum left the booth, Aviva asked him, "OK, Eugene, so after the Aztecs, what?"

"Medical bloodletting, Chinese foot binding, and wars."

Aviva's facial expression showed her utter confusion at his strange answer. While she was thinking of something to say, Dr. Brotbaum, followed by Danny Fleetwood, turned on his heel and left the studio.

*　　　　*　　　　*

On the Saturday after Dr. Brotbaum's show, I had my first date since splitting with Joe. A week earlier Monty had asked me, "Are you dating these days, Eloy?"

"No."

"Would you like to?"

"I don't know. I certainly don't have time for a relationship. It would be nice, though, to have a date from time to time."

"Well, Eloy, how would you like to date a Japanese man? Mr. Takahashi is in his fifties. I'm sure you'll like each other. He has been in this country for only a short time. He's here because of the takeover of Allied Computer Technologies by the Japanese conglomerate Kasegi All Nippon Enterprises. You've probably read about that in the papers. He's the general manager of the American operation."

"How do you know so much about him?"

"He's gay. We've met in Japan. Of course, Mr. Takahashi is a married man. In Japan, you don't get promoted unless you're married. He's extremely closeted. Still, he'd like to meet a discreet young guy occasionally. If he feels comfortable enough with him to be seen in public, he'll take him to the opera, which is his passion. Do you like opera, Eloy?"

"I've never had the money to buy tickets. I'd love to go to the opera."

"I've mentioned your name to Mr. Takahashi. It's difficult to find a suitable date for him because of his awkward English and his terribly rigid Japanese formality. But the two of you have things in common. You can talk about computers.

"You'll learn a lot from him. He's extraordinarily bright, but you'll have to be patient with him. Japanese men hate to make mistakes. If their English is shaky, the conversation moves very slowly while they're making up their minds about the grammar. Fortunately, they're less prone to fuss over their pronunciation. Mr. Takahashi is the Japanese company's man on the spot here, in spite of the fact that his English isn't up to par. From the company's point of view, he was the best choice. In public, he's always accompanied by an interpreter.

"If you're interested, you can meet him next Saturday after work."

"Next week, Monty, I would like to come in late. I'm going to be at the radio station in the morning, listening to Dr. Brotbaum's show. Then I'll have to work until late in the afternoon. I'll be too tired for a date and then the trip back to Berkeley." I had told Monty very little about *Philosopher's Corner*. He knew only that Dr. Brotbaum was my philosophy instructor, and that he had a radio show. "Take the day off. I'll suggest to Mr. Takahashi that you'll have lunch together. I really would like for you to meet him. I'm sure the two of you'll get along fine. I owe him a few."

"Doesn't Mr. Takahashi have a first name?"

"His first name is Jiro. In America he doesn't mind being called Jiro, though for a Japanese, especially in his position, it must be very jarring to be addressed by his first name. Call him Mr. Takahashi. Better, make it Takahashi-san, until he tells you otherwise."

*   *   *

Monty set up the date for Saturday at noon. Jiro lived just a few blocks from Japan Town. From the outside, his building looked like an ordinary San Francisco apartment house. Inside, however, there were two uniformed Asian security guards. One sat at a desk. The other stood by the elevators. He carried a gun in a holster.

I walked to the desk. "My name is Eloy Wise. I'm here to see Mr. Takahashi."

"Do you have an ID?"

I handed him my ID. First, he checked my name against a list. Satisfied, he looked at the photo and compared it to my face. "Please let us keep it. You'll get it back when you leave."

He called over the other guard, speaking to him in Japanese. Accompanied by the armed guard, I took the elevator to the second floor. The guard rang the bell at apartment number two. What ensued was something out of the movies. A handsome, older Japanese man opened the door. He wore a bright, crisp dressing gown. I would learn later that it was called a *yukata*. The guard bowed stiffly and formally. He pointed to me and said something that sounded like, "Wisu-san." Jiro spoke briefly to the guard and then, with the slightest nod of his head, dismissed him. The guard, as if on military parade, stiffly and loudly said, "Hai, Takahashi-san," and then bowed from the waist. Jiro motioned me in and closed the door.

We shook hands. "Please sit down," he said, pointing to a chair. "Would you like a drink?" Actually, when he said "drink" it sounded more like dlinku. In the background, a tape softly played music by Johann Strauss. Jiro started moving toward a wet bar. "Only a soft drink, please. A Calistoga would be fine, Takahashi-san."

"So you don't drink, ha, ha," he said. He sounded amused. "Please, Wisu-san, call me Jiro, American style. May I call you Eloy?" He handed me the Calistoga in a fancy tumbler. "I've ordered ronchu here for one o'clock. Is this OK?"

"Yes, Jiro-san." This seemed more appropriate. I liked formality in older men.

Jiro looked distinguished, and had what Joe would have called a military bearing. He stood just under six feet, and was quite trim. He had piercing brown eyes behind glasses in old-fashioned metal frames. His hair was prematurely gray, turning white in spots. He spoke slowly and deliberately.

"Monty-san tells me that you are studying computer programming, is that so?" I told him that this was accurate. Slowly, mindful of his English grammar, he asked me programming questions. If I did not know the answer, he would guide me gently to help me come up with it. When I could not figure out a problem, he would explain it to me patiently, then look at me and ask, "Is this all queer?" The question took me by surprise the first time around. But then I understood that this was how he pronounced "clear."

He talked a lot about parallel processing in computers, the rage at the time. It was a subject about which I knew little. Jiro would have driven me to distraction with his halting, deliberate English. But what he had to say was of great interest to me. In fact, he was a much better teacher than my college instructors. After an hour or so, the bell rang. A man dressed in a waiter's outfit, accompanied by the same guard who had escorted me, set up our lunch on an ornate dining table.

Jiro handed the waiter a hundred-dollar bill. When the latter tried to make change, Jiro dismissed him with a wave of his hand. The waiter had left a copy of our order on the table. While Jiro went to the wet bar to make a drink for himself, I glanced at it. Had I not done so, I would never have known what I was eating. The first course was vichyssoise soup, followed by a roast beef sandwich with side orders of caviar and artichoke hearts. I had never eaten this kind of food before. The meal cost seventy-one dollars.

I enjoyed the food. We made small talk; I answered Jiro's many questions about my studies at UC. Then, without transition, he asked, "Do you like *bondaji*?"

"I don't know. I've never tried this dish before."

Jiro made one of his ha-ha noises that indicated that he was amused. "*Bondaji* do, not eat!"

I had no idea what he was talking about. I had never heard this computer term before. Surely we were talking about computers, or were we? The look on his face suggested that he may have switched to another subject of even greater interest to him. He repeated the expression *bondaji*, and performed a crude charade of the activity. After watching for a while I asked, in complete disbelief, "Bondage?"

"Hai, so desu," he answered, which I took to mean yes.

As had happened before, I acknowledged to myself the benefits I derived from having attended GIF meetings. On my own, I would never have known that there was a sex-related activity called bondage. Joe had been the most conventional of gay lovers. Neither my late friend Helmut nor Monty had ever talked about such matters. But I did attend, with Joe, a GIF evening devoted to "Exploring S&M and B&D." Never having practiced it, I did not know whether I liked bondage or not. Was I going to be the "bonder" or the "bondee?" I tried to break it down into simple English. "Who'll do the bondage, you to me, or I to you?"

"I do," Jiro answered. His tone implied that this had been an unnecessary question. I should have known the answer on my own.

On the one hand, I looked forward to the thrill of a new sexual experience. Already, during Bruno's spanking scenes in Acapulco, I had became aware of a bit of kinkiness that Eloy harbored (in contrast, José Luis was wild but not kinky, and Harmony was a question mark). On the other hand, I worried about my safety. Idly, I wondered whether, once properly tied up, Jiro-san would torture and kill me, then call his armed honcho and curtly order, "Dispose of Wisu-san's body!"

The guard would bellow "Hai, Takahashi-san," bow from the waist, and take my mutilated body to the nearest dumpster.

Jiro must have understood what was going on in my mind. "Just little sex play." It sounded like sexu pray. "No hurt."

I trusted Monty. He would not have introduced me to a lunatic. But was Monty aware of Jiro's sexual idiosyncrasies?

"All right, then," I said.

We finished our food, and walked into the bedroom. What a surprise! The walls were black. The heavy brocade curtains were black as well, admitting absolutely no light from the outside. On two walls were mounted huge mirrors. There was a large bed in the center of the room, covered with a black leather spread. The only other furniture was a chair and a stool, both upholstered in black leather. A hidden source illuminated the room with faint light changing from one color to another. Blue slowly became green, and then dissolved into orange. Jiro must have flipped a switch because, suddenly, macabre, synthesized music emanated from invisible speakers.

Without speaking, just through motions, Jiro indicated that I should undress and sit on the stool. He took off his *yukata,* and stood there stark naked. His hairless body was lean and muscular. He had a long, thin, uncircumcised dick. From a closet, he took out a motorcyclist's black leather jacket and put it on. His lower body remained naked. From a hidden drawer under the bed, he removed leather straps and a rope. He arranged them carefully on the floor. By now I was naked, sitting on the stool. Jiro motioned me to lie on the bed. He had not uttered a single word since we had entered the room. I lay on the bed, frightened and yet excited at the same time. I was sexually aroused, and had a roaring hard-on to prove it.

Since I had never before been tied up, I could not compare Jiro's handiwork with previous experiences. He tied me up not to restrain but, rather, to immobilize me. My arms, for instance, were tied up along my body. In the end, all I could do was wiggle my toes and fingers and move my head.

Except for the fact that I should have gone to the bathroom before Jiro started the procedure, I felt inexplicably comfortable and relaxed in my mummified state. Then Jiro sat on my thighs, facing me. Slowly he started playing with my nipples. Bruno had done that too, but only briefly. Jiro increased the pressure ever so slowly. Soon, I felt pain. When I winced, he relaxed his pressure, but continued playing with my nipples. The discomfort aroused me. I moaned softly as the pain became pleasurable.

Suddenly, his body moved forward and he thrust his tongue into my mouth. Because I was immobilized, I was unable to control his wild kissing. That, too, pleased rather than frightened me. He kept manipulating my nipples and kissing me simultaneously for quite a while. From time to time, he moved his mouth to one of my nipples and gave it a sharp nip. When I cried out in pain, his tongue immediately returned to my mouth.

Just as the thought popped into my mind that Jiro and I hadn't discussed the subject of screwing, he got off me and moved to one side of the bed. He took off his leather jacket. Then he rummaged somewhere under the bed and came up with two items, which he held close to my eyes: a condom and a bottle of water-based lubricant. "On penis *kondomu* put," he intoned solemnly. Following safe sex guidelines, he poured a few drops of the lubricant into the condom before dressing my dick with it. He applied a liberal quantity of the lubricant to the rubber.

How does he expect me to screw him when I'm tied like a parcel waiting to be shipped? I thought. But even as I was contemplating this, Jiro, facing me in a squatting position, hovered over my erect penis, and then, in one swift maneuver, impaled himself. Immediately, he started moving his body up and down. I don't remember what I experienced. All I know is that I exploded inside Jiro within moments. Our timing was perfect. Jiro climaxed at the same instant, all over my chest.

Methodically, as always, Jiro got off me, removed the condom, and swiftly untied me. "Thank you very much for pleasant occasion," he said. "Now shower take." He led me to a fancy bathroom with an enormous tub. We showered together, and soaped each other's backs. After we dressed, we returned to the living room. The Viennese music was playing softly, just as before. Jiro offered me a glass of sparkling apple cider. Then he excused himself.

He came back after some ten minutes. "This is a very little *purezentu* for thank you saying." He held in hands a small package wrapped in paper with a delicate floral design. "Can we meet again next week for lunch?" he asked.

"I have to work for Monty until about two or three in the afternoon on Saturdays, Jiro-san," I said.

"Can you night sleep in San Francisco with me? We'll opera going in the evening."

"Yes. I'd like that."

"Then, maybe you come here after work, we pray a little, then eat dinner, and then opera going."

In my mind I converted the "pray" to play. "That's fine, Jiro-san. I'll be here by five o'clock next Saturday."

On the way out, I retrieved my ID from the guard downstairs. While waiting for the train back to Berkeley, I opened the package. It was a recently published book about parallel processing.

12

Dr. Brotbaum's Blunder

On the second Saturday of Dr. Brotbaum's philosophical examination of social issues, I arrived early in the morning at the GGLC office in San Francisco. I made myself a cup of coffee and tuned the radio to KLZW.

I am tempted to give here a full transcript of Dr. Brotbaum's segment on social issues. I found it fascinating. What was even more important to me at the time was that he mentioned me, not by name, of course, and even sent me what I took to be a coded signal. However, in view of later events, I will confine myself to a summary of Dr. Brotbaum's discussion, and describe at length his comment, in response to a caller, that Aviva dubbed "Eugene's Blunder."

The "blunder" actually took place before Dr. Brotbaum's discussion on social issues. It happened during the listeners' call-in segment of the show.

A woman identified herself as Cathy from Mill Valley, a first-time caller. Usually, these first-timers rambled. Cathy's question, however, was succinct and to the point. "We human beings can choose whether to eat meat. Other animals cannot. Killing prey for survival is the way this world has been created. Why, then, do so many religions teach that God loves his handiwork; that he watches lovingly over every creature he has created?"

As always, it seemed as if Dr. Brotbaum had spent the entire week preceding the show just thinking of how to answer Cathy's question. "My response to you, madam, will be based solely on a philosophical analysis of your question. For a religious answer, you'll have to seek your clergyman's counsel.

"In the Judeo-Christian and the Islamic traditions, there is an underlying assumption of God's love and compassion for all living things. In the Christian writings, God cares even about a single sparrow, as the evangelist Luke reminds us. But everybody can observe, on a daily basis, that nature is violent. Indeed, the predators must be violent in order to survive. The spider must lure the fly into its web and suck it dry; the tiger must devour the gazelle.

"Even the most eloquent spokesman for God, the prophet Isaiah of the Old Testament, was disturbed by the cruelty and violence that governs creation. He foresaw a time when nature would not be violent. Isaiah prophesied that there will come a time when 'The wolf also shall dwell with a lamb, and the leopard shall lie down with a kid; and the calf and the young lion and the fatling together, and a little child shall lead them.' The prophet goes on: 'And the lion shall eat straw like an ox.'

"This prophecy can be taken as an implied criticism of God, who, speaking in modern terms, could have configured a universe without violence and terror—a universe where the lion could survive on straw—but chose not to do so.

"Philosophically speaking, the most forceful argument against vegetarianism is the present configuration of our world. The fact is that the lion does not, and cannot, eat straw like an ox. Killing prey for food is a matter of survival for him. If killing for food is nature's way, why would human beings exclude themselves from this activity? Logically, it can be argued that human beings do, systematically and methodically, what other animals do when driven by hunger.

"The implied criticism of the prophet Isaiah extends to our propensity for making war. Here again, the prophet suggests that God could have configured a world where peace would be the norm, but chose not to do so. A time will come, says the prophet, when, 'Nation shall not lift up sword against nation, neither shall they learn war any more.'

"You may consider that we call only the most destructive and bizarre occurrences 'acts of God.' In a world configured with love and compassion, there would be no such disastrous acts. It may well be that we ascribe to God not the qualities that he manifests, but the qualities we would like him to manifest."

At the time, I did not pay much attention to Dr. Brotbaum's answer to Cathy. Neither religious questions nor animal rights issues held much interest for me. In any case, I was looking forward to the segment on social issues. I was therefore quite surprised when Aviva called me on Sunday night and referred to that particular answer as a major blunder. With hindsight, her assessment was an understatement.

"On Powell and Market in San Francisco, where the cable cars turn, there are lots of people exercising the American right to free speech. What do they talk about, Harmony?" Aviva asked.

"I don't know. They're just a bunch of religious nuts. Nobody takes them seriously."

"They have the right to free speech precisely because nobody takes them seriously. Americans really believe that everybody has an inalienable right to practice different religious faiths. The right to say that God isn't perfect is much more restricted because there are sanctions against it."

"What sanctions?"

"For one, we may lose our show on KLZW."

"But Dr. Brotbaum didn't say anything that other philosophers haven't said before him."

"This may be so. But they didn't discuss their theories on public radio. Eugene verbalized, on the air, a secret doubt that gnaws at the minds of many. In political science terms, Eugene questioned the quality of divine governance."

Agitated now, she asked, "Do you read the Bible?"

"Not at all, Aviva."

"The book of Job in the Old Testament deals precisely with what Eugene's comment was all about. Job questions at great length whether God governs this world righteously, because the opposite appears to be true. When God finally addresses Job's grievances, the answer is not convincing. Rather than explain to Job why things are the way they are, God browbeats Job. He says to him, 'Since I know everything, and you know nothing, how dare you ask in the first place?' Dr. Brotbaum dared ask. The price will have to be paid."

* * *

After answering Cathy's question, there was a brief station break. Then Dr. Brotbaum resumed his discourse about his own philosophy.

As he did with the Aztecs and their human sacrifices, Dr. Brotbaum gave two additional examples of customs that lasted for many centuries and were detrimental to all concerned: Chinese foot-binding of young girls, which crippled them for life, and medicinal bloodletting in Europe and the Americas.

As always, I was tremendously impressed by the breadth of Dr. Brotbaum's knowledge, and his skill in explaining complicated matters in a few minutes. With the help of these illustrations, Dr. Brotbaum introduced his main theme: warfare. This is where I came into his discourse. "One of my students proposed writing a paper about the philosopher Ludwig Wittgenstein," Dr. Brotbaum related. For the benefit of his listeners, he took great pains to pronounce Wittgenstein the English way. He only half succeeded. It came out as Wittgenshtein. "This philosopher volunteered as a private in the Austro-Hungarian army during the first World War. Later on, though an Austrian citizen, he was forced to live in England as a refugee before and during the second World War. Under Nazi racial laws, Wittgenstein was classified as a Jew because three of his grandparents were Jewish. His parents, as well as the philosopher himself, were Christians."

"Wittgenstein was doubtlessly a genius. He put relatively little into writing, yet succeeded in changing our thinking in the fields of logic and language. My student complained that Wittgenstein, in spite of a powerful mystical experience he underwent as a soldier, had no philosophical insights to offer regarding wars or the other hideous political events of his time, events that profoundly affected his own well-being!

"Rather wisely"—I took this as a coded signal to me—"my student observed that Wittgenstein accepted the madness of the first half of the twentieth century as a natural phenomenon. 'As we,' my student said, 'in California accept earthquakes.' Some philosophers, like Nietzsche, glorified wars. Others, like Kant, gave some thought to achieving perpetual peace. By and large, philosophers have accepted wars as natural phenomena.

"I explained to my student that Wittgenstein probably had nothing profound to say about warfare. This was a satisfactory answer, but in a very limited way. Could the genius Wittgenstein had brought to bear on a narrow philosophical subject have been applied to consider solutions to much more urgent issues? Do philosophers have an obligation to deal with crucial matters before they are permitted the luxury of philosophizing about issues that are, relative to war and extermination, trivial in nature?

"When we focus collectively on a life-and-death issue, as in the case of nuclear weapons, we can sometimes manage to control it. But throughout human history we have chosen to accept pernicious stupidities as the law of nature. Worse, we have often been proud of our follies.

"Philosophers are trained to analyze human institutions and practices. Do they owe a duty to audit the books of human conduct? Would we live more peacefully if we had a think tank with hundreds of philosophers focusing on warfare?"

When the program was over, I turned off the radio and started working. I was proud that Dr. Brotbaum had alluded to me. Naively, I looked forward to his next show.

* * *

I had never been to an opera, and therefore had no idea how I should dress for the occasion. I called Monty on the Monday following my first date with Jiro to ask his opinion. Monty told me right away that Jiro had already spoken to him and told him that he had really enjoyed our date. As to what I should wear to the opera, Monty said, "This is San Francisco, Eloy. At the opera you can see guys dressed in leather sitting next to gentlemen wearing dinner jackets. Nobody cares. Wear one of the neat sweaters Joe got for you."

Monty was probably right. I was not concerned about what society in general would think of me but, specifically, what Jiro would expect me to wear. I wanted him to be proud of me.

Since we split, I had not had much contact with Joe. The few times we saw each other, at my GGLC job, we only exchanged a few words.

From Monty, I learned that Joe's new boyfriend was a student from, of all places, Iceland. Monty told me that Joe, as a result of his work with AIDS organizations, had become an advocate of strict monogamy.

I called Joe, and we chatted for a while. He told me that his new boyfriend, Björn, was a graduate psychology student at Stanford. He talked about him at length, and not once did he refer to him as a twinkie! Monty had already told Joe about my first date with Jiro. Regarding my quandary, Joe said, "If you go out to the opera with Mr. Takahashi, you should wear a suit."

"I don't have a suit."

"Come to think of it, you don't even have a sport coat. Why don't you buy one that matches a pair of nice pants you have. With a sharp tie, that should do the trick."

"I'll need to buy a tie as well. Will you go shopping with me?"

"If you want me to, Eloy."

As always, Joe was accommodating. He helped me pick a preppy sport coat that matched a pair of navy blue trousers I owned. I also bought two neckties. I felt comfortable enough with Joe to confess to him that I did not know how to knot a tie.

We went to Joe's apartment, where he taught me how to make the Windsor knot. "You'll make a splendid escort for Mr. Takahashi," Joe said. "I'm curious to know how he'll handle security at the opera."

"Why does he need security?"

"You don't know? Ever since the Japanese acquisition of Allied Computer Technologies, there have been threats against him. A few months ago, in Mountain View, his car exploded mysteriously. Fortunately, nobody was inside. At the time, there were all sorts of theories about the perpetrators, but nobody claimed responsibility. Now, when Mr. Takahashi appears in public, he's always accompanied by an interpreter as well as a bodyguard."

I told Joe about the armed guard at Jiro's apartment house. "It'll be interesting how he handles dating you. You know, of course, that he's married. Imagine an item in a gossip column stating that Jiro Takahashi was seen at the opera accompanied by a young and handsome Hispanic male!"

* * *

The security routine at Jiro's apartment house was the same. Again, I was asked to leave my ID at the desk. After dismissing the guard, Jiro took me into his arms and kissed me passionately. I had called him from the GGLC office to ask him whether I could arrive as early as four o'clock, to which he agreed. "We have much time before opera going," he said, as he opened a Calistoga for me. He made himself a cocktail.

"Thank you for the book. I enjoyed reading it, though I didn't understand everything," I told him. We talked about his book for a while. In his quaint and cumbersome English, he answered some of my questions. Then, once again without transition, he asked, "Do you like praying banira sexu?"

It took me a few seconds to interpret the three last words as, "playing vanilla sex."

When they talked about S&M at the GIF meeting, I learned that ordinary gay sex was referred to by the S&M crowd as vanilla sex. But never before had I been asked whether I enjoyed that type of sex.

Because I didn't reply immediately, Jiro must have assumed that I did not like it. "I'm sorry," he said, "we don't..."

"It's OK, Jiro-san. Most of the time I do nothing but vanilla sex." I had difficulties visualizing vanilla sex in Jiro's black *bondaji* room. I was in for a big surprise.

The black room had been converted into a bright and cheerful space. The black wall paneling had disappeared. Now there was wallpaper with a delicate floral design. Only the large mirrors were exactly where they had been last time. The bed was covered with a bright green spread. The black chair and stool had disappeared. An antique yellow love seat was positioned in one corner. Through a glass door I could see a small balcony full of potted plants. Soft Viennese music played in the background.

Our lovemaking was tender and affectionate. Much of it consisted of various ways Jiro liked to kiss. This time he did not even touch my nipples. I was surprised by his tenderness. After a long while, Jiro brought out a condom. Once again he showed me the condom and the lubricant. "On penis *kondomu* put," he intoned solemnly. I waited for him to put it on my dick. To my surprise, he slid it on his own.

Jiro had a knack for performing complicated maneuvers flowingly. Seemingly, he managed to turn me facedown, spread my buns, put a finger condom on himself, and lubricate my asshole in a single, uninterrupted movement. Before I had time to give my usual speech about not allowing anyone to penetrate me, Jiro was inside me all the way. It didn't even hurt much!

For a few moments I just lay there, awed by the fact that Jiro had managed to penetrate me all the way. Then my body responded to his thrusts. As he bore down on me, I raised my butt in welcome. I felt great joy that Jiro was inside me, that our bodies were joined together. Jiro was very good at what he was doing. I reached an orgasm spontaneously just as he was climaxing inside me. When it was over, I wondered how it all happened. Why had Joe been unable, however much we both tried, to penetrate me? Maybe, I told myself, Jiro could do whatever he wanted with me because I respected him so much. "Did you enjoy?" he asked after removing the condom.

"Yes, very, very much, Jiro-san. Thank you." I gave him a deep kiss. A silly thought popped into my head. I knew that my body and soul would one day belong to Dr. Brotbaum. But would he be able to perform with the marvelous dexterity of Jiro?

*   *   *

Our outing to the opera was like an episode from a TV soap opera. After dinner, brought in from a fancy French restaurant, Jiro put on a sport coat and a tie. I was relieved that he had not dressed formally. During dinner he had made a few calls, speaking in Japanese.

Downstairs, two Japanese men I had never seen before were waiting for him, as well the armed guard. One of them was dressed in a formal dinner jacket and a black tie, and wore dark sunglasses. They bowed solemnly to Jiro and gave monosyllabic answers to his questions. Accompanied by the armed guard, the five of us went into the garage. A new Lexus was parked next to a nondescript Honda Civic.

To my surprise, "Sunglasses" and his buddy got into the Lexus. The former sat in the back; the other, in the driver's seat. The armed guard pressed a button, and the garage door opened. The Lexus pulled out in a hurry. The garage door closed and the three of us returned to the lobby.

Jiro took out a pack of Japanese cigarettes and offered them around. My ID was returned to me. We sat there and waited for a good ten minutes. Then, escorted by the armed guard, Jiro took the wheel of the Honda and drove out slowly.

He looked at me and smiled. "Security, you understand."

We had a hard time finding a parking space. We drove by quite a few off-street parking lots, but Jiro ignored them. Eventually, we found a space on Ivy and Laguna. Jiro consulted his watch. "We walk around block until opera almost begin." Jiro had timed our entrance to coincide with the dimming of the house lights. Our seats were in the center of the first row. Soon the curtain rose, and I saw my first opera: Verdi's *La Traviata*.

I was moved by the performance. Seeing an opera on stage was not the same as watching it on a TV screen. I felt grateful to Jiro, and discretely took his hand into my mine. He squeezed it gently.

During the intermission, Jiro did not get up. In a low voice he asked, "Do you want to get a drink? Sorry, I cannot go with you. Security, you understand."

I sat with him contentedly. We did not speak. Because we were in the first row, I hardly saw any other patrons. I never even found out how other members of the audience dressed for that occasion. When the performance was over, Jiro made no attempt to get up, even after the many curtain calls. We were the last people to leave the opera house. In the lobby, Jiro made a brief call from a public phone.

He drove to the intersection of Eddy and Gough. Sunglasses waited for us there. Now he wore street clothes, and had discarded the shades. He took over the driver's seat. We got into the back of the car. A block before we reached his apartment house, Jiro laid his head in my lap. As he did so he said, "Sorry, security, you understand."

The Lexus was already parked in the garage. In the lobby of the apartment house I was asked for my ID once again. Jiro said something in Japanese. The reception clerk, or whatever he was, looked embarrassed. He sucked in his breath through his clenched teeth and, apologetically and monosyllabically, spoke to Jiro. After a few exchanges, Jiro said, "Sorry, you have to give ID to him. Security, you understand."

We went back into his apartment, and had a repeat performance of playing banira sexu.

13

Huitzilopochtli

By pure coincidence, Aviva had ordered pager service for me just a few days before Dr. Brotbaum's latest radio program. Aviva experienced computer problems on a daily basis. Once I started working for her, she became dependent on me. She wanted to be able to get hold of me whenever she had one of her computer crises. In those days, pagers were rare and the service costly. It made me feel special to have that gadget. Had it not been for the pager, I would not have become involved intimately in Dr. Brotbaum's life.

* * *

On the Monday after Dr. Brotbaum's program, we heard the first faint rumble of the coming storm. A San Francisco gossip columnist described Dr. Brotbaum's last show briefly and summed up the topic: "In his all-encompassing remarks, Dr. Brotbaum also took God himself to task for faulty planning. We're waiting with bated breath to hear from Rev. Horace Tippit, the indefatigable critic of public broadcasting."

Indeed, everybody at KLZW was waiting for Rev. Tippit's take on Dr. Brotbaum's show. According to Aviva, Tippit had scores, if not hundreds, of monitors listening to public radio and television programs around the clock. If a program offended him, and many did, he would complain to the FCC, the appropriate House and Senate subcommittees overseeing public broadcasting, and the companies funding the offending show. The last were the easiest to intimidate; they did not wish to be involved in controversies.

By Tuesday, the station heard not from Tippit, but from the corporation funding *Philosopher's Corner*. I believe it is against the law, but nevertheless, Aviva taped the conversation with a vice president of New Century Systems, Inc., the sole funding source of Dr. Brotbaum's show. The vice president told Aviva that he had received an overnight package with a audiotape of the program. The sender did not bother to identify himself. Referring to Dr. Brotbaum's answer to Cathy's question, the vice president said, "The CEO and everybody else found his comments offensive. We didn't fund *Philosopher's Corner* to discuss religion one way or the other."

"But much of philosophy involves religion."

"You know the drill, Aviva. If Dr. Brotbaum wants to criticize God, then he needs someone to represent the Almighty. He could have an infamous atheist locking horns with, say, Rev. Tippit, and he, your good Dr. Brotbaum, could referee the show. Equal time, fairness, all that sort of thing. We're funding programs to generate goodwill for our company, not to alienate our customers. Unless you can get your philosopher to work with a panel, rather than spout his own ideas, the funding is over."

Aviva predicted that Rev. Tippit would consider Dr. Brotbaum's blunder a treasure trove. "The obnoxious old geezer keeps repeating the same stuff about public broadcasting. It's always pornography, sexual immorality, abortion, and so on. Eugene's blunder will enable Tippit to add a new dimension to his criticism: sacrilege."

Rev. Tippit struck on Thursday with a prime-time interview on TV-24. Unlike Aviva, the producers at TV-24 knew the drill. They located

Dr. Brotbaum, told him about the upcoming attack on *Philosopher's Corner*, and suggested that they interview him to rebut Rev. Tippit. As a matter of principle, Dr. Brotbaum refused to appear on TV. As an alternative, TV-24 suggested a telephone interview. He declined that offer as well, because the producers told him that they would condense his comments to thirty seconds of air time.

Next, TV-24 approached KLZW for a rebuttal. Aviva asked Danny Fleetwood to take on that task. He was a good speaker, and at least one side of his face looked youthful yet professorial. True to Aviva's predictions, Danny distanced himself from Dr. Brotbaum. "It would be improper for me to defend my own thesis advisor. There may well be a conflict of interests involved," he told Aviva, declining the assignment.

Aviva herself could not come to Dr. Brotbaum's defense. She was sure that Tippit would attack Dr. Brotbaum as a newcomer to these shores. She, too, was a foreigner. The station manager was out of the country. After consulting the manager by phone, Aviva gave the rebuttal job to Leona Jackson, the station's spokesperson. Leona had a lot going for her: she was handicapped and black. Unfortunately, she lacked Tippit's rhetorical skills.

Everybody at the station watched the interview. Rev. Tippit was a soft-spoken, elderly, somewhat stooped gentleman. At first glance, he appeared to be an inoffensive, reasonable person. He managed to convey the impression of a long-suffering, well-disposed man who, under extreme provocation, finally rises to say a few words to set the record straight.

"Our taxes pay for public broadcasting," Rev. Tippit said in a measured tone of voice. "I've often spoken against scandalously immoral programs aired at our expense. But never, never before did I have to utter a word about blasphemy at taxpayers' expense.

“I’m steadfast in my faith.” Here Rev. Tippit lowered rather than raised his voice. “But still, I believe that all people in this great democracy have the constitutional right to worship in their own way. I might not like it, but I would allow,” he lowered his voice some more, “even an atheist to express his opinion.

“What we must not allow,” his voice suddenly became shrill, “is to mock God with taxpayers’ money. At KLZW, a National Public Radio station in Berkeley, California, they have a self-proclaimed Bible expert by the name of Dr. Eugene Brotbaum. He asserts that the prophet Isaiah criticized God rather than praised Him.

“The Berkeley philosopher, Dr. Brotbaum, claims that there is a bug in God’s software program for our world, to use the quaint new parlance, and that the prophet spotted it. According to Dr. Brotbaum, we aren’t waiting for the day of judgment to set things aright. No, we’re waiting for a new, improved version of God’s software.” Here he lowered his voice again. “And yes, Dr. Brotbaum, who came to this country only recently to enjoy our freedom and prosperity, thinks that our military is a ‘pernicious stupidity.’

“We live in a free country. Dr. Brotbaum can say whatever nonsense enters into his philosophical head but,” and here he raised his voice to a shout, “not at our expense. Not at our expense!” Then, dramatically, he lowered his voice to almost a whisper. “We, the taxpayers who finance public radio, demand that Dr. Brotbaum’s show be shut down!”

Leona, her crutches in full view, spoke softly and reasonably. “Dr. Brotbaum is a philosopher. His calling in life is to analyze ideas. At the end of every show, the station states that the opinions expressed do not necessarily represent the views of the KLZW. We believe that Dr. Brotbaum, a philosophy professor at UC Berkeley, is entitled to express his views on KLZW without censorship. We invite Rev. Tippit to do the same. We’ll gladly give him air time. Under pressure, the corporation funding Dr. Brotbaum's program will no longer sponsor his show. As soon as we find another source of funding for *Philosopher's Corner*, it, and Dr. Brotbaum, will be on the air again."

While KLZW would not officially give in to Rev. Tippit's pressure, it did cancel the show. The likelihood of finding another sponsor for the program was nil.

*   *   *

To give a coherent account of the events that took place after Rev. Tippit's TV interview, I'll narrate them chronologically. At the time, I did not have all of the information I am relating here.

On Friday morning, Mrs. McLaughlin, the matronly Irish housekeeper who took care of Dr. Brotbaum's home, was horrified by grotesque drawings of human bodies on the garage door, done in red marker. Dr. Brotbaum, who did not own a car, had not seen the graffiti when he left home to walk to the campus. Unable to contact Dr. Brotbaum, Mrs. McLaughlin took two steps on her own. First she called the police. They were not particularly perturbed by the minor vandalism, though they did take notice of the neatly printed signature at the bottom of the graffiti: "The Hummingbird." An outline of a small, precisely drawn red hummingbird appeared below the signature.

Mrs. McLaughlin then called her daughter. When her grandchildren came home from school, their mother drove them over to Dr. Brotbaum's home. They got rid of the graffiti swiftly, and with great expertise. Dr. Brotbaum never saw it, though Mrs. McLaughlin called him later from her home and told him about it. Unfortunately, she did not describe the drawings in detail.

Saturday night, I had dinner with Jiro. What occupied me most during dinner was guessing what new sexual adventures I would encounter upon entering the bedroom. Suddenly, my pager buzzed. Without looking, I knew it would be Aviva. Only she had the number. I glanced at the little screen on the pager. It displayed Aviva's number at KLZW.

She answered on the first ring. "Where are you, Harmony?" she asked in a tense voice.

"In San Francisco, having dinner with a friend."

"Harmony, Eugene is in real trouble. Somebody shot at his living room window. The police want him out of the house. He'll be staying at my place. The problem is that I can't leave the station until eleven. Please take a taxi to Berkeley. First, stop by the station. Have the taxi wait for you. Pick up my keys from the receptionist. I'm also leaving an envelope with cash to pay for the taxi ride. Get a receipt from the driver. Then go to Eugene's home. Keep the same taxi. Go with Eugene to my place. Stay with him there until I get home. Do you understand everything?"

I was in a daze. "Yes, Aviva. I'll be on my way immediately."

"Oh, one more thing, Harmony. We hired security guards for the station, and there are police with Dr. Brotbaum. I left word to let you through after you identify yourself. Do you carry an ID?"

Damn! I thought. My new driver's license was made out to Eloy Wise. Inexplicably, it did not even have an "H" for my middle initial. "Aviva, my ID reads Eloy Wise, not Harmony Wise."

"What the…I'll take care of it," she snapped. "Be quick, please."

Without making it a long story, I gave Jiro a summary of what I needed to do. He thought for a moment, then said. "You use my car. It is," here he said something I did not understand. "Please wait, I speak to driver."

Five minutes after Jiro's phone call, Sunglasses, minus his shades, appeared at the door. He bowed to Jiro but, it seemed to me, in a perfunctory manner. "You come," he said to me. In the garage we entered the Lexus. He shot out of the garage door at a dizzying speed that he maintained all the way to Berkeley.

Just before we reached the Bay Bridge it became obvious to me that I was riding in an armored car. I had three clues. Looking out of the car's windows was like seeing things through a prism; the exterior of the car was much larger than the interior; and the word I did not understand when Jiro referred to the car must have been "armored," which he had pronounced almoled.

Sunglasses uttered only a one-word question: "Address?" After I gave him KLZW's address in Berkeley, he ignored me. I had no idea how much English he spoke. I was happy not to have to make conversation. I was in a strange state. While I was worried about Dr. Brotbaum's safety, I also felt elated that I was riding to his rescue!

Two uniformed security guards were stationed in front of KLZW. One of them examined my ID carefully, and then let me through. I picked up an envelope containing the keys to Aviva's apartment. In addition to the keys, there was seventy-five dollars in cash for the cab fare.

A Berkeley police car was parked in front of Dr. Brotbaum's home. I went to the entrance door and rang the bell. A black man in civilian clothes opened the door. He was tall, beefy, and in a good mood. "You're Eloy Wise?" he asked.

I took out my ID. "That's not necessary. Impersonating Eloy Wise wouldn't be a wise thing to do. I'm Detective Patterson. Come in," he said. He ushered me into the kitchen, where he had been eating a pizza and drinking a Coke. "It seems your prof here made an enemy. You know someone called 'Hummingbird?'"

I looked at him blankly. "I had a feeling you wouldn't know, but still, it doesn't hurt to ask. Well, then, Eloy…By the way, why does your prof call you Harmony?"

"Harmony is my middle name. He knows me by that name."

"Stick with Eloy, Harmony. As I was saying, someone shot at the prof's living room window. A forty caliber bullet, I'd say from a Berreta semiautomatic. It's a fairly big gun. It may be better for the prof not to stay here tonight. I understand you're taking him to a friend's home?"

"Yes. May I speak to him?"

"Sure. I put him in the bedroom facing the yard. No sense having a target in the living room. Listen, Eloy, I must return to headquarters. Can you get the prof out of here in a hurry? Who owns the Lexus you came in?"

I thought for a moment. I could not tell him that I arrived in an armored car belonging to a Japanese VIP. "A friend of mine is driving us."

"OK, let's get going. Give me the address you're taking the prof to."

He jotted down Aviva's address and phone number. I went across the hall. As I knocked on the bedroom door I said, "Dr. Brotbaum, it's Harmony."

"Come in."

Dr. Brotbaum, wearing a T-shirt and baggy pants, was packing a suitcase. He looked terrible. "Good evening, Harmony," he said.

"Aviva asked me to take you to her place, Dr. Brotbaum. I have a car outside. The detective wants us to leave right away."

"I'm just about finished here," he said. He sounded drained.

A few minutes later, the three of us were outside the house. We entered the car, and Sunglasses started the motor. Detective Patterson was copying the Lexus' license number from the front bumper. A shot rang out. I could hear a ping coming from the car's rear window.

"Down, now," ordered Sunglasses. He had spoken so authoritatively that it gave me the courage to do the unthinkable. I put my arms around Dr. Brotbaum's neck, and pulled him down with me. Sunglasses took off and executed a series of crazy maneuvers. We must have rounded a corner driving on the sidewalk, and then rounded another corner much too fast. Then we drove at a crazy clip on College Avenue. "OK to sit up now," Sunglasses said.

During the entire time, less than one minute, I had been holding onto Dr. Brotbaum's neck. Though it was fairly dark inside the car, once we sat up, I saw that Dr. Brotbaum was shaken. He mumbled incoherently. Maybe it was not in English. Looking at the rear window I could see a large indentation in the glass.

"Address?" Sunglasses asked. I wondered whether he was capable of uttering a whole sentence.

I gave him Aviva's address. "Do you know how to get there?" I asked.

"Yes." He drove directly to Aviva's building. Protectively, without speaking, he accompanied us from the curb to her apartment. I opened the door and let Dr. Brotbaum in. Sunglasses motioned me not to follow. In perfect American English he said, "I'm going to stop at the Berkeley police station to make a report about the shooting incident. The car is registered in my name, Glenn Tanaka. If you're asked, say we're friends, that we know each other from GIF. Don't get Mr. Takahashi involved."

I was flabbergasted. Jiro's security service had checked me out! They learned that at one time, I had been a GIF member. How much did they know about the rest of my life? What about my Acapulco caper?

*　　　　*　　　　*

Dr. Brotbaum and I sat in Aviva's living room just looking at each other. After a long silence, Dr. Brotbaum asked, "What do you think I should do?"

Though his tone did not betray fear, the question indicated how dramatically our roles had changed. I was there with him not as his student, but as an employee of KLZW temporarily in charge of his security. For the moment, he was not my professor but my responsibility.

"I don't know," I said. "I'm sure that the police caught the person who shot at us." I really believed that to be true, since the shooting took place while Detective Patterson was looking on.

I felt uncomfortable sitting and staring at a despondent Dr. Brotbaum. I gave some thought to suggesting that we prepare a meal, but it occurred to me that he would be more at home at Aviva's place than me. Eventually, I turned on the TV but I did not really watch the program. It allowed us to sit in silence.

At about nine thirty, Detective Patterson arrived. "You're a lucky guy, Eloy Harmony Wise," he said as soon as I let him in.

"How so?"

"Had you not been in an armored car, your head would have been blown off. The bullet hit the rear window right where you were sitting."

Until that moment, I had not given any thought to my personal safety. I assumed that only Dr. Brotbaum's life was in danger. Even now I was not afraid.

Detective Patterson sat down and addressed Dr. Brotbaum. "We were unable to obtain any description of the perpetrator. We're consulting with the FBI. We, in Berkeley, believe that the person who shot at you on two occasions is the same individual who vandalized your garage door.

"We now know that your garage door was vandalized sometime between five and seven on Friday morning. It appears that whoever did it isn't afraid of being apprehended. He shot at your car twice—he missed the second time due to the evasive skills of your driver—though he must have seen the police car in front of your home. We have to assume that he seeks a violent confrontation.

"If the same individual committed all three crimes, then we must find out what the hummingbird signature is all about. You have any clues, professor?"

"Hummingbird? Why a hummingbird?" Mrs. McLaughlin had not told Dr. Brotbaum about that. Detective Patterson described the graffiti on the garage door in detail. Dr. Brotbaum considered the question. He lowered his head and closed his eyes. After a while he opened them, and looked at the detective. "Huitzilopochtli," he said.

Patterson gave him the strangest look. Maybe he thought that, under the tremendous stress, Dr. Brotbaum was losing it. "I beg your pardon?"

"Huitzilopochtli was the chief god of the Mexica who are, interchangeably, also called the Aztecs. His name is derived from their word for a hummingbird, *huitzilín*. The hummingbird was associated with human sacrifices."

"I understand that the Rev. Tippit is mad at you," Detective Patterson said. "Would an Aztec war god, whatever his name is, also have reasons to be mad at you?"

"Yes," I said. "Dr. Brotbaum criticized the Aztec religion, specifically, human sacrifices. It was one show before the program that so upset Rev. Tippit."

"Does anyone still practice that religion?" asked Patterson.

"Evidently so," replied Dr. Brotbaum.

*   *   *

Aviva arrived just as Detective Patterson was about to leave. The police had already informed her about the latest incident. The last thing that Detective Patterson told the three of us was, "Professor, don't leave this place at all. I'm sure that the driver of the Lexus wasn't followed, so you'll be safe here. I start my day at two in the afternoon, and I'll be over here tomorrow around three. We'll see how we can deal with the Aztec you offended."

"I must return home Sunday night to prepare for my Monday classes," Dr. Brotbaum said.

"Professor, that hummingbird dude may be one crazy bird, but he's determined to bump you off. Right now, your most pressing business is to stay alive. So do me a favor and let the police tell you when it's safe to go home. Hopefully, we'll have the hummingbird in a cage by tomorrow."

Once the detective left, I was impressed by the way Aviva handled the situation. She did not say, "I told you so," or even insinuate it. She concentrated on practical matters. "Have you eaten, Eugene?"

"I'm not hungry."

"What about you, Harmony?"

"Don't worry about me, Aviva. I'll get a bite to eat on the way back to San Francisco."

"Harmony, please sleep here tonight. I have to return to work and finish up. I don't want Eugene to be by himself. I'll come back late, catch some sleep, and go to the station early tomorrow morning. Can you stay here on Sunday until I return? I'll be back before Patterson comes by."

I loved my new role as Dr. Brotbaum's bodyguard. I had planned on doing some homework Sunday morning, but being with Dr. Brotbaum was more important and much more exciting.

"Do you like pizza, Harmony?"

"It's OK."

"I'll order a pizza for all of us. You'll have to eat something, Eugene. And you'll sleep in my former roommate's bedroom. When she moved, she took the folding bed. Where shall I put you, Harmony?"

With all her postmodern furniture, she did not have a couch in the living room. "I'll sleep on the floor," I said.

In the most nonchalant manner, Dr. Brotbaum said, "The bed is large enough for two. Harmony can sleep with me rather than on the floor."

My heart skipped many beats. Aviva did not comment on Dr. Brotbaum's suggestion. When the pizza arrived, I went downstairs to pick it up, rather than buzz in the delivery man. I paid with the money Aviva had left for me at KLZW, and gave the remainder to her.

We had beer with the pizza. Aviva and I drank one bottle apiece. Dr. Brotbaum drank two. This was only the third time in my life I'd had beer. It made me feel light-headed and slightly nauseous. During the meal there was only one sharp exchange between Aviva and Dr. Brotbaum. Momentarily, they switched to another language—I assumed it was Hebrew—but then they dropped the subject.

It seemed odd to me that Dr. Brotbaum and Aviva hardly discussed the new hummingbird angle. Later on, when I thought about it, I understood why. Huitzilopochtli would make for good reading in a mystery paperback. For them, the "hummingbird dude," unlike Rev. Tippit, was just a madman not worth the expenditure of mental energy.

Once we had eaten, Aviva gave me sheets and blankets to make the bed. "Don't wait up for me. I'll be back in a few hours. I have to go back to the station early tomorrow morning. Eugene, please prepare breakfast for yourself and Harmony. You know where things are. I'm leaving some money on the table, Harmony. There's a Chinese take-out place around the corner. Buy lunch for the two of you. Don't let Eugene leave the house."

After Aviva left, Dr. Brotbaum went to the bathroom to take a shower. I called Jiro and told him that I would not be back. Then I busied myself preparing the bed and thinking. I was still light-headed from the beer, but I was absolutely certain that once I shared a bed with Dr. Brotbaum, things would happen. I wondered why he had suggested that we sleep together. Did he want to have sex with me?

I assumed, though I was not sure why, that I was the more experienced of the two of us. On the one hand, I did not wish to seduce Dr. Brotbaum. I certainly did not want to add to his worries by introducing the subject of homosexuality on this particular night. On the other hand, I desired, above everything else, to be physical with my teacher.

Until I met Joe, I had always slept in my underwear. Joe considered that an unsanitary practice. He gave me the choice of spending the night with him in the nude or in pajamas. Naked, I felt cold. So Joe bought me a few pairs of pajamas. From that time on, I always wore pajamas in bed. But here, at Aviva's, except for the clothes I wore, I had nothing with me. So how was I going to sleep with Dr. Brotbaum—in the buff, or in my underwear?

When Dr. Brotbaum came out of the shower wearing a nightshirt, I went into the bathroom. While showering, I remembered a classic, unsuccessful seduction scene where the teacher rebuffs his student.

Plato narrates the story. Socrates and a group of students are guests at a symposium in Agathon's house. There they drink and philosophize all evening. One of the students, the very handsome but conceited Alcibiades, tries to cajole Socrates to share a bed for the night. Gently, Socrates makes fun of him. Alcibiades tells of a similar occasion, when he was also mocked by Socrates. On that occasion, he had managed to sleep on the same couch with Socrates. He forced himself on Socrates, and spent the entire night embracing him. In the morning, he rose from the couch as if, in his words, "I had slept with my father or brother." Socrates had not succumbed to his beauty.

Unfortunately, I forgot why Socrates had refused to get it on with Alcibiades that night. Of course, I did not fancy myself an Alcibiades, but I saw many similarities between Socrates and Dr. Brotbaum. Would he reject me as Socrates had rebuffed Alcibiades?

14

Sexual Congress with Dr. Brotbaum

I left my underwear on. I felt it would be improper of me to lie naked next to Dr. Brotbaum. The reading lamp, on his side of the bed, was turned on, but the professor lay on his back with his eyes closed. I walked over and turned the light off. From his shallow breathing I knew that he was not asleep.

Each of us kept to his side of the bed, leaving a wide space between us. Like Dr. Brotbaum, I lay on my back with my eyes closed. I also pretended to be asleep, though I was wide awake. I wondered whether we would spend the entire night like this.

It took thirty minutes, maybe more, before Dr. Brotbaum asked in a barely audible voice, "Are you awake Harmony?"

"Yes," I said. My own voice was so tense that the word sounded awkward.

"It's difficult for me to fall asleep. This day has created a certain amount of tension in me."

"I know. I feel tense too."

"Harmony, why is your identification card made out to Eloy Wise?"

"My first name is Eloy; my middle name is Harmony. I used Harmony for the first time in my life in your class."

"Why did you do that?"

"I thought that Harmony would be a better name for a serious philosophy student." Once I said that, I was compelled to continue. "When I started using Harmony, I realized that my personality had two aspects: Eloy and Harmony. Later, I discovered that there was a third aspect, a José Luis."

"When you say 'aspects,' do you mean multiple personalities?"

"Something like that."

"How do your personalities differ from each other?"

"Well, Eloy is the oldest of my personalities. He's intelligent, but shy and lacks a sense of direction. Harmony is much more focused on future goals and is assertive. José Luis is wild and crazy. You know, José Luis understands the hummingbird."

"Oh?"

"Well, José Luis is a Mexican—I'm Hispanic on my father's side—and can identify with an Aztec whose religion you have slighted. The hummingbird is just as mad at you as Rev. Tippit, but doesn't have access to the media."

"You certainly have interesting insights. Detective Patterson might learn something important from José Luis's insights. Tell me, what are Harmony's future goals?"

"Harmony's future goals? For one, to major in philosophy and minor in computer science." That choice of subjects was news to me. A minute earlier I did not have that information. Then it came: "And Harmony loves his philosophy professor!"

The most profound silence descended upon the room. The statement was out there. That which was said could not be unsaid. I made my move and now it was Dr. Brotbaum's turn. Finally, he broke the silence. "In what manner does Harmony love his philosophy professor?"

"In all manners. Intellectually, spiritually…and physically. Harmony wants to be one with his professor."

"Must the love Harmony feels for his teacher be physical, as well as intellectual and spiritual?"

"Yes! Intellect and spirit are abstractions; the physical union of two bodies is concrete." As I said this, I experienced an instant erection.

"I've never before been with a man or a woman. Physically." Dr. Brotbaum stated this with complete nonchalance.

"Why not?"

"There hasn't been the occasion."

"Would tonight be such an occasion?"

Dr. Brotbaum thought my question over. After a long while he said, "For many reasons, I've chosen celibacy for myself. The Hindu concept of *brahmacharya* has always appealed to me. It refers to one who renounces sexual pleasures and can therefore dedicate himself entirely to a life of contemplation. Sexual renunciation affords one much more time and energy for spiritual and intellectual pursuits."

Each of us needed time to digest the answers of the other party. My erection was getting even more rigid, if that was possible. I considered my next question to be too forward but, still, I needed to ask it. "You may have been able to have full control over your actions, but what about your imagination? What about…" Here I paused for a moment, but finally dared utter the word, "Lust?"

"When I was an adolescent, and even a young man, I had carnal thoughts. They were confusing to me because I had difficulties making out, in my mind's eye, the objects of my desire. They were spectral rather than well-defined women or men. Then, over a period of many years, I learned to distract myself from carnal thoughts altogether. I believe I've been the better for it."

"Would tonight be an occasion to indulge in lust?" I took note of the fact that Dr. Brotbaum, in his reply to my question, had avoided the word "lust." As I asked that, I was furious with myself for having brought up the subject.

By now, both of us had shifted our positions. The distance between us was the same, but at least we faced each other. "Have you read Plato's *Symposium*?" Dr. Brotbaum asked.

"Yes, but I don't recall all the details."

"Do you remember the reason Socrates gave Alcibiades when he rejected his sexual advances?"

"No, I was thinking about that dialogue earlier on, but I forgot Socrates' reasoning."

"Socrates says to Alcibiades, who pretends to be drunk when he arrives at Agathon's symposium, 'You, Alcibiades, praise me for my great beauty, and you wish to spend the night with me. If I am as beautiful as you say, then you will have a great advantage over me. You will have my great beauty, whereas I fail to see the beauty in you.' Alcibiades accuses Socrates of being 'ironic.' After all, he is famous for his beauty. But Socrates is referring to the inner beauty, virtue, in which Alcibiades is lacking. In the end, Socrates suggests that their host, Agathon, rather than Alcibiades, spend the night with him.

"Tonight may be the night, Harmony, because ever since I've laid eyes on you, I've coveted you physically, even while admiring you intellectually. Your attraction to me must have stirred dormant and suppressed desires. I've seen the virtue in you which Socrates sought in all his lovers.

"I've never before been shot at. I shall suspend my *brahmacharya* and, for once, behave as other mortals do. Tonight you will be my Agathon." Saying this, Dr. Brotbaum turned toward me, his arms outstretched. I let him engulf me.

*   *   *

I had never been kissed the way Dr. Brotbaum did it. Joe, a former navy pilot, had a strict kissing drill: He puckered his lips and expected me to do likewise.

A few seconds later, our tongues touched, and both of us relaxed our jaw muscles simultaneously. Jiro, the kissing acrobat, was always showing off new and innovative techniques. But in his novice's fumbling manner, Dr. Brotbaum was the best kisser of all.

In our lovemaking, I was the teacher and Dr. Brotbaum became my student. In the beginning, he made love like an inexperienced teenager, awkwardly but enthusiastically. Soon it became obvious that he was learning to imitate my techniques, and would become a good sex partner in his own right. Above all, I desired Dr. Brotbaum to penetrate me. It was more than a physical need. I wanted to be possessed by Dr. Brotbaum's body and spirit. That wish confronted me with two immediate problems.

The first one was how to communicate that wish to Dr. Brotbaum. No way would I say to him, "Please fuck me." But if I used an elegant circumlocution like, "You may enter me when you're ready," he might not quite understand what I had in mind. I came up with an expression I thought was both decorous and descriptive, and said, "I'd like you to penetrate me tonight."

As usual, Dr. Brotbaum had a dissertation on the subject of penetration ready, just waiting to be delivered. "There is evidence, Harmony, that the ancient Greeks practiced intercrural intercourse. That is, the older partner would insert his member between the upper legs of the younger one. We know this from the many Greek vases where such scenes are depicted. But the poetry of the period strongly suggests that anal penetration did take place at times. I believe that in our case, full sexual congress would, indeed, be the right and proper form."

Having solved one problem, I turned my attention to the next issue. It was practical rather than semantic. Unlike many other gays, I never carried condoms with me because there would be no occasion for using them. Now that I needed one, I was not prepared.

I fully believed Dr. Brotbaum when he said that he was a virgin. Therefore, he could not give me AIDS. I myself had been examined at the beginning of the school year. I specifically asked the doctor to check me for AIDS. As they did in those days, he examined my lymph nodes and assessed my general health. He pronounced me free of AIDS. I reviewed my sexual activities since September, including my trip to Mexico. The likelihood that I had become infected with AIDS since then was infinitesimal. I believed it would be safe for us to have unprotected sex.

But we still needed a lubricant. We could use any suitable substance, since we did not have to worry about the condom breaking. But I did not know where Aviva kept things. I decided that we should use cooking oil. That would be the easiest item for me to locate in her apartment. I said, "Dr. Brotbaum, we need a lubricant. I'm going to dash into the kitchen and see what I can get hold of."

I found Aviva's cooking oil almost immediately. It was virgin olive oil, which would go well with our Greek motif. In a moment, Dr. Brotbaum and I were going to have, in his words, sexual congress. I felt that before we commenced the congress, I'd need to get his permission to call him by his first name. It would be comical to tell him, "Penetrate me now, Dr. Brotbaum." When I returned from the kitchen, I asked timidly, "Dr. Brotbaum, before we do it, may I call you, in private, Eugene?"

"Harmony, you may call me whatever you wish."

Being penetrated successfully by Eugene was of greatest importance to me. Even though Jiro had performed that feat successfully only a week earlier, I was worried about my ability to handle Eugene. His penis was not as long as Jiro's, but it was much thicker. Also, I discounted my experience with Jiro because of his great sexual expertise. Rather, I was thinking about my failure as a bottom with Joe. If I had such serious problems with him, who had a thinner dick, how would I be able to handle Eugene's equipment?

At that moment, all the teachings of my old textbook, *Upping Your Anal Pleasure: The Yoga of Anal Penetration*, came back to me. As Eugene inexpertly rammed his penis into me, I concentrated on my breathing, pushed down against his thrust, and let my mind relax completely. For a few seconds I felt a searing pain, which, as I had been taught, signaled me to relax even more. Then Eugene was inside me.

That was the moment Aviva chose to come home.

Both of us froze. I assumed that our bed, like all beds, made its own peculiar creaking noises when people engaged in sexual activities. Would Aviva hear these sounds? Our room was next to the bathroom at the end of the hall. Though Aviva was now in her own bedroom, she would be likely to use the bathroom before going to sleep.

More or less the same thoughts must have crossed Eugene's mind. He just lay on top of me, caressing me and gently kissing the nape of my neck every now and then. Amazingly, he stayed hard. I felt no pain whatsoever. After a while, I was so relaxed that I almost fell asleep with Eugene's cock inside me.

Aviva was quick about getting ready for bed. It took her less than a quarter of an hour. When the apartment became completely dark once again, and we did not hear Aviva walking about any longer, Eugene resumed his thrusting. It was like nothing I had experienced with Jiro.

Eugene possessed me, because I wanted to be possessed by him; he took me, because I wanted to be taken by him; he impregnated me with his essence, because I wanted his spirit to dwell within me.

* * *

Both of us woke up early when we heard Aviva leave.

"I have to get up," Eugene said.

"No, we have absolutely nothing whatsoever to do here until Detective Patterson arrives. Go back to sleep, Eugene!" Later in the day, it struck me that I had spoken to Dr. Brotbaum as if we were boyfriends. How things had changed in less than twelve hours!

Both of us got up around nine. "I'll prepare breakfast," Eugene said. For some reason I have always regarded Eugene as helpless in practical matters. But, having lived alone all of his life, he must have known how to feed himself. He made breakfast while I took a shower.

Eugene's breakfast was different from any breakfast I had ever eaten before. He prepared a mixed green salad, finely sliced, with lots of black olives and tomatoes. There was an assortment of cream and yellow cheeses, herring in sour cream, slices of a delicious rye bread, and two pieces of halvah. For dressing, Eugene put out oil and vinegar cruets. Last night's lubricant was now on the table. "Do you take tea or coffee in the morning?" he asked.

"Coffee," I said. "What sort of breakfast is this?"

"Oh, more or less an Israeli breakfast. That's what Aviva and I eat in the morning."

After breakfast, I cleaned up the bedroom and put the sheets in the washer. I thought of calling the police station. But what would I ask them? "Is the hummingbird in the cage already?" This sort of question, I was sure, the police would dismiss as a nut call. Instead, I called Aviva to find out whether KLZW had received word from the police. She was unavailable. All I could do was leave a message. By tacit agreement, neither of us referred to the events of last night. I knew that the subject would be discussed sooner or later, but I preferred Eugene to broach it. After cleaning up, I looked forward to Dr. Brotbaum discussing his personal philosophy. But he had a different agenda. "Last night you told me that you were Hispanic on your father's side. Do you speak Spanish?"

I told Eugene how I learned Spanish. When I finished, to my great surprise, he addressed me in that language. "Let me propose to you that we spend some time this morning speaking Spanish with each other. Of course, you'll have the inconvenience of speaking with someone who does not have your mastery of the language. Is that agreeable to you?"

"Of course."

Eugene, speaking in Spanish, told me that he had started his studies of that language because he wished to read the poetry of García Lorca in the original. Lorca, Eugene said, was man of many artistic talents: playwright, director, musician, and poet. He was executed early in the Spanish Civil War by Franco's soldiers, still a young man. "Do you know that García Lorca was what is now called gay?"

"I know nothing about Lorca."

"If you were to look him up in encyclopedias you would still not know that he was…gay." Eugene definitely did not like the term "gay."

"Why?"

"The contributors to encyclopedias usually, not always, know that the person about whom they write is, or was, a homosexual. But unless homosexuality is obviously what the person's work is all about, like the French author Jean Genet, or played a crucial role in his life, as in Oscar

Wilde's case, they'll suppress that information. They think they are protecting their hero."

Eugene's knowledge of Spanish was impressive. Using a grammar textbook and listening to tapes, he had managed to learn quite a bit of the language. He spoke it with extreme formality, and followed the grammar and pronunciation used in Spain rather than in Latin America. I don't know whether his formal speech was a result of his textbook, published between the World Wars, or his personal preference.

As in English, he did far better with grammar and vocabulary than with his pronunciation. As for all non-native speakers, trilling the Spanish double "r" was the most difficult feat for him. It made me laugh when he attempted it. He sounded as if he had a real frog in his throat.

Later on in the morning, Eugene switched to philosophy and spoke in English. As always, even in his present condition, Eugene was eager to philosophize. He must have become aware of the incongruous behavior under the circumstances. "You probably compare me, in your mind, Harmony, to Socrates. He, too, philosophized at inopportune times. Do you know that in the end, he did not sleep with Agathon on the particular night we mentioned yesterday?"

"I remember now. But why?"

"As Plato tells it, 'Agathon arose in order that he might take his place on the coach by Socrates, when suddenly a band of revelers entered and spoiled the order of the banquet.' Everybody got very drunk. Agathon and Socrates had their hands full with the guests and revelers. Neither of them got any sleep. In the morning, Socrates, who could out drink his students, was still discoursing to whoever was awake. Though the students were inebriated and could hardly understand him, he went on and on, wanting them to admit that there were great similarities between tragedy and comedy.

"This is, Harmony, what philosophers are supposed to do: philosophize. Socrates died philosophizing!"

*　　　　*　　　　*

At noon, I picked up two Chinese lunches to go. During our meal, Aviva called to make sure we were all right. She said she had not heard from the police.

She came back about two in the afternoon. The three of us were talking when, accidentally, I referred to Dr. Brotbaum as Eugene. Without comment, Aviva gave me a withering look. I wondered what she thought about our sleeping together last night. How much did she know about Eugene's love life or, more accurately, the lack thereof?

At three o'clock on the dot, Detective Patterson arrived. "I have good news and bad news," he said right away. "The good news is that we've located a DBA under the name Huitzi Painting in Oakland."

"What is a DBA?" Eugene asked.

"Doing Business As," Detective Patterson said. "To use a fictitious name for a business, an ad has to be placed in a newspaper notifying the public of it. Then the fictitious name is registered at city hall. The owner of Huitzi Painting uses a hummingbird with a long beak as his logo. Unfortunately, nobody took photos of the graffiti on your door, Professor. But your housekeeper, Mrs. McLaughlin, sees a likeness between the logo and the graffiti."

Detective Patterson glanced at his notes. "The name of the owner of Huitzi Painting is Marcos Montoya. He's described by neighbors as a Hispanic male with a fairly light complexion, long black hair, and a short beard. He's about thirty years old, over six feet, and quite thin. He answers to Huitzi. None of his neighbors know what the name Huitzi stands for. We obtained a warrant and searched his place this morning.

"Apparently, the suspect only stores his equipment at that address. It is a one-room cottage adjacent to a rundown house. We've not yet interviewed the suspect's landlord, who may be out of the state at the moment. In addition to brushes, some cans of paint, turpentine, and the like, we found a Berreta semiautomatic gun in a tool shed. We also found a stack of calling cards with the hummingbird logo. The telephone listed on his card is a voicemail number. We're checking that out. We've issued an all points bulletin to detain him. What makes it difficult is that though he drives an old Nissan pickup, no vehicle is registered to him."

"So what now?" asked Aviva.

"Now we wait until the hummingbird flies into our trap," said the detective.

"I have to go home to prepare for tomorrow," Eugene said.

"Professor, you aren't going anywhere. Huitzi is our only suspect. We may be wrong about him; there may be other accomplices. Who knows? In the meantime, you're safe where you are. If you want to move to a hotel, one that we'll choose for you, we can arrange the transfer. Most important is for you not to be seen in public, and for the two of you," he pointed at Aviva and me, "to keep mum about the professor's whereabouts."

"Detective, I have classes to teach."

"No, Professor, you have a life to save. Your own. Hummingbird may be crazy, probably is, but he's as dangerous as they come. If you need to go home to pick up clothes and personal stuff, we can arrange this with enough notice. We can secure your house for an hour with five officers. Even if we had the resources, which we don't, we couldn't protect you on campus. For that you would need the Secret Service."

Eugene was about to say something when Detective Patterson raised his hand to stop him. "I know what you're going to ask: 'How long?' Nobody can answer that. We may apprehend Hummingbird as soon as he returns from work, if he is at work, or in a week, or in a month. Then we have got to prove to a court of law that we have probable cause to detain him. It's a nuisance, I know. But, Professor, your life is at stake!"

* * *

After the detective left, Eugene went into the bedroom and closed the door behind him. Aviva and I sat in the living room feeling dejected. Finally, Aviva said, "It's very likely, Harmony, that I'll have to resign. The powers that be blame me for having given Eugene carte blanche to say that which must not be said."

"Is it really such a big deal, Aviva? I mean, Rev. Tippit has an ax to grind, and Hummingbird is crazy, but Dr. Brotbaum didn't say anything terrible. What about free speech, and all that sort of thing?"

"We've already discussed that, Harmony. Your great hero, Socrates, was sentenced to death just for asking questions! Dr. Brotbaum didn't play the game according to the rules. I was his accomplice. Both of us must be punished. I'm changing the subject. I know Eugene. He won't agree to stay under some sort of house arrest. Do you have any suggestions?"

I entertained briefly the fantasy of Eugene and me fleeing to Acapulco. There we would live incognito, speaking Spanish. I would work on Angel's relative's boat and support both of us. In the evenings we would philosophize, and at night we would make passionate love. Wrong fantasy, I said to myself. We cannot stay among Huitzilopochtli's people after having insulted their chief god. "Right now, Aviva, I can't think of anything constructive."

We busied ourselves reading the Sunday paper. Eventually, Eugene came out of his room. "I feel pretty restless, Harmony, I must take a walk. Would you like to accompany me?"

15

The Hummingbird Is in the Cage

Both Aviva and I were startled by Eugene's desire to take a walk. "Don't you understand, Eugene, that there's someone out there who wants to kill you, and that today you cannot take your walk?" Aviva asked in an almost shrill voice. She stopped for a moment, and then added sarcastically, "You know, Eugene, this is not Königsberg in the eighteenth century, and you are not Dr. Immanuel Kant taking his daily constitutional. This is California in 1985."

Nonchalantly, Eugene replied, "If Huitzilopochtli's follower doesn't know that I'm at your apartment, then he is not likely to know that I'm taking a walk."

"For heaven's sake, Eugene, we don't even know for sure if it's Hummingbird who's after you. Your photo has been in the papers. Many people in Berkeley will recognize you."

"Then I shall walk at the Redwood Park in Oakland."

I had heard that occasionally Dr. Brotbaum liked to take his students to a park and, while walking, philosophize with them. In this practice he emulated the peripatetic Aristotle. I had never been invited to such a foray.

"And how, pray tell, will you get to the park?"

"Could we borrow your car? Maybe Harmony will drive us." I thought it was ironic that Dr. Brotbaum, in spite of his immense erudition, did not know how to operate an automobile.

"Harmony," Aviva asked me, "do you have a driver's license?"

"I do," I said proudly. At that moment, I did not think it would be advisable to mention that I had driven only once without an instructor at my side. I had operated a car by myself a total of fourteen blocks, shuttling between Monty's offices. Even that had taken place quite a while ago.

"I still think the whole thing is crazy," Aviva said.

"I'll drive your car into the garage," I told Aviva, "and Dr. Brotbaum can lie on the back seat for a few blocks. This way, nobody in this neighborhood will know that he's around. We'll follow the same procedure on the way back. I believe Dr. Brotbaum will be safe at the park."

"Since when are you a security expert?" Aviva asked.

"Oh," said Eugene, "Harmony brought me here in an armored car."

Aviva gave me one of her withering looks. "Had my life been seriously threatened, I wouldn't be taking walks in a park. I think both of you are crazy." She went to her desk, separated her car keys from the rest, and, disdainfully, handed them to me. When Dr. Brotbaum had left his home the previous day, he had prepared himself for a walk. He brought with him a pair of sturdy hiking boots and a wide-brimmed khaki hat. I was glad that it was not his cowboy headgear.

* * *

I had never before been to Oakland's Redwood Park. All I remember of scenery during our long hike in that park is a large herd of goats that we saw just after leaving the parking lot. I believe they were there to keep the ground clear, to prevent fires. Eugene, who knew the trails well, was a surprisingly fast hiker and walked uphill without getting winded. I, on the other hand, breathed heavily at times.

As soon as we started our walk, he said in a nonchalant tone of voice, "Of course, Harmony, we shall never again be able to indulge in romantic activities. I hope you understand that it must be so."

I had a premonition that Eugene would reach such a conclusion. Just for practical reasons, it would be impossible for me to be intimate with him, even verbally, in Berkeley. Again, I fantasized wildly: Renting a small apartment in San Francisco for our meetings. Traveling together to Switzerland during the summer vacations. But I only asked, "Why does it have to be this way, Eugene?"

"Why do you think, Harmony, that there's so much said and written against smoking cigarettes nowadays?"

Eugene's Socratic method of teaching was great fun in class. At the moment, I was not interested in playing philosophy games. I failed to see the connection between smoking and dating. Without much thinking I said, "It's not good for you. Heart, lungs, cancer, surgeon general's warnings, that sort of stuff."

"Do you think that a hundred years ago, smokers didn't have that knowledge?"

"I would think not. If smokers had known then what we know now, they would've quit long ago."

"Dostoyevsky's *Crime and Punishment* was published in 1866. The police inspector who interrogates the hero, Raskolinkov, exclaims, even as he smokes: 'I smoke too much. It is killing me. My doctor tells me that I must stop. But I cannot.' People have known for a long time that smoking is bad for them. They must have known this from empirical observations.

This is why they've always forbidden their children to smoke. What they lacked were only the statistics to prove it scientifically.

"You see, Harmony, fashion and not fact, dictates what we consider good or bad. For instance, if health considerations mattered at all, women would not wear shoes with high heels. When the high-heel fashion changes then, suddenly, it will be common knowledge that wearing high heels is bad for women's feet. Of course, women and their doctors know now how bad it really is. As long as wearing high heels is in fashion, the health issue will be ignored."

Here Eugene paused for a few seconds, and then continued. "I daresay that what's now called 'gay liberation' is also dictated by fashion. But let's not dwell on too many politically incorrect subjects in one afternoon.

"Carnal relationships between a teacher and his students were quite acceptable, even desirable, in Socrates' Athens. The older partner was expected to be a role model and teacher for his young lover. In *Symposium*, Plato assigns the duty of educating the younger partner to the older one. We know less about females in Greece because there isn't an extensive enough record. As far as Sappho of Lesbos is concerned, we have only fragments of her writings. Some scholars have even speculated that there were two Sapphos."

I found it maddening to discuss the future of our love life as if it were a history lecture full of obscure scholarly observations. I did not care how many Sappho look-alikes had been spotted. But Eugene, after his learned asides, went right back to the main body of his lecture.

"Romantic intimacy between instructors and students was ignored at Cambridge in the twenties and thirties, as you know from researching Wittgenstein. In Berkeley, in the eighties, such relationships are completely out of fashion. Since they are out of fashion, and only because of it, they're viewed as immoral."

"But we've already done the deed."

"Yes, but under extraordinary circumstances."

"Do you think, Eugene, that you'll hurt me by being physical with me?"

"In the short run, it won't hurt you at all. It may even benefit you. However, in the long run it may very well cause you some damage. You might need, ten years hence, to consult a psychiatrist or psychologist. Once the therapist discovers that you have had a romantic involvement with your professor and tells you that, whether you are aware of it or not, you were terribly damaged by such a liaison, then you may indeed feel injured by it.

"For centuries masturbation was considered a morbid practice to which children were especially prone. In and of itself, it didn't harm the children physically or psychologically. But adults kept telling the younger generation that what they were doing would result in terrible consequences. For some of them, bad things did happen, just because of the dire predictions.

"The English philosopher John Locke said, 'What humanity abhors, custom reconciles and recommends to us.' In Berkeley, at this point in time, romantic involvement between instructors and their students is abhorred. A decade from now, it may become a fashionable custom."

"Out of curiosity, Eugene, would my romantic involvement with you be bad for you?"

"I've given this subject a great deal of thought. I must put it in words that won't hurt you, yet will be completely honest. For me, last night's experience was exciting, even exhilarating, but extremely undisciplined. Harmony, I'm not cut out for the role of a lover. My calling is intellectual rather than romantic. This morning was the first time in over two decades that I prepared breakfast for another person. Your generation calls what would happen between us, if we were to continue, a 'relationship.' For this one needs time, patience, dedication, maybe even a vocation. All of these attributes I do not have.

"Even if romantic involvement between instructors and students were tolerated at the university, I would not permit myself this luxury. You yourself are better off not having me as a lover."

"What about a philosopher like Socrates? He had lots of time for both philosophy and romance."

"It is kind of you to compare me to Socrates. But, unlike Socrates, I'm just an ordinary mortal who happens to be a philosopher. Socrates may well have wanted you as his lover. Many a philosopher would. But I cannot afford this luxury."

"Could we be together just in the summer months? We could meet in Zurich. I have a friend there. I could stay with him and we could meet somewhere."

"Harmony, I'm not a person who has trysts or assignations in remote places."

"What will become of me then, Eugene?"

"I'm sure that you'll study hard and find your own vocation. I hope that you'll continue studying philosophy with me. I would rather be your scholastic mentor than your sexual companion."

We stopped talking and walked silently, each of us busy with his own thoughts. We must have walked like this for almost a mile. Eugene was walking ahead of me at a steady pace, not slowing down when walking uphill. It occurred to me that he must have done some mountain climbing in the Alps when he was a student in Switzerland.

I did not know what else I could say to change Eugene's mind. A great sadness engulfed me. Of course, I could always find companions and sex partners. There were enough foolish, mature gentleman at GIF to satisfy my own physical needs. That was not the point. I needed and wanted only my Dr. Brotbaum. I knew that if my love for Eugene were selfless, I would let go of him. But, I thought, the only love that was ordained by nature to be selfless was that of a mother for her young. I loved Dr. Brotbaum with the same possessiveness and jealousy that Benjie displayed toward Monty.

Silently, I started crying. I don't know how Eugene noticed this—the trail narrowed at that moment, and he was walking briskly ahead of me. But notice he did. He turned around, stepped backward, and put his arms around my shoulders. "*The Book Of The Dead*, the ancient Egyptian text, not the Tibetan one, was written to assist the dead on their passage into the afterworld. In it, the soul declares its innocence by stating, 'I have made no man cry.' And, behold, Harmony, I caused you to shed tears!"

I snuggled against Eugene. Almost instantly, but very gently, he released me and said, "It's time for us to go back." We turned around and walked in the opposite direction.

*   *   *

We followed safety precautions on our way to Aviva's apartment. I was exhausted. The hike had tired me, the dismissal by Eugene had crushed me, and the effort of driving made me tense. I just wanted to go home and be by myself.

A little before six, we were back at Aviva's apartment. She appeared more cheerful than before. "Detective Paterson is due at any moment," she told us. "He called and said that Hummingbird was in the cage." By now I was sick of the hummingbird. I wanted to open the cage and wring his neck.

The detective arrived at 7:30, just after we had finished supper. "As I've told Ms. Harari," this was Aviva's surname, "Hummingbird is in the cage. The Oakland police arrested him this afternoon when he returned to the cottage. They found an unlicensed Berreta semiautomatic handgun and some LSD in his tool shed. He was turned over to us and, during interrogation, admitted that he was the perpetrator of the graffiti on the professor's garage door. Then he asked for a lawyer and the interrogation came to a halt.

"This is where things are at. Tomorrow he'll be arraigned on three charges: possession of an unregistered weapon, possession of an illegal substance, and malicious damage. We have to match his gun with the bullets for more serious charges. Most likely, he won't be able to post bail. So unless I notify you to the contrary, Professor, you're safe for now. What happens in the long run, since he's not going to get life, is another matter. The court, of course, will issue a restraining order to keep him away from you."

"Why did he vandalize my door?"

"Well, Professor, we don't know whether the guy is crazy or not. My guess is that he has done too many LSD trips in his life."

"What's the Aztec business all about?" asked Aviva.

"Well, we're still checking him out, but he seems to be here legally, unless he showed us a phony green card. He kept saying that he was born in—" Patterson consulted his notes, "Tenochtitlán."

"Tenochtitlán is the original name for what is now called Mexico City," said Eugene.

"Well, the hummingbird dude has a thing about it. He claims that he's an Aztec citizen. So, Professor, you can return home. Mr. Hummingbird will be out of circulation for a while. If we can match the bullets, he'll be doing hard time. We'll let you know how things develop."

* * *

It was almost nine o'clock when Aviva drove Eugene and me to our respective homes. She dropped off Eugene first. I asked Eugene, in Spanish, so Aviva would not understand, "Do you want me to stay the night? Just so you won't be alone?"

He understood my rapid Spanish perfectly. *"No es posible,"* he said in his strange accent, *"la gente va a murmurar."* Of course he was right. It was not possible because "people would murmur."

When we were alone in the car, Aviva asked me furiously, "What's going on between the two of you? Why did Eugene want you to spend the night in his bed? Why have you started calling him by his first name? Since when do the two of you speak Spanish to each other?"

"I've been in love with Eugene from my first day in his class. He, too, is in love with me. But nothing will ever come of it!"

"What did you expect, Harmony? He's a tenured professor at the university. He doesn't need the aggravation of a young student sexually harassing him! Why don't you pick on someone your own age?"

I was shocked. It was not only what Aviva had said; it was also her tone of voice. I sat silently in the car until we reached my home. I was just about to get out of the car when Aviva spoke in a soft voice. "I'm sorry, Harmony. It has been a long, hard weekend. I'm worried about Eugene. I don't think that this episode is over. Now I need to worry about you as well. Eugene has never discussed sexual matters with me, though he knows, of course, that I'm a lesbian. Most of the time I thought that he was…asexual."

"Harmony, let's get a good night's sleep and talk about all of this when our heads are clearer."

I was emotionally drained. I was sure that I would not be able to fall asleep. But the hike with Eugene must have exhausted me physically. I fell asleep immediately, and I slept soundly until the alarm woke me up.

16

The Revenge of the Hummingbird

Monday was a hectic day for me. I had to catch up on all the schoolwork I had neglected during the previous weekend. I called KLZW and told the receptionist that I would come in the following day.

My philosophy class took place from eleven to noon on Tuesday. Dr. Brotbaum wore his customary dark suit and nondescript tie. In spite of his ordeal, he did not look any different. He received a short ovation when he entered the lecture hall. Illogically, I was angered by it. What were the students applauding, the suspension of *Philosopher's Corner*, or the fact that their instructor had been shot at? He taught his class as he usually did, without referring to any subject unrelated to the topics under discussion.

Ronnell came in halfway through the lecture. When it was over he approached me and said, "Harmony, can we talk?"

"Not now, Ronnell. I have another class. Then I've got to work at KLZW." It took us a while to come up with a time that would suit both of us. We agreed to have a dinner at a restaurant on Dwight Way.

*　　　*　　　*

The beginning of my conversation with Ronnell was quite scary. When he told me that he wanted to know "everything that happened between you and Dr. Brotbaum," I assumed that he was referring to our having been intimate. A bit later, I understood that Ronnell alluded only to the shooting incident and the aftermath.

I told Ronnell the entire story as I had witnessed it. I omitted any mention of the armored car, which had not made the news, and my physical involvement with Eugene. While telling the story, I wondered how Ronnell would have taken the whole truth. Like my mother with her Hindu gurus, the student circle around Dr. Brotbaum also regarded him as a kind of "lay guru." I was the only one who wanted an intellectual as well as a physical union with him. Upon reflection, was I really the only one? Maybe there were others of whom I was not aware.

We had almost finished our dinner when my pager beeped. It displayed a phone number I did not recognize. Since only Aviva and Jiro knew the number, I was tempted to ignore the beep. But I had a premonition that it was not a wrong number. I dialed the number, and a deep, irritable voice answered on the first ring. "Lieutenant Littlejohn."

"Did you page me?"

"What's your name?"

"Eloy Harmony Wise."

"Hold on."

The next voice was that of Detective Patterson. "Eloy?"

"Yes," I said, feeling a sense of foreboding.

"This is Detective Patterson. We're at your professor's home. I'm afraid I have bad news for you. Very bad news.

"What happened?" I asked, my legs almost buckling under me.

"I'll let you talk to Miss Harari."

"Harmony?" It was Aviva's voice.

"Yes."

"Dr. Brotbaum is dead. He was murdered. Please come over to his home right away." She hung up the phone.

Somehow, I must have been able to walk back to where I had been sitting with Ronnell. He asked, “Harmony, are you OK?”

I spoke slowly and deliberately. “Dr. Brotbaum was murdered. I must go there. Please give me a ride.”

*   *   *

I coped with the next twenty-four hours by disassociating myself from the situation. I became an observer rather than a participant. Though part of me had been destroyed, outwardly I functioned efficiently.

To make the narration more orderly, I will reconstruct here chronologically the events that took place before the murder. My own memory of what I had witnessed and what I read later on is hazy. The media, including a number of lengthy magazine articles, covered the crime extensively.

Dr. Brotbaum’s murder happened on Tuesday afternoon, while I was still working at the radio station. By the time Ronnell and I arrived at Dr. Brotbaum’s home, Eugene’s body had already been removed. For reasons I never understood fully, Aviva had been summoned to identify the body, though that had already been done by Detective Patterson.

It was a real donnybrook. Only police officers and witnesses to the crime were supposed to be in the house, but there were lots of other people on the premises. Everybody was talking at the same time, and a uniformed cop kept yelling, “Don’t disturb the crime scene.” But not disturbing the crime scene would serve no useful purpose. Dr. Brotbaum was dead, and the criminal had been apprehended red-handed. It was Hummingbird.

*   *   *

Hummingbird had been arrested on Sunday while Dr. Brotbaum and I were staying Aviva's apartment. The public defender who was assigned to Hummingbird's case had been on the job for only one week. He was young, fresh, and eager. He soon discovered that the weapon the police found had not been in Hummingbird's cottage, but in a free-standing tool shed. At Hummingbird's arraignment on Tuesday morning, he argued that though Hummingbird had a key to the shed's padlock, it had not been rented to him by the owner, nor was it part of the cottage. The search warrant covered only the cottage itself. By breaking the lock of the tool shed and searching it, the police had gone beyond the warrant. The judge agreed, and suppressed that piece of evidence. The fact that the bullets discharged at Dr. Brotbaum's home and Jiro's car matched the gun found in the shed did not matter any longer.

All the district attorney was left with was Hummingbird's confession to malicious damage. Guided by the public defender, Hummingbird retracted his statement, pleaded not guilty, and requested a jury trial. With surprising efficiency, the district attorney and the public defender worked out a plea bargain. Hummingbird pleaded guilty to disorderly conduct. He received a thirty-day suspended sentence and a hundred-dollar fine. By early afternoon, Hummingbird was out of the cage. Detective Patterson learned about Hummingbird's release a few hours after he started his afternoon shift. He drove immediately to Dr. Brotbaum's home.

The entrance door to the house was ajar. Patterson called for backup. With drawn guns, four cops barged into the house. By then, Dr. Brotbaum had been bludgeoned to death and Hummingbird, holding a huge carving knife, was about to cut out his heart. He had used a marker to outline his cuts on Eugene's chest. When he saw the cops, he turned on them. He was shot in the right arm, disarmed, and arrested.

Detective Patterson summoned me into the kitchen, the only space available to speak privately. "He fell through the cracks," he kept saying, by way of apologizing. He asked me a few perfunctory questions dealing with the very last time I had contact with the deceased. Then he said to me, "Eloy, in the next hour this case will turn into a real media circus. Do you want to be interviewed dozens of times, having to answer the same dumb questions over and over again?"

"Why me?" I asked.

"Because of your special relationship with the victim."

For a moment I thought he was referring to my intimate relationship. But, forcing myself to think clearly, I understood that I had witnessed the previous attempt on Dr. Brotbaum's life. That alone made me a worthy interview. "I don't want anybody to ask me anything."

"Then get out of here as soon as possible. You may even want to leave Berkeley for a few days."

Aviva was being questioned by two policemen in civilian clothes. She was in tears, and looked pinched. I did not want to wait until they finished with her. When I saw Ronnell being ushered out of the building, I joined him. Silently, we walked to his car. As soon as I was inside, I broke down and cried uncontrollably. Ronnell did not start the engine. Eventually, he touched me gently on my arm. "Harmony, where am I taking you?"

I had to get out of Berkeley. I did not want to go back to school, speak to other students, or be interviewed by reporters. "Can we stop at a public phone?" I asked Ronnell. Jiro had given me his personal number. It had a call forwarding feature. He answered on the second ring. "Ah, Eloy, I've heard about your teacher. I'm very sorry."

"Jiro-san, I'd like to be out of Berkeley for a while. May I stay with you?"

Without hesitation he replied, "Yes. I will send driver to pick up you. Where are you?"

I gave him my home address, and had Ronnell drive me there.

*   *   *

I packed a small suitcase. By the time I was finished, Glenn Tanaka, driving the battered Honda, rang the bell. As always, Glenn was taciturn, which, on this occasion, I appreciated greatly. From the time he picked me up in Berkeley to the moment he discharged me at Jiro's building, he uttered only one sentence: "Hello, Eloy, I'm very sorry about your instructor."

This time my reception was different. The guard, who had previously accompanied me to Jiro's apartment, photocopied my ID and returned it to me. He issued me a small badge with Japanese writing and a plastic cover. Across the badge the date was stamped in bright green. Then he told me, "Today's pass. Tomorrow we give new pass. Every day new pass. Takahashi-san not here. Please follow me." He took me to the second floor and ushered me into an apartment. Like a bellboy at a hotel, he handed me the key, bowed formally, and left.

The one-bedroom apartment was cheerfully decorated, but impersonal. Not knowing what to do with myself, I examined each of the rooms. The kitchen was equipped with a dishwasher and a state-of-the-art microwave, in addition to a modern electric stove. The cabinets were full of all sorts of cans with Japanese labels. The refrigerator contained fresh fruits, milk, eggs, and lots of Japanese beer bottles. The freezer compartment was full of Japanese TV dinners.

The desk in the living room featured a phone, a fax machine, and a PC. The room also had an expensive stereo system and a TV with a VCR.

In one corner stood an elegant bar with a large selection of alcoholic beverages. The bedroom was decorated with a multi-colored bedspread and a yellow curtain. Incongruously, a pink telephone in the shape of a duck was positioned on the night stand. I assumed that the apartment was for the use of out-of-town visitors.

I felt numb. I had no plans for the present or the future. I turned on the TV and absentmindedly watched a Spanish *telenovela*. After a while the phone rang. It was Jiro. "Hello, Eloy. Are you comfortable?" he asked. Jiro had great difficulty with words like "comfortable" which contained the letters "l" and "r" in close proximity. He had to repeat it twice before I understood what he said.

"Thank you. I'm fine."

"Sorry, cannot see you tonight. Tomorrow please have dinner with me. I come to your apartment maybe seven in the evening."

I had almost twenty-four hours ahead of me to be by myself. At that stage, enforced loneliness was what I wanted.

*   *   *

I spent the night fitfully. In the morning, I made myself a breakfast of cereal and fruit, and decided to go out for a walk. At the last moment, I remembered to take my pass with me. The receptionist downstairs took the pass from me and exchanged it for another one, in a different color, stamped with the current date.

For a while I walked around Japan Town, looking at the sights without really seeing them. Then I took the bus to Golden Gate Park. For a few hours I wandered around the park in utter apathy. Eventually, I reached the beach at the western end of park and bought myself a take-out lunch. As I was leaving the delicatessen, my eye caught the huge headline in the afternoon paper: "Controversial UC Professor Murdered," and, in smaller print, "Aztec Sacrificial Ritual Suspected." I bought the paper, and took it with me to the park. I forced myself to eat my lunch before reading it.

There were four different articles dealing with the murder. The first one, on the front page, was the lead news story. Much of the information came from interviews with Aviva and Detective Patterson. The last paragraph was Rev. Tippit's reaction to the murder. "When a man, or a woman, offends God, they open themselves to the powers of Satan. Once you are in his power, he will toy with you like a cat with a mouse. The professor's own blasphemy brought about his horrible death. How accurately the Bible predicts what will happen to people like the benighted Berkeley philosopher: 'Be not deceived; God is not mocked: For whatsoever a man soweth that shall he also reap.'"

The second item was an interview with Danny Fleetwood, identified as Dr. Brotbaum's associate. It was the story of Dr. Brotbaum's life and teaching career and, of course, Danny's own contributions to the professor's work. Danny ended the interview with this statement: "I admired Dr. Brotbaum's great intellectual courage and, needless to say, mourn his loss terribly. I believe that, on the *Philosopher's Corner*, he had lost the objectivity of a scholar toward the end and took up a more pedestrian approach."

The third feature was a gory description of Aztec human sacrifices. It contained a lot of sensational information about the sacrifices, but very little about Hummingbird himself. The connection between Huitzilopochtli, represented as a hummingbird, and the murderer, Marcos Montoya, was noted. The reporter's conclusion was that Hummingbird was clinically insane.

The fourth story was titled, "How Could It Have Happened?" How could Hummingbird have been released without precautions? The phrases "He fell through the cracks," and, "It fell through the cracks," kept repeating themselves. By the end of the article, it was not at all clear whether it was Hummingbird, Dr. Brotbaum, or the case itself that had fallen through the cracks.

All the interviewees agreed readily that the matter had been mishandled by the authorities. A leading criminal lawyer said that the judge should have issued a restraining order enjoining Hummingbird from coming within a hundred and fifty yards of Dr. Brotbaum. Sagaciously, the reporter commented that a deranged criminal like Hummingbird "would probably not have obeyed the court's order."

*   *   *

Back at the apartment, I turned on the stereo and listened to classical music. I must have fallen asleep, because the phone woke me up. "May I come over for visiting you?" Jiro asked.

When I let him in, he addressed me solemnly. "I'm so sad about terrible death of your teacher. Please accept my deep sorriness." Then he took me in his arms and held me tightly.

We ate a catered dinner at my apartment. As usual, it was brought in by a waiter accompanied by a guard. It was my first exposure to sushi, which I really liked. When we finished, I took the few dishes we had used to the kitchen to wash them. "Not necessary," Jiro said. "Tomorrow maid do." Indeed, I noticed that the apartment had been cleaned and the refrigerator restocked while I was out. I had made up my bed before leaving for my walk. Most likely, it was not necessary. The maid would have taken care of it.

"When will you go back to university?"

“I don’t want to continue my studies. I’ll probably get a job with Monty. I can’t go back now.”

“I know that you’re very sad. But you must go back to university; to honor your dead teacher.”

In my misery, I never asked myself what Eugene would have wanted me to do. Of course Jiro was right. Eugene would have insisted that I go on with my studies.

I was certain that Jiro would not impose upon me, and would leave me in the apartment by myself. But I did not wish to be alone. “May I sleep with you, Jiro-san?” I asked.

“Of course. We go back my apartment.”

Jiro was extremely gentle and loving with me. He did not perform any sexual acrobatics. His body language conveyed to me his great empathy. Unable to sleep, I clung to him throughout the night. Toward morning, I drifted off. When I woke up, Jiro was gone. He left me a note saying that we would meet for a late dinner at my apartment.

I spent the rest of the week at Jiro’s. Sunday morning he had Glenn drive me to Berkeley to prepare for school.

* * *

Childishly, I assumed that with the death of Dr. Brotbaum everything would come to a stop. I did not call the radio station because, however foolish that sounds now, I believed they would mourn Dr. Brotbaum and shut down. I also neglected to notify Monty that I was taking a few days off.

On Monday afternoon I went to KLZW. Two security guards were still posted there. I showed them my ID. Instead of letting me in, they had me wait outside in a light rain. One of them went into the building. After a long wait, Violet, the bookkeeper, came out with one of the guards. She was holding an envelope in her right hand. Because she was in charge of payroll, she was considered the head of a nonexistent personnel department. "Hello, Harmony," she said. She appeared to be mulling over a problem in her mind. It took her a few seconds to invite me into the station.

There was no lobby in the building. Violet took me into the first room from the entrance door. It was the station engineer's office, but he was out. Violet was a petite woman in her late fifties. We had always gotten along well. She was a heavy smoker, and usually spoke in a raspy, deep voice. Trying to speak softly, she said, "Harmony, you haven't been here for the last few days. Have you been in touch with Aviva?"

"No."

"Then you wouldn't know. Aviva was fired on Thursday. You've been laid off."

"Why was she fired?"

"The board of directors feels that Aviva has not exercised adequate control over *Philosopher's Corner*. Because of what has happened, they also regard her as a security risk. Neither she nor you are allowed in this building." She added sadly, "I have your last pay check ready for you," and handed me the envelope. I believe she would not have invited me into the building had it not been raining.

I was so shocked by this development that, as soon as I left the station, I called Monty from a pay phone. I fully expected him to tell me that I was fired.

"Eloy, where have you been? We've been so worried about you."

"We?"

"Joe keeps calling me because he's anxious about you. He knows that the death of your instructor would be a terrible shock for you. I've been trying to get in touch with you for days."

"I stayed with Jiro. I'll be at the office next Saturday, and I'll explain everything. I really don't want to talk about it now. Please tell Joe not to worry. I'll be all right. I'll call him in a few days."

After I hung up I wondered whether I would ever again be all right.

*　　　*　　　*

I dialed Aviva from home. "Harmony, are you calling from work?" she asked.

"No, from home. I was laid off."

"We have a lot to talk about, Harmony. Will you have supper with me on Friday? Now that we don't work, you can come early. How about five?"

"Thanks, Aviva. See you on Friday. And Aviva, please call me Eloy, not Harmony. My real name is Eloy."

She was silent for a long while. "I'm not sure I understand, but it's all right," she said. "I'll see you on Friday, Eloy."

The next person I called was Ronnell. "Where have you been, Harmony?" he asked. "I called and called. I don't know your pager number. Are you OK?"

"I had to sort things out. I stayed with a friend in San Francisco. I'm all right now. I need to talk to you as soon as possible. And, Ronnell, please call me Eloy, not Harmony."

My sudden name change did not faze him at all. "Will do, Eloy. I'll come by this evening around eight."

For the last few days, I had been thinking about switching my major from philosophy to computer science, and my minor from German to Spanish. With Dr. Brotbaum dead, I had little motivation to continue studying philosophy. If I changed my major, there would be no reason for me to learn German. I had given up on the European trip.

Spanish was a different matter. I was like a baby abandoned at a church. I had no past. The Harmony in me had died with Eugene. As Eloy, I could trace my line back only as far as my mother, and there was nothing of her in me: neither my intellect nor my physical appearance. José Luis was an inner voice bidding me get in touch with my undeniable Hispanic roots. My facial features and the color of my skin reflected my heritage. To heed that voice, it was mandatory that my Spanish be perfect.

*   *   *

I made Ronnell a cup of tea. Then we spent the evening talking. It pleased me that he did not comment on my name change. He called me Eloy without once reverting to Harmony. We spoke a lot about Dr. Brotbaum. "What I liked best about him," Ronnell said, "was his love for teaching. Most instructors prefer graduate students to teach their classes while they write books or do research. Dr. Brotbaum wanted his students to enjoy philosophizing."

I told Ronnell that Dr. Brotbaum's murder was the catalyst in my decision to change majors. I summed up the case for getting out of philosophy by saying, "I don't see that philosophy contributes to human happiness. With all his genius, Wittgenstein was an extremely unhappy person who also made others miserable. Why, then, spend my life in this field?"

"Ideas," said Ronnell, "are the driving force behind all human endeavors. Some people like to play with them just for the sake of the game. It hones their intellects, but is not at all related to happiness. Philosophizing, in and of itself, won't make you into a more fulfilled person."

"What will do that?"

Without a moment's hesitation, Ronnell answered, "Being true to yourself."

*   *   *

Danny Fleetwood took over Dr. Brotbaum's class. He taught correctly and dully. A few times he tried to imitate Dr. Brotbaum, but did not quite manage to pull it off. Eugene's great gift as an instructor was his complete spontaneity when he toyed with ideas. To do that, an instructor needed phenomenal knowledge as well as tremendous mental agility. Danny did not possess these qualities.

Since I do not wish to return to this subject again, I may as well write here what happened to me at the end of the semester. Accepting Dr. Brotbaum's suggestion, I had started working on a paper discussing the philosopher's social responsibility. But I did not wish to share those ideas with Danny. To satisfy the requirements of the course, I wrote a ho-hum term paper. During my four years of college, I received nothing but A's. The exception was a B I earned in the late Dr. Brotbaum's philosophy course.

17

José Luis of the Desmadres

As the second semester of my sophomore year was coming to an end, I resolved to spend the summer in Mexico. In preparation, I read as much as I could about Mexico, both in English and in Spanish. Nobody had taught me how to read Spanish, but since it is a phonetic language, it was a pretty easy task to master.

My first inclination was to revisit Acapulco. I would have loved to swim in the Pacific Ocean once again. Monty dissuaded me from going there. According to him, both the Atlantic and Pacific coasts of Mexico were much too warm to visit in the summer. It was he who came up with the idea of a trip to the Silver Cities.

"For good climate and unpolluted Mexican attractions, visit the Silver Cities," Monty said. "The Spaniards looked for gold in Mexico but found only silver. The mining towns, before their decline in the nineteenth century, were the richest and most opulent urban centers in Mexico. I'm speaking of places like Querétaro, Guanajuato, San Miguel de Allende, Zacatecas, and…"

I interrupted Monty. "I once watched a *telenovela*. That's a Mexican soap opera. It was called *The Strange Return of Diana Salazar*. Diana lives in modern-day Mexico City but, simultaneously, relives a past incarnation. In her previous life, she is a beautiful young maiden living in

Zacatecas. There she is accused of being a witch, and is about to be burned at the stake. As I remember it, Zacatecas looks like an outdoor museum."

"I myself have never been to Zacatecas," Monty said, "but I've read that it's one of the most beautiful colonial towns in Mexico not yet on the tourists' path. I believe that you can fly there directly from San Francisco."

I had told Monty only that I wanted to take a trip to Mexico to practice my Spanish. As soon as he mentioned Zacatecas, I knew that city would be my summer destination. Like Eloy with José Luis, modern-day Diana coexists with another manifestation of herself in Zacatecas. Also, Zacatecas would not be full of foreign tourists. In Acapulco I wound up sharing my bed with a Swiss tourist. This time, I wanted to be just with my own kind—with my father's people.

Which name would I assign to myself in Zacatecas: Eloy or José Luis? In as much as I could control these things, I would prefer being Eloy. It would certainly save a lot of trouble not to have the bother of a fictitious identity. The disadvantage would be that as the Chicano Eloy, I would be considered a gringo expatriate rather than an authentic Mexican.

There was a big difference between a Chicano, who could legally earn a living in the United States, and an ordinary Mexican native. My hustling caper in Acapulco had been an ordeal. But it was the real thing for Angel. Unlike me, he would not have been able to refuse to be penetrated without a condom by the abominable Ricardo. I wanted, just for the summer, to rub elbows with ordinary Mexicans—to be one of them.

There was something else about not being Eloy. He excelled in calculus, understood some of Wittgenstein's philosophy, and had mastered hundreds of German verb conjugations, but he was a loner. In contrast, José Luis had an extroverted personality and would make friends easily in Zacatecas.

I knew that it was not good for my mental health to indulge in my multiple-personality games. Planning whose identity I would take in Mexico could not serve any useful purpose. However, I had a burning desire to deconstruct my José Luis personality and to observe all its facets. Once I understood the complexity of this personality, maybe I would be able to let go of it.

If it could be done, it would make sense to fuse José Luis and Eloy much of the time, rather than separate them completely. Most importantly, I did not wish to repeat my Acapulco fiasco by confusing people, like hotel desk clerks, about my true identity. Also, Monty wanted to keep in touch with me while I was in Mexico in case he came up with an assignment there. I could not tell him to ask for José Luis Herrera when he called me.

It occurred to me that I could tell people in Mexico that I went by two names: Eloy and José Luis. I suspected that José Luis would continue with his *desmadres*—wild and crazy stuff—just as he had done in Acapulco. But he needed to clean up his act and become less scruffy, in order not to be an embarrassment to Eloy.

Mexicans are fast to judge people by the way they dress. I could pose as a struggling young man who barely had the money to dress decently. With this in mind, I went shopping at a thrift store. There, I bought my second-hand Mexican wardrobe: four pairs of jeans, six shirts, and a hooded sweatshirt, since nighttime in Zacatecas could be cool. For my footwear I would take pairs of old tennis shoes. These outfits would make Eloy and José Luis look respectable and, at the same time, indicate their strained economic circumstances. Naturally, I would also pack the wooden cross with the bronze Christ. When I wore it, I would become José Luis of the *desmadres*.

It dawned on me one day that the real José Luis, the one who hustled in Acapulco's *zócalo*, could make only brief appearances without giving the show away. One day, for practice, I wrote my grocery list in Spanish. I discovered that I did not know the word for shoelaces. Once I gave the subject some thought, it became obvious that there were scores of common Spanish words that I did not have at my disposal. These were terms that had not come up in conversations or in *telenovelas*.

I was unsure whether I could exercise enough control over José Luis to stop him from holding the stage indefinitely once he was out of the bottle. In his lengthy performance in Acapulco, José Luis may have fooled Angel. More likely, Angel did not worry about mundane matters like a grown-up who did not know simple words in his native tongue. Most people would think it odd.

Before leaving Berkeley, I made a two-night reservation in a Zacatecas hotel for Eloy H. Wise. That would give me time to find a room in a private home for the two months I intended to stay there.

* * *

Incredibly, I located the room even before I got a chance to look at the city. When I checked into the hotel, the desk clerk, a young woman by the name of Isabel, took a liking to me. We chatted for a while, and I told her that I needed to find a room for the summer. She made a phone call to a señora Serrano. Before she hung up she said, "Yes, I understand. I'll tell him to take a taxi and be there as soon as possible. His name is Eloy Wise."

"You're lucky," Isabel told me. "Señora Serrano has a vacancy until the last week of August. It has already been seen by two other persons. You could walk—Zacatecas is a small town—but you must be there immediately to put a deposit on the room. I'll order you a taxi. The room is across the square from the Cathedral. It has the prettiest view in town. Do you have Mexican currency?"

I exchanged fifty dollars at the desk. Isabel called a taxi for me. While riding in it, I only had a brief glimpse of Zacatecas. It was just as magnificent as in the *telenovela*. The taxi stopped in front of an old, but recently painted, three-story building. The door of an apartment on the second floor was opened by a tallish, lanky woman who must have been in her late forties. Her excessive makeup worked against her; it accentuated her wrinkles. Señora Serrano extended her hand, and said, "You must be *joven* Eloy. It gives me great pleasure to make your acquaintance."

"The pleasure is mine," I said as we shook hands. She ushered me into a somewhat musty living room adorned with religious paintings. As soon as we sat down, I said, "My legal name is Eloy Wise, Señora Serrano. It is the name my mother gave me. Here, in my late father's *tierra*, I prefer to be known by the Spanish name he wanted me to have, which is José Luis. You see, my mother is American and, I'm afraid, not very friendly toward Mexicans."

"Has your father passed on?"

"Yes, señora."

"Poor *joven*," she said, putting her hand gently on my forearm. "It's proper for you to use your Spanish name when you're among your own people in your father's *tierra*. I myself am of Spanish, not Mexican, origin. My parents came here at the end of the Civil War in Spain."

I had already noticed that señora Serrano pronounced her *c*'s and *z*'s the way Spaniards do, similar to the English *th*. For a briefest of moments, I remembered with sadness that Eugene attempted to speak Spanish the same way. While, señora Serrano talked, she eyed me flirtatiously. Her hand kept caressing my forearm ever so slightly. "Why do you wish to spend your summer here?" she asked.

"I want to live for a while in my late father's *tierra*, among his people. I wish to learn more about the culture of my ancestors. Unfortunately, I don't know where in Mexico my father was raised. I chose Zacatecas because I had seen the Diana Salazar *telenovela*."

For the next twenty minutes we talked about the *telenovela*. Finally the landlady said, "Let me show you the room before the two señoritas who had already looked at it earlier claim it."

Señora Serrano led me up one flight of stairs. The small room she showed me, one of the four she rented out, was furnished plainly. The walls were painted a light green. In addition to a large bed, there was an assortment of colorful plastic chairs and a rickety bridge table. The view from the window was incredible. As in a picture postcard, I could see part of the cathedral in the center, framed by the mountains in the distance. The intricate facade of the cathedral appeared pink in the afternoon sun.

The landlady urged me to rent the room. "It has been my experience, *joven* José Luis, that gentlemen make better tenants than ladies. It is a strange fact that men are tidier than women. And also more amusing."

We agreed on a weekly rent that amounted to just over twenty dollars and included breakfast. I declined to take my dinners with the señora's other tenants. I wanted to be free to come and go.

Then my new landlady made a little speech. "Things in this town, *joven* José Luis, aren't what they used to be. When I first came here, some twenty-five years ago, I never locked the doors, nor was I afraid to walk about the streets. Now if you forget to lock up, your place will be cleaned out. Low-class people will even try to rob you in the main street! Therefore, you must always be very careful." She positioned her index finger where the lower right-eye lid touches the cheekbone, which, for Spanish speakers, emphasizes the need for caution. "I know that in your heart you are a Mexican, not a gringo, but still, you may be mistaken for one. People often assume that all gringos are rich and will try to take advantage of you.

"Your Spanish is so good that you can tell everyone that you're a native of this country. That may help to protect you. Here, in my house, you have nothing worry about. I rent my rooms only to high-quality people. Please remember that if you need advice or help, I'm always available to you, *joven* José Luis."

We stood up. She was quite a bit taller than me. It was easy for her to put her hand on my head in a gesture that could have been interpreted as a benediction. To me it felt more like a subtle sexual overture.

I moved to señora Serrano's home the next day.

*　　　　*　　　　*

Zacatecas is an overwhelming town. It really is an outdoor museum of the Spanish colonial period. My choice of a room, though, turned out to be a mixed blessing. The endless tolling of the cathedral bells was difficult to get used to. But I enjoyed the incredible view from my window. Sometimes, I would just stand there and stare at the cathedral and the hills behind it.

Apparently, señora Serrano liked to surround herself with young men. The day I moved in, my landlady invited me to dine with her and her three male tenants. The most likable one, and the one who took most interest in me, was Dr. Alfredo Chang, the son of a Chinese immigrant father and a Mexican mother.

Dr. Chang had just graduated from medical school and was fulfilling his obligatory year of social service. He worked at a small clinic in a pueblo about a forty-five-minute drive from Zacatecas. By GIF standards, he would be considered an alpha twinkie. Though he was twenty-five years old, he looked like a teenager. He had a hauntingly melancholy face, combining perfectly the Chinese and American-Indian features he had inherited from his parents. He had a somewhat androgynous appearance but, fortunately, spoke in a deep baritone. Were it not for his voice, it would be hard to imagine him as an authority figure to his patients.

The other two tenants, both young men, were employees of a local bank. I occupied the room of the fourth tenant, a priest on a sabbatical, who had gone to the Holy Land for the summer. Except for the José Luis tall tale, I gave my fellow tenants a truthful account of myself. I am sure that they must have deduced that my father had been a gentle Mexican without proper documentation, who got mixed up with a heartless gringa vixen. That woman, my mother, alienated his son from him and tried to make him into a gringo like herself.

The two bank employees were impressed with my computer background. We talked a lot about this subject. Their bank was in the process of switching from mainframes to PCs and utter chaos ensued. After dinner, Alfredo invited himself to my room. He brought with him an unopened bottle of tequila and two ordinary glasses. In my José Luis role, I did not object to Alfredo's suggestion that we get drunk to celebrate my moving to señora Serrano's home.

Actually, Alfredo never mentioned getting drunk. To indicate his intention, Mexicans make a particular motion with their right hand. They fold the three middle fingers while extending the thumb and the pinkie, shaking the hand close to the mouth as they say *"demasiado."* Unlike Eloy, José Luis wanted to be one of the gang. Tonight he was going to have a few drinks too many—*demasiado*—with his new friend, Dr. Alfredo Chang.

After setting the bottle and glasses on the table, Alfredo went back to his room and returned with a small saucer filled with salt and a few slices of lemon. He poured tequila almost to the top the glasses. Then he folded the index finger of his left hand into the thumb, creating a fleshy area. He sprinkled a dash of salt on it and licked it as he raised his glass. I followed his example and licked some salt myself. We stood up, touched glasses and said, "Salúd!" Alfredo drank his tequila in one gulp, and then bit into the lemon peel. I drank half the tequila in my glass. It gave me an colossal jolt. For a moment I thought my head would explode. Then, momentarily, I was unable to breathe. Finally, when I set the glass down on the table, I felt that I was going to pass out. Through all of this, I managed to follow Alfredo's example and also bit into the lemon. Then I plopped into the chair.

However José Luis differed from Eloy, neither of them could handle alcohol. I have absolutely no recollection what Alfredo was talking about for the next five minutes. As soon as I came to my senses, I tried to find a way to dispose of the drink without offending Alfredo. I came up with a simple solution. My head was still spinning, but with some difficulty I stood up. Holding the glass in my right hand, I walked about the room carrying on a conversation with Alfredo. He sat in the chair facing the window. The sink was in a little alcove in back of him. Surreptitiously, while pacing, I poured the tequila into the sink. Alfredo refilled my glass as soon as he saw that it was empty. I kept repeating the maneuver until we ran out of tequila. Alfredo never caught on. But then, why would he? Why would a normal person pour good tequila down the drain?

My hidden agenda, getting rid of the tequila shots, kept me pretty busy. After a while, I noticed that Alfredo, too, had a hidden agenda. Fairly rapidly, he moved the topic of the conversation from our respective fields of study to sexual matters.

He introduced the subject by gossiping about the young priest in whose room I lodged. "In the morning, he never uses the bathroom on this floor. He says that señora Serrano allows him to use the facilities on her floor so he can get ready for mass. However rushed he is to attend mass—he's on a sabbatical so he doesn't celebrate mass here—he always takes his breakfast with us. We're convinced that he spends the nights with our landlady. Well, everybody needs sex, the priest, our landlady, and me. Let me tell you about my *novia*."

Alfredo's fiancée, Antonia, a plain Chinese girl, lived in Mexico City, studying dental hygiene. He saw her only once a month, and even on these rare occasions she would not satisfy him fully. God willing, they would get married as soon as he finished his social service. She wanted to stay a virgin until then. "As I've told you, Antonia isn't all that pretty. But she's a good person and her family is well-off." Politely, he stopped his monologue to inquire whether there was a young lady in my life.

"I also have my problems," I said, as I walked about the room carrying the tequila glass. "As you know, Alfredo, women control men by not letting them have what they want and need most. They always manipulate the time so intercourse happens when they want it. In the end, it usually happens at an awkward time for the men." That profound observation I had heard from Monty; I knew nothing about such matters.

Maybe gringo Eloy could have told Alfredo that he was a gay and gotten away with it. From my reading, I knew that the Mexican José Luis had the privilege of performing homosexual acts only as a macho heterosexual who did *travesuras* under the influence of alcohol. "My girlfriend lives in Japan Town in San Francisco and my university is in Berkeley. When I manage to come to the city, she often isn't in the mood, or has her period, or some other excuse."

"Is your girlfriend an Asian?"

"Yes, she is Japanese. Her name is Michiko. She's studying art and she's very pretty." Michiko was the name of Jiro's eldest daughter.

"So you like Asian women, do you?"

Something in his voice alerted me. I sensed that with one or two additional refills, he would want to know whether I also liked Asian men. I had a gut feeling that whatever would develop between Alfredo and me could only take place between two *normales*, the term Mexican gays use for straights. Ordinarily, such "normal" males have sex with females. However, when circumstances force them to abstain from sex with their womenfolk, or while drunk, who would fault them if they did *travesuras* with other men?

I was quite attracted to Alfredo. José Luis's taste in men was quite different from Eloy's. If Alfredo propositioned me, I would welcome it. He had one more drink. By now we had all but finished the bottle. In spite of all his drinking, he appeared to me to be reasonably sober. But he definitely tried to covey the impression that he was tipsy. He took something out of his pocket and put it on the table.

"Now I'm really drunk," he said. "Look," he added, summoning me from the other end of the room. "Do you know what this is?"

I examined the object. "A condom?"

"Yes, a condom. You know about SIDA, don't you?"

"A little bit, yes. It's a very bad disease."

"Well, I'm a doctor. I know how to protect myself. To protect both of us."

"And how will you do that?"

"Well, I'll put the condom on my *verga*. Then, when you give me a *mamadita*, I'll be protected." He thought for a moment and added, "And you will be protected from my ejaculation."

Of course, Alfredo wanted only a little blow job. Had he asked for a full *mamada*, a macho man like me would have had to refuse. But, between friends, a little blow job was not a big deal.

"Will you give me a *mamadita* as well?" I asked.

Alfredo considered my question gravely. "You know, I'm going to get married pretty soon. What you want is difficult in my circumstances."

"I understand that perfectly. But, if I give you a *mamadita* and you don't reciprocate, I'll feel awkward. It'll make me feel like a *maricón*."

"But, hombre, you certainly aren't a *maricón*." Alfredo squeezed my shoulder to emphasize that a little blow job between friends wouldn't make me into a queer. "Tell you what. You do it first, then me."

I could guess what would happen once Alfredo got his rocks off. He would pretend to be drunk and would want to sleep it off. "Let's toss for it," I said.

We did, and I won.

*   *   *

I spent the next day sightseeing. At night, I ate alone in a restaurant. Then I walked about town, but there was little to see or do. Zacatecas folded up at night. I felt pretty lonely. Unfortunately, Alfredo was on night duty at his clinic; he would not return until the evening of the following day. I thought it would make more sense for me to take my dinners at my landlady's with her other tenants. I went back home early to negotiate a new arrangement with her. Señora Serrano was delighted with my request to take my dinners at her place. She raised my weekly rent by about ten dollars.

When I came in, Omar, one of the bank employees, greeted me warmly. "José Luis, I'm glad I can speak to you now. I told our *jefe* about you and he would like you to come in tomorrow morning, to see whether you can fix our computer problems. If it works out, the boss will offer you a job for a few weeks."

"But I'm in Mexico as a tourist. How could I work here?"

"Don't worry. Such things can always be arranged."

I agreed to go along with them the following day.

It took me less than an hour to solve the immediate problem. After that, I spent the morning simplifying the system. I made a big impression on the assistant bank manager, señor Cabrillo. By the end of the day, he suggested that I tutor his employees. This might eliminate their long phone calls consulting computer experts in Mexico City.

"It'll be too complicated for us to put you on our payroll," he told me. "Legally, you aren't even supposed to work here. What we can do is pay your rent. I understand that you are staying at the same boarding home as our employees."

"Yes."

"Well, if you're agreeable, we'll pay your rent and give you a lunch voucher for the days you work at the bank. I'll call your landlady and ask her to refund the money you've already paid her. It isn't a spectacular wage. But you'll work only four hours daily."

I accepted his offer enthusiastically. It was not just the money. I would not have known what to do with myself all day long without the job. Also, going to work every morning helped me feel like a resident of Zacatecas rather than a tourist.

I had to fill out various forms, giving my real name. Still, everybody at the bank kept calling me José Luis. I cannot explain why, but José Luis felt authentic, as if it had been my real name. I could have called myself Juan or Jaime, but it would not have felt the same.

I had always known that I was a handsome man, at least for those who liked my type. But as José Luis, I also exuded a sexual magnetism. On the streets, young women flirted with me constantly. If I had been open to it, señora Serrano would have seduced me in no time. As José Luis, the focus of my sexual interests had shifted from older men to guys my own age. I was smitten with Dr. Alfredo Chang!

When he had lost the toss for the *mamadita*, Alfredo seemed crestfallen. He immediately excused himself to go back to his room to get another condom. He had not planned on exchanging blow jobs. When he returned to my room, he was surprised to see me lying on the bed in my underwear. "Like that?" he asked.

"Like what?"

"Why aren't you sitting up?"

"Because the chair isn't comfortable." And because, I added silently to myself, we're having sex rather than performing a medical procedure.

Before he did anything, he looked at me earnestly with his melancholy, soulful eyes. "You understand that I'm going to do this *de mala gana* just because I'm a man of my word, and we've made an agreement."

"Of course," I said, as I took off my underwear.

Willingly or not, after a few tentative, mechanical sucks, Alfredo lay on the bed and went about his job with great dedication. I climaxed pretty fast and removed the condom. I would have liked to hold and kiss him. But I knew that this would be the wrong moment. I needed to bide my time. I immediately put a condom on his *verga*, ready to reverse roles. While doing so, I admired his beautiful dick. It was long and thin and, though it was uncircumcised, the foreskin was barely noticeable. Alfredo climaxed in a blink of an eye. I wished we would lie together just holding each other. But, his face as melancholy as ever, he put on his clothes, shook my hand formally, and went to his room.

Three nights later he invited himself to my room again, bringing with him a bottle of tequila and two glasses. He went back to bring the salt and lemon peels, as well as a brown paper bag which he set on the table.

"Alfredo," I said, "I have to go to work tomorrow morning. I can have only a small sip of tequila."

He appeared to be happy with my reluctance to get drunk. "I, too, shouldn't have too much alcohol. It gives me a headache," he said. He poured us a drink, and gulped his down immediately. It took me a moment to reach the alcove and dispose of mine discreetly.

"I feel tired," Alfredo said abruptly. "It was a busy day. I think the one shot of tequila got me drunk." He hesitated for a moment, then asked, "May I lie on your bed for a while? It's the only comfortable piece of furniture in this room."

"Of course."

He took off his shoes and lay on the bed for a few minutes. "It's a chilly evening," he said. "May I get under your blanket?"

"Sure."

He took off his clothes and lay under the blanket, stark naked.

"I also feel chilly. May I join you?"

"It's your bed!"

I took off my clothes. Just as I was ready to crawl under the blanket and join him, Alfredo said, "Please bring the paper bag with you."

For a while we lay next to each other, barely touching. Then, quite suddenly, Alfredo turned sideways, embraced me forcefully, kissed my face, disengaged himself, and lay still next to me.

Without talking, we continued lying next to each other. I had taken the brown paper bag with me and put it on the floor. Now I pickled it up. Inside was one condom and a tube of K.Y. lubricant. I took the stuff out of the bag, held it up for Alfredo to see, and asked, "Who is supposed to screw whom?"

Alfredo blushed at my question. "If you allow me, I would like to penetrate you. You know that I'm not like this, but with you it's different. I want to be inside you."

Alfredo's lines would not have gone over well in California. He appeared very much "like this." He was one of us. But Mexico was not California, and our standards should not be applied to another culture. Alfredo may have been bisexual or even homosexual, yet when the time came, he would marry the wife his parents had chosen for him and have children by her. Nonetheless, if, after his marriage, I would happen to visit Mexico City, and he could squeeze me into his schedule, he would want to get inside me again.

I had been with Jiro every weekend before my trip to Zacatecas, and he screwed me on a regular basis. Tutored by Jiro, I had learned to relax my sphincter. I was certain that I would have no problem with Alfredo. Actually, I was looking forward to it.

"I'll allow you to penetrate me," I said to Alfredo. "But before you do it, I want you to show me that you desire me, not just my ass."

"How?"

I rolled on top of him and gave him a deep kiss. "Like this, Alfredo!" I said. He responded lovingly when our tongues touched inside his mouth.

"José Luis, this is so difficult for me. What happens if this thing grows on me? What happens if I fall in love with you?"

"You cross the border on a dark night and come to the California to live with me forever. Alfredo, this isn't your first time with a man. Am I right?"

He blushed, thought for a moment, and then said, "No. But it has never been like this. On the other occasions, I was drunk, and I didn't care for the person I was with. I love you, José Luis."

—

"Look, Alfredo, let's just enjoy this moment. We don't need to justify what we're doing."

I gave myself wholeheartedly to Alfredo on that occasion. As he climaxed inside me, the church bells tolled the hour. It felt good to alleviate his melancholy a bit. Sex was different with him than with the others. I felt something that Eloy could not have experienced: the bonding, body and soul, of two men in their prime.

Around ten at night, Alfredo put on his clothes and returned to his room. After that night, he always brought an alarm clock with him so that he could spend the night with me, and be back in his room before our fellow tenants got up. "I'm only a doctor, not a priest," he said. "I have my reputation to worry about!"

18

A Bar Brawl in Querétaro

On my second Sunday in Zacatecas, Zacatecas (meaning the city of Zacatecas in the state of Zacatecas), señora Serrano's tenants invited me to attend mass with them. They took it for granted that I was Roman Catholic. Even though I was quite ignorant about Catholic services, I had enough *telenovelas* under my belt not to embarrass myself at church. Actually, as José Luis, I felt at home there.

I fell into a groove in Zacatecas. Five days a week I worked until two-thirty in the afternoon. When I got off, I explored the city. I did a lot of touristy stuff. I took the spectacular cable car sky ride, went to the municipal market, and walked through the picturesque squares and parks. On weekends, I went by bus to outlying places. Once I visited the clinic where Dr. Alfredo Chang worked. That was a pretty depressing experience, because of the poverty of his patients and the rundown appearance of the pueblo. I spent the evenings with my landlady and her tenants. We dined at eight thirty. After dinner, except when he was on duty at the clinic, Alfredo spent the night in my room.

Soon I found out that, for a price, any type of document was available in Mexico. Had I wanted to assume the persona of José Luis Herrera W., I could have obtained an *acta de nacimiento* stating that I was born in Mexico, and a *cartilla*, to prove that I had discharged my military obligations. With these documents, I would be able to find a computer-related job and live comfortably in Mexico.

But that would not have solved the mystery that came with the name José Luis. There was more to it than just fascination with the *tierra* of my forebears. Like the reincarnated Diana Salazar, I was looking for some undefined link to an unspecified event in my past.

Until now, José Luis had been pretty tame. He and Eloy were almost identical in all aspects. The only real difference was José Luis's romantic involvement with young Alfredo. The fully Mexican José Luis had not yet had his day in the sun. Even without seeking links to the past, like any other tourist, I wanted to travel around the country. Following Monty's suggestion, I decided to explore the Silver Cities lying south of Zacatecas: San Luis Potosí, Guanajuato, and Querétaro. I would start out on a Friday morning, and be back at work on Wednesday of the next week.

I proposed to my boss that for two weeks I would work full days and, as compensatory time, be given three days off. Señor Cabrillo was only too happy to oblige. I had already put in many more hours than I had been paid for.

When making my plans, I came to the conclusion that I probably would not have enough time to visit all three cities. I decided to go directly to Querétaro. It is the cradle of Mexico's independence, and also the place where the hapless Austrian Maximilian—made Emperor of Mexico by Napoleon III—was executed. After visiting Querétaro, if time permitted, I would take in additional Silver Cities.

I left Zacatecas by bus early in the morning on a Friday and arrived in Querétaro in the late afternoon. Around my neck I wore José Luis's cross, symbolizing my complete separation from Eloy. As José Luis, I sought out a cheap hotel catering to ordinary Mexican travelers.

I checked into a small, rundown hotel right by the bus depot. My accommodations did not matter since I did not plan on spending much time at the hotel. My room had what I needed: a comfortable double bed and a private bathroom. I took a shower, put on a clean shirt, and left the hotel. I managed to explore the Plaza de la Independencia before it turned dark. Nearby, I found a small restaurant and had supper there. When I finished my meal and walked out, I spotted a cantina across the street.

The way I understood it, the Mexican cantina is an ordinary bar that caters to the masses. More refined folk frequent real bars. I was perversely tempted to go into a cantina and rub shoulders with the common people. I say perversely because I had already proved to myself as José Luis that I could not stomach alcohol. And I was certain that I would make a spectacle of myself if I ordered a soft drink at the cantina.

But spotting that particular cantina in Querétaro gave me an inspiration. Aviva had served me cognac at her home in Berkeley and I had tolerated it well. I would order a cognac at the cantina, and, most likely, it would agree with me.

There was one problem with my plan. José Luis was a native Mexican, who could not make silly mistakes in his native tongue. I had never heard the noun "cognac" spoken in Spanish. I worried that I would mispronounce it. The English noun "champagne," for instance, is pronounced completely differently in Spanish. But I was willing to take a chance. Boldly, I entered the cantina.

I was so intent on getting my order out of the way that I barely noticed my surroundings or the people at the bar. As soon as I caught the bartender's eye, I ordered un coñac.

The bartender understood my order but was amused by my request. His broad smile displayed a mouthful of rotten teeth. "This here place, *joven*, isn't for people of your high-class social circles. We don't stock coñac because nobody here would be able to afford it! Does the señor wish to order some other drink?"

Damn, I thought. Now what? Then I remembered that cognac was just a fancy French brandy. "Would you have brandy?" I asked.

"Sí, señor, of course, immediately!" the bartender said, with mock deference.

I hesitated before sipping the drink he set in front of me. Would I react differently to it than to the cognac? But once I tasted it, I tolerated it as well as I had the cognac. Actually, I liked the taste of it.

Now I looked around me. The cantina was not a fancy place. It was decorated gaudily, full of tobacco smoke, and unpleasantly noisy. The jukebox was playing mariachi music, and a boom box by the bar blared a rock number. While there were few people at or near the counter, there were more playing pool at the back of the cantina. I sensed a movement to my left and, out of nowhere, a tall young "lady" materialized next to me.

Drag had never interested me much. I knew that most drag queens claimed that they looked like real women. The fellow standing next to my stool certainly did not look like a young woman. But, given his physical limitations, he was doing a damn good job of it.

"She" was well over six feet tall and quite broad-shouldered. Fortunately, she was slender. It would have been better had she not worn high heels, needlessly exaggerating her height. Standing next to my bar stool, she towered over me. Her pretty facial features were ruined to a large extent because, like my Zacatecas landlady, her makeup was grossly overdone. Her wig was a simple affair: just very long black hair running below her shoulders. On second thought, it may have been her natural hair. I know nothing about women's clothes, but to me, her turquoise dress seemed elegant. Her long neck was adorned with a heavy necklace laden with semiprecious stones. She addressed me in a seductive falsetto. "Hello, handsome. You're new here, aren't you?" Her right hand caressed my left thigh ever so lightly.

"Yes, this is my first time here. I am from…Zacatecas, Zacatecas."

"I am Katya. What's your name, *mi amor*?"

"My name is José Luis, querida." If she wanted to call me "my love," I, too, could be intimate.

"Treat me to a drink, love," she said while rubbing her upper leg against mine. I ordered a tequila for her. She drank it in one gulp. Katya kept rubbing her leg against mine and her hand drifted to my crotch. In my nervousness, I finished my brandy much too fast. Seeing my glass empty, the bartender asked, "Another brandy for the caballero?"

I ordered a refill. The brandy acted like a potent diuretic. I felt I had to empty my bladder immediately or I would pee in my in pants. The issue became even more urgent because Katya was about to unzip my fly. I mumbled an excuse and went to the restroom.

It was difficult for me to pee. I was unsteady on my feet, my head felt heavy, and I had a hard-on. It took me a while to do my business. Returning to the bar, I saw the back of a big man, wearing a sombrero, with one arm draped around Katya's shoulder. He was speaking to her with his mouth almost touching her ear. As I approached them I could hear Katya laughing at something the man had said. Obviously, he was amusing rather than annoying her. When I reached the bar, I noticed that the man had taken my seat. My second shot of brandy was on the counter, indicating clearly that this particular place was occupied.

As a schoolboy I had been involved in precious few fights. I had been a strange child, good-looking and bright, but shy and withdrawn. The other kids pretty much left me alone. I suppose I could have held my own because I was a strong boy, but I had no need to prove the point. Now, in Querétaro, of all places, I was about to be challenged to a fight.

Eloy would have beaten a hasty retreat. Katya would have mattered none to him, and the brandy even less. José Luis was a different story. His machismo had been challenged, and blows would have to be exchanged to prove to his woman how manly he was. Standing at the bar, I got a clear picture of my rival. He was a heavyset man in his late thirties or early forties. He seemed to be pretty drunk.

I sat next to Katya. She was flanked on the left by my rival and on the right by myself. I reached across her and retrieved my brandy, snarling a *con permiso* that was meant to be menacing rather then polite.

The man locked eyes with me for a long while, and then said, "*Hijo de puta*, if you want your fucking drink, all you need to do is to ask for it. You don't grab for it in front of a lady."

Now that my mother's honor had been called into question, José Luis had only one option: kill the bastard. I stepped back from the bar so Katya would not be in the way. She winked at me, conveying the impression that she was pleased that I took up the challenge. My rival also stepped back. He was much taller and heavier than me, but tottering from the alcohol. His beady eyes were bloodshot, his face red. Clumsily he swung at my jaw. I sidestepped and he missed. Apparently, he had taken it for granted that his fist would make contact with my face. When it failed to do so, he lost his balance. As he fell, he pulled Katya off her bar stool and landed on top of her.

Stupefied, I watched the spectacle I had created. I saw the cantina patrons rushing to form a circle, waiting for the fight to begin. The bartender said something I did not catch. Then somebody grabbed my forearm so strongly that I winced. In heavily accented English he said, "You must leave right now. It's very dangerous for you." Then, emphatically, he added the imperative, *"Vámnos!"* Clinging to my forearm, he dragged me out. The moment he spoke to me in English, I switched from José Luis to

Eloy. Once outside the cantina, I felt very frightened. My hard-on deflated like air rushing out of a punctured balloon.

We could hear a big commotion inside the bar. Somebody was shouting that he would get the *hijo de puta* and his *maricón* friend and kill them both. My new friend said in English, "We've got to run!" He sprinted away, and I followed. We ran hard for a few minutes. Eventually we slowed down because we were both winded. "There's a hotel here with a nice bar. Let's have a drink," the stranger said in Spanish, pointing across the street.

Now I saw the speaker clearly. He was a short guy, a little pudgy, about ten years my senior. He wore a rather elegant sport coat but no tie. His designer glasses suggested that he was well-off. As we went inside the hotel he said, "Forgive me for not having introduced myself. My name is Ernesto Flores."

"I'm pleased to meet you, Ernesto. My name is Eloy Wise." It was as if José Luis had vanished into thin air. We entered an intimate, elegant bar and sat at a table. "What will you drink?" asked Ernesto.

"Just a bottle of mineral water," I answered. After Ernesto ordered whisky for himself and Vichy water for me I asked, in Spanish, "Why did you speak to me in English?"

"I didn't want the others to understand my warning."

"But how did you know that I spoke English?"

Ernesto considered my question for a moment. "I don't know. It's noticeable that you aren't a Mexican. Maybe you are the son of Mexican parents who emigrated to the United States. Certainly, your Spanish, which you speak as we do, is excellent."

"But how did you know that I was American?"

"I have no idea. I just knew."

"Are you a detective?"

"Close. I'm a lawyer. A prosecutor, as a matter of fact. I interrogate witnesses. That is how I knew, *joven* Eloy, that you were being set up."

"Set up? How?"

"The drunk who took a swing at you was supposed to hurt you, not himself. Then, once you were on the ground, he would take your watch and wallet, rough you up some, and he and his *travesti* accomplice would split. At least that is what I suspect. I'm from Mexico City, not from Querétaro."

"But wasn't the drunk a local? What would happen if I went to the police?"

"This is Mexico. If you went to the police and told them that you were carrying on with a *travesti* and were mugged by her boyfriend, they would tell you that it served you right for being a fool. Everybody knows that *travestis* are bad news.

"If you persisted in making a fuss, and seeing that you're a foreigner, they'd accompany you to the cantina, only to be told that nobody had ever seen or heard anything. And who is this gringo who is saying bad things about their cantina? They'd acknowledge that you had been there, but left drunk out of your mind. Who knows what happened to you on the street after you had left?

"Most likely, the man who tried to punch you gives the bartender a cut every time he robs someone at the cantina. Naturally, he and his *travesti* pick only on out-of-town strangers."

"What about you yourself. Aren't you a stranger here?"

"Yes, of course. But the *sinvergüenzas* know how to pick their victims."

I must have looked puzzled. "Well, you know," Ernesto said. "A horse shies when he spots a snake. How does the horse know that snakes are dangerous for him? It's in his blood, or genes, or what have you. Like animals, the shameless ones know instinctively all they need to know." Then, as if the cantina incident needed no further elaboration, he changed the subject: "Where in the United States do you live?"

"Berkeley, California. I work in San Francisco. Do you know that city?"

"Very well. I used to take my vacations there. In the evenings, first I would go to the opera or the theater, and then to one of your many fabulous bathhouses. Now, because of SIDA, the baths are too dangerous. I understand that some of them have been closed. How sad!"

He paused for a moment and then, looking straight at me, asked, "Are you an *internacional* or a *mayate*?"

I looked at him uncomprehendingly. I did not know what *mayate* meant. Not until I returned to home did I find out that it was the Spanish word for dung beetle.

"So there're words in our language that you are unfamiliar with," he said with a smile. "An *internacional* is a gay," he spoke this word in English, "who's both active and passive."

"Why 'international?'" I asked.

"Because the internationals recognize no borders; they respect no limits. You have to understand that in traditional Latino culture, homosexual roles are defined precisely. At the fabulous baths of your city, I met men who enjoyed playing both the active and the passive roles with the same partner. As a rule, that doesn't happen here. Or, more correctly, it didn't use to happen. Things have been changing in Mexico."

I thought of Alfredo. "Doesn't this rule become more flexible under the influence of alcohol?"

"Everything becomes more flexible when one is drunk. That is, after all, why one gets drunk in the first place. But I'm speaking about sober people."

"And what about the *mayate*?"

"It isn't a complimentary term. But many Mexican men like to penetrate other men. If they limit themselves to that activity they get the reputation of being, shall we say, 'different,' rather than *maricones*. Often they do it for money, which makes it even more permissible."

"Well," I said, "I'm an international."

"Good," Ernesto answered. "So am I."

*　　　*　　　*

Ernesto, who was on business in Querétaro, stayed with a cousin. I proposed that we go to my hotel. Now I was sorry that I had checked into such a cheap place. It certainly had not been for lack of money. José Luis wanted it that way. But for what we were planning to do, my hotel would be adequate.

When I asked for my key, the reception clerk, who had not registered me, asked my name. Just as at the El Faro in Acapulco, my companion for the evening knew me by one name and the desk clerk by another. I was terribly embarrassed. "José Luis Herrera," I whispered.

"Mande usted?"

I had to speak up for the clerk hear me. He checked the registration form and said, "Señor Herrera, your room is registered to one person. If you wish to bring in a visitor, you must pay a fifty percent surcharge."

Ernesto said, "I'll take care of it."

When we entered the room he said, "In a hotel of this category you can do anything you want to as long as you pay the surcharge. Oh, by the way, I thought your name was Eloy?"

"If you don't mind, let's talk about it later."

"All right," he answered.

*　　　　*　　　　*

As José Luis, I was attracted sexually to handsome Mexicans within my own age range. For José Luis, Ernesto was a bit too old and pudgy. But once I reverted to being Eloy, Ernesto held no sexual appeal whatsoever for me; he was much too young. Nevertheless, I did not want to disappoint Ernesto, who had saved me from serious bodily harm. We behaved like true *internacionales*, each of us taking turns being the active and passive partner. Our sex was mechanical, lacking in passion. I sensed that Ernesto was more focused on demonstrating that he could play both roles than on having a good time. It was over in less than thirty minutes. The fact that José Luis had neglected to pack condoms and lube was mind-boggling. Fortunately, Ernesto was properly prepared for the occasion, carrying with him a selection of these items.

Though our sex was humdrum and mechanical, I felt comfortable with Ernesto. Because he had saved me from harm, I had *confianza* in him. In Mexico, it is the degree of trust between people that defines their friendship. And neither Ernesto nor I were playing mind games. That was not the case with Alfredo, however much we liked each other. Alfredo had assigned to himself the role of the normal and had me play the *maricón*.

As a medical doctor, Alfredo was more qualified than Ernesto to deal with my multiple personality disorder, assuming that was what afflicted me. But I would never have discussed that with him. He was too conservative, and we were too involved with each other.

Now I really needed to talk about my problem with Ernesto. Not only because I had promised him that I would tell him about my two sets of names, but also because he was handy. That evening in Querétaro, I finally realized that I had reached an impasse. Every time I tried being the “real” José Luis, I got myself into serious trouble and, on top of it, was unfailingly exposed as an impostor.

I had spoken about my problem with only one person, the late Dr. Brotbaum. Now I wanted to unburden myself by talking to Ernesto about it. He was a good candidate: an educated person, a stranger whom I would never see again, and a Mexican like José Luis. I never entertained the thought that he would not be interested in the subject.

We were resting in bed after we climaxed. I assumed that Ernesto would stay the night. But after a few minutes, he looked at his watch. “Oh, it’s getting late. I’m staying with my cousin’s family and shouldn’t return home too late.”

“Ernesto, I’d like to talk to you. To explain everything. Could we meet tomorrow sometime?”

“Of course, Eloy. Tell you what. Meet me at Jardín de la Corregidora tomorrow at ten. We can spend the day together. If you want to, we can do some sightseeing.”

* * *

I got up bright and early. I deliberately did not hang the wooden cross, José Luis’s talisman, around my neck. After breakfast, I made my way to the Jardín de la Corregidora, strolling briskly through the well-kept streets.

The Jardín de la Corregidora was dedicated to the wife of a city alderman who warned Hidalgo, the father of Mexico’s independence, that the Spaniards were on his trail. A few days later, on September 16, 1810, Hidalgo proclaimed Mexico’s independence from Spain.

In that historical setting, I waited from ten until noon for Ernesto. At eleven, I called my hotel to see whether Ernesto had left a message for

José Luis Herrera or Eloy Wise. There was none. By noon it became clear to me that I had been stood up.

Why, I wondered, would a gay man, who had gone out of his way to help me at great risk to himself, stand me up? Had he been dissatisfied with my sexual performance? Was he angry that I had given him a false name? Did he just want me for sex, but not for friendship? Was he embarrassed to be seen with me in public because of my less than elegant clothes? Was the subject of my two names of no interest to him?

At GIF meetings, I had heard that being stood up by people one met in bars and made dates with was a common occurrence. That sort of thing had never happened to me before. Ernesto's behavior frustrated me because it made no sense. But then, nothing that had happened, from the moment I entered the cantina until noon the next day, made any sense to me.

19

Eloy Is One

At noon I gave up on Ernesto. I found a restaurant and ate lunch. I had absolutely no idea what to do with myself. Since I had time on my hands, I thought I should visit Guanajuato. But I really had lost interest in the trip.

Two men sitting at the next table were discussing a business matter of some sort. One of them asked something, to which the other replied, "It's in León, Guanajuato."

León is an important industrial city in the state of Guanajuato. Originally, I chose it as José Luis's place of birth because it was Maximiliano's hometown. I had learned from him that there was nothing of interest there except a considerable shoe industry. But upon hearing the name of the city, I was immediately drawn to it. Maybe, in Jose Luis's birthplace, I would discover something new about myself.

I went to the bus terminal and made reservations for the 8:00 AM bus to León on Sunday morning. There was no direct service; I would have to change buses in Guanajuato. I spent the rest of Saturday doing the Querétaro tourist sights with little enthusiasm. I spoke to others only when it was absolutely necessary. By ten, I was asleep at my hotel.

I arrived in León just before noon the next morning. I had asked a fellow passenger for the name of a decent hotel in León. I was given the name of a place near the bus depot. It being a Sunday, there were few people about. I was searching for the hotel's name when a man stopped in front of me and asked, incredulously, "Eloy? Are you Eloy from Fairfax, California?"

It was Maximiliano, my mother's lover of years ago. He had grown quite fat and his hair had turned completely white. He shook my hand and, a moment later, gave me an enthusiastic *abrazo*, the formal Mexican hug. "What a miracle! It's so good to see you. What're you doing here, *hijo*?"

Good question. The correct answer would have been, "I'm visiting the putative birthplace of one of my personalities." But I said, "It's wonderful to run into you like this, Maximiliano. I'm spending the summer in Zacatecas, Zacatecas. I have a part-time job there. I took a few days off to tour the Silver Cities. Since you told me so much about your city, I decided to pay it a visit, though it is not one of the Silver Cities. I came here from Querétaro."

Maximiliano, as a matter of fact, had spoken very little about León. He had told me much more about Guanajuato.

"I'm so very happy to meet you once again, *hijo*. And how's your mother?"

My mother? I thought. How does she tie into any of this? After making the correct mental connection, I said, "She's very well, thank you."

"*Joven*, you must stay with us for a while. You know, I have a large family here. I now have eight grandchildren." As he said that, he seemed suddenly troubled about something. He thought for a moment and then said, "Let's have a cup of coffee. We can't talk in the street."

He took me to a small cafe. "Maximiliano," I said, "I owe you a lot. Because of your influence, I've continued to study Spanish."

"Yes, I was going to comment on it. You could tell people that you're from León, and nobody would think that you were lying."

After a bit of reminiscing, Maximiliano came to the point. "You know, *joven* Eloy, things sometimes get more complicated than we want them to be. I first went to California in the late sixties. I simply walked across the border from Tijuana. I needed to earn a lot of money fast so my family and I would be able to improve our lives. I soon realized that without a green card I was a nobody. With the card, as a legal resident, I'd be able to earn good money because of my trade.

"To make a long story short, I married a gringa and got the green card. After living with her for a few years, I divorced her. That is when I met your mother. I'd visit my family here, in León, only twice a year. It's not easy for a man to live by himself, especially not in an unfriendly place like California. That is why, or how, your mother and I..." His voice trailed off. "Two years after your mother and I separated, I took all my savings and went back to my family. And, thank God, I've been living here peacefully.

"My señora doesn't know all the details about my life in California. I don't want to hurt her, because she's a sensitive person. Do you think that you could keep confidence, I mean about your mother and me?"

"But, Maximiliano, of course."

"Well then, *joven* Eloy, let's go to where you will have your home while you're in León, Guanajuato."

*　　　*　　　*

Margarita, Maximiliano's wife, was considerably older than my mother and not as pretty. She was a big, easygoing woman, dedicated to caring for husband and children. Of her five sons and two daughters, only one boy still lived at home. But she was looking after one teenage grandson, two granddaughters, and a ten-year-old godson who preferred living with Maximiliano's family.

Maximiliano's youngest son was named Pepe, though everybody called him Pepín. He was an intense eighteen-year-old with lively, dark brown eyes. In contrast to his father, he was thin and sinewy. He was full of bubbly happiness that was contagious.

Bringing a guest home must not have been an unusual occurrence in Maximiliano's household. He presented me as the son of a close amigo from California, whom he had run into earlier that morning. I arrived just before the family took their lunch. Margarita made sure that I ate more than enough. I was happy that no *caldo de pollo* was served. I certainly did not want José Luis to pop up. Maximiliano was the one person in all of Mexico who would know for sure that I was not José Luis Herrera.

Maximiliano, now an assistant to the president of a large shoe factory, had come up in the world. He owned the four-bedroom house where we were having lunch. The well-worn furniture must have been bought over many years, and was utilitarian rather than elegant. The walls were adorned with prints of saints and Catholic posters. They made me remember how much Maximiliano had worried about my lack of religious education. The kitchen was fairly modern and featured a new microwave. I saw three TV sets in the house; there may have been more.

Pepín took great interest in me. He had recently graduated from high school. Before starting college, he wanted to go to California, work there for a while, and come back with some money of his own. This was a bone of contention between Maximiliano and Pepín. "I crossed illegally and suffered many hardships so my son wouldn't have to go through the same thing," Maximiliano told us while we were eating.

"Papá, I want to have my own money. You worked hard enough not to have to support me."

"Do you know, Pepín, how hard it is, how dangerous it is, how desperate it is to work illegally in California? When I was there, at least I had a trade and a green card. You'll be standing on some street corner waiting for day-labor jobs. Sometimes the boss won't pay your wages. At other times one of your own people will steal your money and beat you up. On a really bad day, the migra will catch you and bus you across the border to Tijuana!"

I suspect that Pepín wanted to go to California as a rite of passage as much as to make money. After lunch, he kept asking me questions about the United States, and even spoke some English with me. Just as he had done with me, Maximiliano encouraged Pepín to learn a second language. He paid good money for Pepín's private English tutoring. I spent a pleasant day with Maximiliano and his family. Visitors came and went, neighborhood children ran in and out of the house asking for this or that, and the family had to be fed. All of these functions were handled cheerfully by Margarita.

Pepín's bedroom also served as a guest room. Pepín offered to sleep on the floor while allowing me to use his bed. I was tempted to accept his offer. Firmly established as Eloy, I was not the least bit sexually interested in Pepín. However, who knew what sexual urges lurked in Pepín's heart? But, of course, courtesy dictated that I ask Pepín to share the bed with me. I need not have worried. As soon as we went to bed, Pepín bade me goodnight, and a moment later he was fast asleep.

Maximiliano had suggested that Pepín drive me to the city of Guanajuato on Monday and show me around. Since visiting Guanajuato had been my original plan, I accepted his suggestion gladly. The upcoming trip also pleased Pepín. He wanted to spend the next day talking to me. Pepín was the proud owner of a Ford pickup, which was as old or even older than he was.

We started out early in the morning. Pepín drove the old jalopy carelessly, as if it were an old nag that knew her way and just needed a slight tug on the reins. While he drove, he gesticulated freely with his hands, and kept looking at me instead of at the road. He had an insatiable curiosity about California in general, and San Francisco in particular. I did the best I could to answer his questions. I must have disappointed him at times. To me, Fairfax, in Marin county, where his father had lived with my mother, was an OK place, not an enchanted town. I did not share Pepín's opinion that everybody was wealthy and happy there.

* * *

Guanajuato is not as imposing as Zacatecas, but more intriguing. In addition to its colonial style, it has an endless web of mysterious narrow alleys and enchanting tiny parks.

After lunch, Pepín took me to the Museo de Panteón on the outskirts of the city. It turned out to be an exhibit of mummified cadavers that were perfectly preserved due to the properties of the local soil. The mummified bodies, with their gaping mouths, seemed angry at the visitors. When I left the exhibit I felt shaken.

Pepín had to run an errand. Rather than drive with him, I sat on a bench in a small plaza, waiting for him to come back. "So, José Luis," I spoke silently to myself, "you've finally returned home. Would you be satisfied to live in the state of Guanajuato with your people?" José Luis chose not to reply. But, for Eloy, the answer was clear. I liked Maximiliano's family and they, like my friends in Zacatecas, were hospitable to me. I spoke the language and had a good a grasp of the culture. But I was not a Mexican. What was I? Probably that which I had always refused to acknowledge: an American, a Californian, a Chicano.

Genetically, I was only half Chicano. It was my skin color that forced me into their camp, rather than into the Jewish side of my mother. But I had always felt that Chicanos were not my people. I may have bought into American society's low esteem of Chicanos and internalized this racist attitude. The mythical connection I felt to Mexico was just the head game of an unhappy adolescent. My *tierra* was the United States. I was the son of Gitel Weiss and Domingo Herrera, a uniquely American mixture. If I wanted to be at peace with myself, I had to learn to accept who I was, rather than pretend to be someone else.

* * *

That evening, sleeping next to Pepín, I had the strangest dream. I saw the beginning of a procession, led by Bruno, and I knew it was a funeral. It was winding its way down the main street of León. When the casket came into view there was a skeleton, like the ones I had seen at the Museo de Panteón, inside. Around its neck hung José Luis's wooden cross. In the procession I recognized Alfredo, señora Serrano, and other Zacatecas acquaintances. Walking in a separate group was Angel, M. Darlan, and people I had met in Acapulco. At the grave site stood Dr. Brotbaum, wearing his cowboy hat.

"Dearly beloved," he intoned, "we come to bury José Luis in the city where he was born. Like Socrates, he took the cup of hemlock with dignity. Like the great Greek philosopher, he accepted his death sentence. He too…"

His speech was interrupted by a woman's voice shouting, "José Luis is dead," and a man's voice answering "Rong riv Eroy." I turned in the direction of the voices and saw Aviva and Jiro.

Frantically, I looked for Bruno. I urgently needed to know why Harmony had not been laid to rest. When I caught up with him, I knew I had to speak to him in German, but I had forgotten the word for "buried." I performed a pantomime. Finally, he understood me, and said, "Ach, ya, him we buried in Berkeley."

As soon as he said that, my UC zoology instructor, Mrs. Hedge, stood next to him. In her prim voice she rebuked Bruno and said, "But he carries the Brotbaum gene."

Bruno seemed startled by her statement and replied, "But, my dear lady, the dead don't carry genes."

"You wouldn't know, would you, you're just an undertaker," Mrs. Hedge said to him huffily. "I tell you, the boy carries the Brotbaum gene!"

I woke up with a sense of great relief. I knew that José Luis had died and was buried in the *tierra* of his native town. Harmony, too, was at peace. But the Brotbaum legacy would be with me always.

I looked at my watch. I could barely make out the digits. It was 5:50 in the morning. I knew my business in Mexico had been accomplished, and I could go back to California.

I had seen signs on the road pointing to the León airport. I could probably fly to Mexico City from there and catch a plane to San Francisco. Then I remembered that the late José Luis had taken a few days off from his job in Zacatecas, and that his belongings were still there. I could not go back to Zacatecas calling myself Eloy. Nor could I pretend to be José Luis, because he was dead.

In Zacatecas, when I had packed my overnight bag, something made me put my passport, tourist card, ticket, and traveler's checks into my fanny pack. The personal belongings I had left in Zacatecas consisted only of clothing. I could afford to lose these items. My first thought was that I should disappear from the scene. This way I would never have to deal with anyone in Zacatecas.

But that would be unfair to the people who had befriended José Luis. They would be worried enough, I was sure, to file a police report if I did not return from my trip. I knew that the Mexican police would come up with nothing. That would worry my friends even more. I had to perform one more brief task while pretending to be José Luis.

During our trip to Guanajuato, Pepín and I stopped at the central bus terminal to make a bus reservation to Zacatecas for the next day. I had told Maximiliano and his family about my job in Zacatecas, omitting the José Luis part. I could not call from their home to tell my landlady in Zacatecas that José Luis was abandoning his stuff and then, as Eloy Wise, make flight reservations to San Francisco.

To do all of these things, I needed to be by myself. The bus to Zacatecas would make a stop in San Miguel de Allende. I would get off there and, from a hotel, make all travel arrangements. Most likely, I would take a bus to Mexico City from San Miguel, and catch a flight home.

San Miguel had not been on my original itinerary for my trip through the Silver Cities because it was so heavily populated by Americans. Now I welcomed that fact. It would be easier to make arrangements from there. The travel agents would be more experienced with flights to the United States.

*　　　*　　　*

The hotel in San Miguel was expensive. But everything was more expensive in that town because of the many foreigners who lived there. Through a local travel agency, I arranged to rewrite my airline ticket to depart from Mexico City. I booked a direct evening flight to San Francisco for the following day. I found out that there was daily train service from San Miguel to Mexico City, and decided to go this way rather than by bus.

It was late in the evening when I called my landlady in Zacatecas. I was determined not to mention the name José Luis, hoping that señora Serrano would recognize my voice. It pained me that I would have to play to role of an impostor.

My landlady did, indeed, recognize my voice when I asked for her. "José Luis, how nice of you to call. How has your trip been?"

"I have had some very bad news, señora Serrano. My mother is ill. I'm afraid I shall have to return home immediately…"

"You mean to say that you won't be returning to Zacatecas? Not even to collect your things?"

"I'm afraid there's no time for that. At the moment, I'm in San Miguel de Allende. I'll take the train from here to Mexico City and, from there, fly to San Francisco."

"But your things…"

I thought for a moment. Alfredo was taller than me. My clothes would not fit him. "If any of your tenants wants my clothes, they can have them. Otherwise, please give them to *niños pobres*." Suggesting giving stuff to "poor children" just meant donating it to some charity.

"But José Luis…"

"I'm afraid, señora Serrano, that I have to go now. Please give my best regards to Alfredo and the other tenants. Ask my friends to apologize for me at the bank. Thank you so much for all your kindness." I hung up the telephone. I felt terribly guilty for betraying the trust of José Luis' friends.

As I packed my bag I came across José Luis' cross. For a moment, I toyed with the idea of throwing it into the wastebasket. But tossing a cross would be a sacrilege in Mexico. Maybe, I could wrap it up in newspaper.

Then it occurred to me that I needed to perform a ritual to lay José Luis to rest. I would bury the cross! This would add a touch of reality to my dream. I went to the dining room and borrowed a soup spoon. I waited until it was dark. Carrying the cross in a paper bag, I walked into the large garden that surrounded the hotel. It had rained earlier in the day, and the ground was still soft. In a secluded spot, hidden by a shrub, I dug a grave for the cross. I laid it inside the little trench I had dug, and covered it with dirt. I stood up, looked at the grave, and said audibly, "Rest in peace, José Luis. Adíos, *hermano mío*." I asked myself what José Luis would have done had he laid Eloy to rest. The answer came to me in a flash. Solemnly, I crossed myself.

* * *

There were many gringos on the train ride to Mexico City. I pretended to be asleep; I did not want to speak to anyone. In my mind, I reviewed my Mexican adventure. My dream in León revealed that my fractured psyche had fused; that I had become wholly Eloy. It was like one of those cryptic messages on a computer screen. It stated that something was reconfigured without explaining how this had been brought about.

Now that only Eloy remained, it was necessary to work out a plan for him—for me—to become a grown man. It was time to get out of the twinkie mode, the Helmut lifestyle, the protégé state. I had to become financially independent as soon as possible. If ever there would be an older gentleman in my life, we would be equal partners. I did not want to be dependent on a Joe or a Bruno.

Monty had told me I would earn a substantial salary as a skilled programmer. I was determined to pursue that career. There was no way that I, as Eloy, could become a successful philosophy professor like Danny

Fleetwood. Certainly, as a programmer, I would be on the road to material success faster than as a fledgling PhD in philosophy.

What about Dr. Brotbaum's legacy? Had I not desired him to impregnate me physically and intellectually? To become one with his body and his mind? The dream in León alluded to the "Brotbaum gene" I carried. How would Eugene's legacy affect my life?

I must have fallen asleep for a while. When the train came to a stop, I woke up and knew how I, as a gay young Chicano, would apply Dr. Brotbaum's philosophy to my own life. An observation that Monty had made a long time ago made it possible for me to associate my future life with Dr. Brotbaum's teachings.

"Until I was in my late forties," Monty said to me during one of his philosophical ruminations, "homosexuality was still against the law. Even walking in drag was illegal. Men who dressed like women were busted as 'female impersonators.' As a matter of fact, the gay freedom movement was started by drag queens. They were the ones who risked arrest, and they were the first ones out of the closet.

"A few years later, these dainty queens decided that instead of having big boobs, they wanted huge muscles. And, voilà, the same feminine queens went to the gyms in droves to become, or at least attempt to become, well-built men.

"It's strange that when we were totally oppressed, we wanted to look like women. Now that we have experienced liberation, we try to look like an exaggerated version of our former oppressors."

I never really knew how factual Monty's anecdotes were. But regardless of the veracity of these observations, such abrupt zigzags were interpreted by Dr. Brotbaum as blindly following the dictates of fashion. What was all right at the beginning of a decade might become abominable in less than ten years. Fashion, with no rhyme and reason, dictated what was good and acceptable. Carrying the Brotbaum gene, I knew that I would not be a slave to capricious fashion. Like my teacher, I would use my logic to analyze new fads and customs, and make up my mind whether to follow them.

Of course, being an outsider and a loner, I had always disregarded what was fashionable. But I had not considered that trait to be a virtue. Now, thanks to Eugene, it was all right for me to be what I wanted to be, as long as logic supported my actions.

I would be Eloy, only Eloy, and nothing but Eloy!

*　　　*　　　*

My ticket was waiting for me at the airport. The airline clerk had me fill out an official form. On the first line, I was asked to give my full name. I printed "Eloy H. Wise." The second line asked for my hometown. I wrote, "Berkeley, California, USA." The third line asked for my occupation. I put down "student." My entire being believed that these were true and correct assertions.

To communicate with the author
please write to authorinsf@yahoo.com

978-0-595-39846-1
0-595-39846-4

Manufactured by Amazon.ca
Bolton, ON